Stephen D'Agata

POPE DREAMS

Pope Peter
the improbable

First published by Busybird Publishing 2022

ISBN
Paperback: 978-1-922691-98-9
Hardback: 978-1-922691-99-6
Ebook: 978-1-922954-00-8

Cover design: Busybird Publishing

Layout and typesetting: Busybird Publishing

Busybird Publishing
2/118 Para Road
Montmorency, Victoria
Australia 3094

To my late wife Maria,
for supporting me in this endeavour
despite her reservations.

Preface

'Welcome back to Radio One's broadcast of the Holy Father's Angelus live from the Vatican. You're with Patrick Delaney and the time is five minutes to eleven. With me is Vatican correspondent for *The Irish Times*, Mr Declan O'Reilly. Well Declan, it was a truly stirring Angelus from Pope Anthony today!'

'Yes Patrick, the Holy Father has once again provided us with a wise assessment of world affairs. One hopes that the world leaders are paying attention to his advice. Today's Angelus was directed to the on-going conflicts in the Ukraine, but his words on how it is the hard work of negotiating peace that produces truly great leaders should resonate throughout all conflict zones.'

'And this Pope is not one to shy away from controversies within the Church itself. He has actively supported the prosecution of clergy accused of child sexual abuse and has initiated an open investigation on how such scandals were able to continue for so long.'

'I believe, Patrick, he will also be ensuring that any senior clergy accused of concealing such crimes will also have to answer to the courts in the countries where they reside.'

'But today's message was world peace. To symbolise the importance of this message, the Holy Father will be releasing a dozen white doves from the window of the papal apartments.'

'Yes, and he will be ably assisted in this important task by two youngsters, Elizabetta and Paolo Bonetti.'

'Two very lucky children indeed to be sharing this task with His Holiness. Do we know how they were chosen, Declan?'

'I believe they are the niece and nephew of the Vatican press secretary. So perhaps it wasn't as much luck as good connections that got them the job. But they are also from Pope Anthony's hometown of Padua, which was also the home of Saint Anthony – who, of course, the Pope honoured in the choice of his papal name.

'And now we can see His Holiness returning to the balcony of his apartments with his two young charges and a wicker basket, which I presume contains the doves that are to be released. I know the Holy Father is not a tall man, Declan, but he is not much taller that the two children joining him. How old are they?'

'I believe that Elizabetta is eleven, and Paolo is only eight. And yes, the Pope's most distinctive physical feature is his short stature. In fact, he stands only one hundred and fifty-three centimetres tall.'

'But when he stands at the papal apartment window, he seems to be a similar height to his predecessors.'

'I'll let you in on a little-known Vatican secret there, Patrick. Pope Anthony is so short that he could hardly be seen from the window if he was standing on the floor of the apartment. So, his staff have provided him with a wooden box to stand on. The children must be standing on the box with him today, so he can't hide his stature.'

'That certainly explains a few things. While we're waiting for His Holiness to release the doves I would like us to describe to the listeners the wonderful view of Piazza San Pietro from the RAI television helicopter. We can see the piazza filled with locals and tourists, and the sunlight glistening off the fountains.'

'Oh, it looks like His Holiness is ready to release the doves now, Patrick. He's undone a catch on the basket and is allowing the two children to lift the lid that will release the doves.'

'And off they fly. Always a thrilling sight to see doves released from their cage to spread their message of peace throughout the world.'

'Well Patrick, it doesn't seem that their message is going very far today. The doves have flown about twenty metres away from the window and have now all settled back on the sill immediately below.'

'I'll have to say, those birds seem quite happy just to hang around. And the children are looking very disappointed.'

'Yes, but His Holiness is not about to let some recalcitrant birds ruin their day. He is now leaning out of the window trying to shoo them away.'

'Each time the Pope manages to get a bird to move off its perch, it just flies out a couple of metres and returns, resulting in waves of laughter from the multitude below. The crowd below seems to find this a bit comical.'

'But His Holiness is very determined to move these birds on, Patrick, he seems to be reaching out further and further each time he tries.'

'It seems that his charges have had enough though, they are being ushered inside by Vatican staffers.'

'I can see them stepping off the box now as His Holiness has one last go at getting the birds to move on and … oh my God, he's fallen!'

'It can't be true! The Holy Father has fallen from the window of his papal apartment!'

'It's at least ten metres from the window to the terrace below! Do you think he is okay?'

'We're getting some images from the RAI helicopter now and I can see the Holy Father's motionless body wedged inside a planter box on the lower terrace.'

'This doesn't look good at all, Patrick. His surplice is draped over his body, exposing his bare legs and … are they Juventus boxer shorts?'

An ordinary Catholic

Peter MacDonald was woken by his two-year-old daughter, Suzanne, who had crawled onto his bed and was now trying to prise his eyes open with her fingers.

'Hi Dadda!' she said as he opened his eyes.

'Good morning Suzie,' was his tired reply.

He turned to look at the clock on the bedside table; it showed 9.46. He had slept in, but there was still plenty of time to get everyone ready for eleven o'clock mass.

Suzanne was the youngest of his six children who lived with him and his wife Mary in a four-bedroom detached home situated in a smart suburb of Dublin.

He picked Suzanne up and held her above him at arm's length. Suzanne giggled in anticipation. Peter swung her around as if she was flying and then would let go momentarily so that she could freefall for a split second. Suzanne squealed with delight and encouraged him to do it again and again.

The sound of water running in the en-suite bathroom indicated that Mary was already in the shower. 'Daddy has to get ready for mass now, Suzie,' he said. But the look of disappointment on her face compelled him to continue playing their game a couple more times before he made her crash land beside him on the bed, gave her a quick tickle, crawled out of bed and headed towards the en-suite.

'Morning darling,' he said as he pulled the shower curtain aside far enough to give Mary a peck on the cheek.

Mary, at thirty-nine years of age, was a few years younger than Peter. It was a credit to the strength of their sixteen-year marriage that, at the sight of his wife's naked form, Peter still felt the urge to jump in the shower with her. Sadly, the days of spontaneous amorous encounters had long since disappeared. With six sets of little eyes always lurking, privacy was in short supply.

'Can you get Suzie her breakfast?' Mary called from the shower. 'And make sure that the boys have got everything organised for football.'

'Are they all up?' Peter replied as he splashed water on his face.

'Mike and the twins are already downstairs, and Lauren should be getting dressed.'

'What about Brydie?'

'I've called her twice already but she's probably still in bed.'

'Right-o.' Peter knew the Sunday morning drill well. He needed to get breakfast organised for the younger children and make sure that the three boys had their gear organised for their football matches.

He picked up Suzanne to take her downstairs. They walked past the bedroom that she shared with nine-year-old Lauren, who was inside buttoning up her best party frock.

'Good morning my darling, what are you all dressed up for today?' Peter asked.

'It's Ebony O'Shea's birthday today, Daddy. She's having a party at her place.'

'Well, you look very pretty. Just make sure you don't mess up your frock while having breakfast.'

'Okay Daddy.'

Lauren's such a peaceful and delightful child, he thought as he walked towards the stairs. Her older sister Brydie was also peaceful and delightful … when she was nine! But now she was fourteen and had developed into a cantankerous, self-obsessed teenager.

He knew that he'd have to try to get Brydie out of bed. Not having the courage to take her on himself, he opened the door and set Suzanne to the task, as Brydie was less likely to lash out at her younger sibling.

Suzanne dutifully went up to Brydie while Peter watched at a safe distance. She pulled at her sister's hand which was dangling off the side of the bed. 'Up Briddy, Briddy up,' she called, only to have her sister roughly pull her hand away, nearly knocking Suzanne off her feet.

'Go away Suzie,' Brydie grumbled.

Peter then entered the room to rescue Suzanne before she got overly upset. 'Take it easy Brydie. You almost pulled her arm off!'

'Humph!'

'It's time to get up,' Peter added. 'You've less than an hour to get ready for mass.'

There was no reply save for a muffled groan.

Peter picked up Suzanne and left the room. Brydie was his and Mary's first experience with a teenager. He shuddered at the thought that there were another five such creatures that they would have to deal with. The future looked very bleak indeed.

Peter carried Suzanne down the stairs to the entrance hall. This hallway separated the two front rooms, one of which was the boys' bedroom, while the other was their sitting room. He entered the kitchen, which was directly behind the sitting room and large enough to also serve as their dining room, to find his three boys – eleven-year-old Mike and five-year-old twins Patrick and Connor – tucking into their breakfast cereals. Some of the cereal had found its way into their bowls but a good portion of it was on the table. A crunch underfoot revealed that the floor had got its share as well.

'Can you boys be more careful please?' he pleaded. 'Look at the mess you've made.'

He could have been talking to the walls for all he knew. The boys continued to stare at the Sunday morning cartoons.

As he strapped Suzanne into her highchair and prepared porridge for both of them, he decided to turn the conversation to football. *This should get some response from them.* 'Who are we playing this week Mikey?' he asked.

'St Martins,' Mike replied.

'What are our chances?'

'Dunno, we beat them three-zip last time, so I think we'll do okay this time as well.'

Peter and his sons had a good relationship. Together they sought refuge from the cantankerous Brydie. Peter also knew that he could get out of doing things around the house if he said he needed to spend time with Mike or the twins.

Peter had almost finished preparing Suzi's porridge when Lauren entered the room. She sat down in her usual chair next to Patrick. Almost immediately, she jumped back to her feet and turned to look at the back of her party frock. 'Daddy, Daddy!' she cried, 'Look what Paddy's done to my dress!'

Patrick roused from his television-induced daze, gave his father a puzzled look, turned to his sister and said, 'I didn't do anything to you!'

Lauren was now in tears. 'Yes you did! You spilt your cocoa puffs all over my chair and look what it's done to my dress!'

Peter could see that a damp stain had formed on Lauren's dress. Although he was not an expert in the laundry, Peter knew that it was the sort of stain that would not easily wash out. Then, when Patrick and Connor saw the stain on the dress, they spontaneously burst into laughter.

'Daddy!' she cried out in anguish.

'You apologise to your sister, Paddy,' Peter said sternly.

'But I didn't do it on purpose.'

'I know you didn't, but you were being careless. And if you can't eat breakfast without making a mess, I'll switch off the TV!'

Lauren, however, was not waiting for an apology. Instead, she ran out of the kitchen and back up the stairs in tears, crossing paths with Mary.

'What's wrong with Lauren?' Mary asked when she reached the kitchen.

'Paddy dirtied her dress,' Connor volunteered.

'I did not!' protested Patrick.

'Yes you did! You spilt cereal on her chair!'

Mary turned her gaze to Patrick. 'Did you just, Patrick MacDonald! Well, I don't think you should be eating breakfast while watching TV then.' With that she picked up the remote and switched off the television.

'No Mammy!' cried both Patrick and Connor. 'That was our favourite!' But Mary's rule was law in the MacDonald household and the boys knew that they couldn't change her mind. Instead, Patrick looked accusingly at his twin. 'Why did you have to tell her?'

'Daddy would have told her anyway,' Connor replied.

Mary said to Peter, 'You know they're not meant to watch TV while having breakfast!'

'Coffee, dear?' Peter asked.

Mary scowled at him but then had to turn her attention to the washing machine, while Peter checked that Suzie's porridge was at the right temperature and handed her the bowl. He then prepared a coffee plunger for Mary and himself, quickly finished his breakfast, and went back upstairs to get himself ready.

While climbing up the stairs he built up the courage to try rousing Brydie again. 'Brydie! It's time to get yourself ready for mass.'

'Not going!' was the reply.

'Yes you are! We're all going and that's final,' Peter commanded.

He walked past Suzie and Lauren's room to find Lauren sulking on the bed. He paused for a second at the doorway before walking in. 'I'm sorry about what happened to your dress, darling,' he said, 'but I'm sure that you have a lot of other pretty things to wear.'

'But that was my favourite,' she sulked, 'and the rest of my clothes are all fugly!'

'Fugly? Where did you learn such a word?'

'Brydie uses it all the time.'

That was yet another problem with Brydie. Peter knew that colourful language was part of the teenage vernacular, but she'd been told more than once that she needed to watch her mouth around her younger siblings.

'I'm sure there's something in here,' said Peter as he started rifling through her wardrobe. He found a blue floral dress and pulled it out. 'How about this one?'

'Oh, that's a brand new one!' she exclaimed. 'Can I wear that?'

'Sure you can,' he chuffed as he handed his daughter the dress. 'Just mind where you sit this time.'

'I will Daddy, thank you.'

Peter was very pleased with himself. *Another problem solved by Super-Dad,* he thought to himself as he proceeded to the en-suite for a quick shave.

Peter was not a vain person, but he liked to maintain a pleasant appearance and thought he looked good for a man almost in his mid-forties. He had played around with beards and moustaches in his younger days but was now always clean shaven, mainly because it was hard to conceal grey facial hair. He'd been able to conceal the flecks of grey in his hair, which was a thick and lustrous black and contrasted with his deep blue eyes.

By the time he finished his grooming, got out of his pyjamas and into a clean pair of jeans and check shirt, it was twenty to eleven. They'd better get a move on if they were going to make it to mass on time.

St Stephen's church was an easy five-minute car trip or fifteen-minute walk from their home. They always planned to arrive at mass on time, but there was always something that held them up: last minute nappy changes; the twins forgetting to put on their socks; a misplaced set of car keys. Thankfully, their nappy changing days would soon be over as Suzanne was about to commence toilet training and Peter was booked in for a vasectomy operation a week from Monday.

As he started back towards the stairs, Peter noticed that Brydie was still in her bed. 'Brydie!' he yelled, 'It's time to go! You have to get up now!'

'Not going!'

'Yes you are. Now get out of bed!'

He reached the entrance hall. Lauren's cries of 'But Daddy said I could wear it!' stopped Peter in his tracks. He'd been in trouble before for letting the children wear the wrong things, so he thought it best not to enter the kitchen right away.

'Well, Daddy didn't realise that this is a summer dress. It's too cold outside today so you can't wear it. Now go upstairs and take it off. I'll be up in a minute to find something else for you.'

As a sobbing Lauren ran past him, Peter plucked up the courage to enter the kitchen. 'So, are we ready to go to mass?' he asked sheepishly.

Mary glared at him as she unbuckled Suzanne from her highchair. 'Here, clean her up while I go upstairs and sort out another one of your messes.' With that she handed him the baby and left the room.

'Sorry, dear!' he feebly called out after her.

He took off Suzanne's bib, wet it in the kitchen sink and used it to wipe the porridge residue from her face and hands. Then, addressing the boys he said, 'Get your football things together and go to the car.'

'Do I have to go?' asked Mike.

'Don't you start,' Peter barked back at him.

'But Brydie's not going.'

'Oh yes she is! And you're meant to be confirmed this year so there is no way you're going to miss mass.'

By the time the boys got organised and into the car it was five to eleven. There was no way now that they would make it to church before the start of mass. He could only hope that they would not be too late.

He carried Suzanne with him to see how Mary and Lauren were getting on. A still-sulking Lauren passed him on the stairs wearing a pretty blue dress, white tights and a white cardigan. 'Oh, that is nice,' he said cheerfully.

Lauren didn't answer and headed straight outside to the car.

Mary was still upstairs, taking on the Brydie beast single handed. Brydie was screaming at her mother. 'Why should I! It's all a load of rubbish! All we learn at school about religion is fecking fairy tales about miracles, and how if you pray God will give you what you want! Well, I've prayed loads of times, and nothing has come of it. So why should I keep going to mass?'

'Because it's what we believe in!' Peter answered as he entered the room.

'It's what *you* believe! Not what I believe!'

Mary chimed in: 'Going to mass on Sunday is part of what this family does! We've all been going to mass together since you were a babe in arms. The parish house was like your second home. Fr Mick has been like a grandfather to you.' But Mary's conciliatory tone soon gave way to frustration, and she added, 'If you want to be part of this family then you have to come with us!'

'Well, Fr Mick isn't there anymore, is he? And I hear how you and Dad talk about Fr Damian. Dad even called him a fecking idiot the other day!'

Peter, who had found it more and more difficult to speak favourably of the hapless Fr Damian in recent times, couldn't refute Brydie's statement but simply replied. 'We don't go to Mass for Fr Damian's sake, Brydie, we go for our own sake to celebrate the Eucharist with our community.'

'It's not my community anymore. None of my friends go to mass now that they're in high school, and half of your friends don't go either since Fr Mick left.'

'Fine, we'll go without you. You'll have to stay home on your own and there'll be no internet and no television.'

'But I promised Daphne that I'd face-time with her this morning.'

'I don't care what you've promised. There'll be no internet and no TV and that's final. If you're to stay home, you can do your homework.'

'But I don't have any homework.'

'I don't want to argue anymore. You've already made the rest of us late again. Just read a book or something.'

They left Brydie to her own devices and went to the car. Peter had just turned the key in the ignition when the music signalling the start of the eleven o'clock news came over the radio. The tone of the announcer's voice grabbed Peter and Mary's attention before the words:

'Breaking news from Rome: Pope Anthony is dead!'

Peter immediately screamed at the kids to be quiet as Mary turned up the volume.

'Tragedy in Rome this morning as Pope Anthony was killed in a freak accident. The Holy Father had just completed his Sunday morning Angelus at the window of his papal apartments when he was seen to fall from the window on to the terrace some ten metres below. Details of the incident are sketchy at this stage, but His Holiness is thought to have been killed instantly.'

Peter and Mary just looked at each other for a few seconds before Peter spoke. 'Jaysus, that's one for the books. How could the Pope just fall out of his own window?'

A concerned Lauren called out from the back of the minivan, 'What's happened Daddy?'

'The Pope just died.'

'Oh, that's sad,' Lauren replied.

Peter was distraught. The election of Pope Anthony almost nine years ago was a beacon of hope for progressive Catholics like Peter after almost three decades of conservative rule. Still in a state of shock, Peter backed the car out of the driveway and the family proceeded on their way to church.

No-one spoke in the car during the short drive, but they were so late that when they finally arrived at St Stephen's, Fr Damian was well into his homily. As they took their places, Peter noted Fr Damian's words and demeanour. It was clear that the priest was not aware of the tragic news about the Pope. Peter shuddered at the thought of having to interrupt Fr Damian in the middle of mass to fill him in. But as the mass progressed without any reference to the tragic events in Rome, Peter felt compelled that he would have to intervene so that Fr Damian could at least make an announcement to the congregation before mass ended.

Fortunately, the burden of being the bearer of bad news was lifted when Brenda O'Halloran, who'd been counting collection money in the Presbytery, ran into the church and whispered something into Fr Damian's ear just before he led the congregation into the closing prayer. Fr Damian reeled away from Brenda with an incredulous look on his face. Brenda held the priest's right hand in both of her hands and continued to whisper into his ear. Fr Damian reeled back again, and this time raised his free hand to his mouth. *Now she's told him how he died,* Peter thought. He observed people muttering to each other, obviously wondering what was going on. However, they all fell silent when Fr Damian returned to his lectern and faced the congregation again.

Fr Damian's first attempt to address his flock resulted in muffled croak. So, he cleared his throat and began again. 'Dear parishioners,' he began, 'Brenda has just passed on some very sad news.' His voice was now wavering, 'It appears that our beloved pontiff, Pope Anthony has died in tragic circumstances this morning.'

Gasps of astonishment emanated from the congregation. Some of the older parishioners crossed themselves while others just stared at each other in disbelief.

Fr Damian cleared his throat before addressing the congregation again. 'It appears that his death was accidental, but no doubt we'll find out more information from the media as the day progresses. But now I would like you all to join me in praying the rosary for the repose of the soul of our leader.'

The praying of the rosary was entirely appropriate, but it meant staying in church for another twenty minutes. The children gave soulful looks to their parents, hoping that they could be permitted to sneak out, as others appeared to be doing every time Fr Damian bowed his head in prayer. However, to their dismay, Peter and Mary showed no sign of wanting to leave. In fact, Peter would have liked to stay back even longer to discuss the ramifications of the news with some of their friends.

At the conclusion of the Rosary, Fr Damian invited people to stay behind for silent prayer, but this was too much for Mike, Patrick and Connor, who had football games get to, and they proceeded to drag their parents out of the church.

Farewell to the good Pope

In the week following the unfortunate demise of Anthony, the manner of his death had been transformed from what was essentially a clumsy accident, to a virtual ascension up to heaven. The official Vatican line was that although his mortal body had fallen to the ground, if one looked closely at the footage his soul could be seen being carried up to heaven with the doves he had encouraged into flight. Despite the Pope's massive head trauma, the undertakers had excelled themselves to the point that, with the help of the papal mitre, Anthony's appearance was almost unchanged.

The papal funeral itself was another great media success for the Vatican with record television ratings worldwide. Despite the increasing irrelevance of the Catholic Church in modern society, people were still fascinated by the pomp and ceremony surrounding the papacy.

The event was attended by heads of state from many nations. Those who could not come themselves sent their delegates, and religious leaders from all Christian denominations attended along with representatives of many other faiths.

But for the cardinals charged with presiding over the ritual and solemnity of the papal funeral, the decision on who would be the next to fill the shoes of St Peter was at the top of their minds.

Just over nine years ago, they had gathered in the Sistine Chapel to elect Cardinal Federico Bontempi to the highest office of the Church. Bontempi was not considered by any papal observers to be a favourite for the job despite arguably having the best theological credentials. Over more than two decades, his predecessors had worked to restore traditional Catholic values by winding back some of the hard-won reforms achieved via the Second Vatican Council. In the process, the College of Cardinals had become increasingly conservative. A progressive Jesuit theologian like Bontempi was considered a rank outsider.

However, the hand of the cardinals was forced by the ever-deepening scandals of clergy involvement in child sexual abuse and clear evidence that Church leaders had been protecting alleged offenders from investigation and prosecution. Insinuations that Pope Anthony's predecessor had re-assigned several priests later convicted of child sexual abuse may have even led to the stroke that ultimately claimed his life.

Therefore, they were limited to choosing from candidates who were not tainted by such scandals. Federico Bontempi was duly elected and became Pope Anthony, first of his name.

Pope Anthony immediately set about trying to ensure that victims of abuse were given proper justice. In his nine years in office, despite substantial resistance from cardinals and bishops trying to protect their own reputations, he had managed to restore a lot of the respect and credibility in the Church that had been lost by his predecessors.

Many conservative Catholics were grateful for this fact. But now that the Church was back on track and Pope Anthony was out of the way, the process of returning the Church to traditional values could re-commence.

Pope dreams

The ceremonies associated with the funeral of a Pope would be exhausting for most men, let alone elderly cardinals. So, after an indulgent post-funeral dinner, Cardinal Francesco DiMattina was more than eager to return to his hotel room for a well-earned rest. He barely had the strength to change into his night clothes before collapsing on the bed and immediately falling into a deep sleep.

He was now in a football stadium, and it was the national finals! The commentators could barely be heard above the roar of the enthusiastic crowd. The two teams vying for the honour this year were Flamengo from Rio de Janeiro and the Sao Paulo Corinthians. As the number one ticket holder for the Corinthians, Cardinal DiMattina was seated in a prominent position just above the coach's box.

It was twenty-nine minutes into the second half and the scores were tied at one-all. The determination of both sides to win had resulted in a high attrition rate, so when the Corinthians' key striker fell after a heavy tackle and dislocated his shoulder, there were no more fit players available to substitute. This meant that the Corinthians would have to play on with a player down. The Corinthians' fans cried in anguish.

How could Cardinal DiMattina stand by and watch his team play on at such a disadvantage? He looked up to the coach's box to find the Corinthians coach looking back at him in utter despair. Instantly he knew what he had to do. With a wink back to the coach, he jumped out of his private box and ran onto the playing field. He would take the place of the injured striker himself!

His presence on the field, resplendent in his black and crimson robes, seemed to intimidate the opposition players. They initially were reluctant to tackle him.

Within seconds of coming on to the pitch, he sprinted towards a Flamengo striker who had possession of the ball. The speed of his approach took the striker by surprise, and DiMattina had no trouble intercepting to take the ball for himself. He was, however, only metres away from the Flamengo goal square and therefore had almost the entire length of the pitch between him and the Corinthians goal.

In what seemed like one fluid movement, he managed to weave his way past all the Flamengo defenders and soon found himself directly in front of the goal with only the Flamengo goalie between him and certain victory for the Corinthians. To confuse the goalie, he began to juggle the ball from one foot to the other and bounced it a few times off his head as well. Meanwhile, he sensed that the Flamengo defenders, who he'd left for dead in his sprint for the goal, were about to catch up to him. So just before he was challenged, he kicked.

The ball sailed high to the right of the goal, but his confusion tactics had worked. The goalie jumped left. Unfortunately, the kick was a bit too high, and the ball hit the top bar, bouncing back into play. Not one to let the opportunity pass, he ran forward to head the rebounding ball into the net. The crowd erupted, and the roar echoed throughout the entire city.

In celebration of his goal, he lifted his cassock over his head and ran around the ground, revealing a complete Corinthians team uniform underneath. This excited the crowd even more. In the midst of this adulation the referee had blown his whistle. He had won the game for his beloved Corinthians and would be joining the rest of the team for the presentation of the Coppa Nationale!

He shed tears of joy as the team's anthem played over the loudspeaker system. Tears also flowed freely down the cheeks of the team's coach and all the other players. He found himself being lifted upon the shoulders of his teammates and carried towards the presentation dais.

At the dais stood the president of the Brazilian Football Association, the president of the Republic, the president of the World Soccer Federation and a bevy of buxom beauties in full Mardi Gras regalia.

He wondered which of these dignitaries would be the one to present him with the coppa. The President of the Brazilian Football Federation then approached the microphone and announced: 'No one present on this dais is worthy enough to honour the amazing feat of sporting prowess displayed by His Eminence.'

The crowd went silent in anticipation of his next words.

'There is only one man who is worthy enough to congratulate this great man. Ladies and Gentlemen, please welcome His Holiness …'

At that point the crowd roared, and he looked to his left to discover that the special guest was none other than the newly appointed pontiff! The pope himself was making his way up the stairs. But the cheering of the crowd had drowned out the President's words, so he did not hear the name of the new Holy Father.

He was so humbled that he dropped to his knees immediately as the Pontiff approached him. He reached out to kiss the papal ring as he had done so many times before, but when he looked up he was surprised to see the face of a relatively young man with jet black hair and deep blue eyes – who was definitely not one of the men he had expected would become Pope.

He was even more intrigued when the Pope said in a broad Irish accent, 'Good on ya, Freddie! To be sure you'll go a long way in this game.'

The cardinal awoke, startled by the image and voice of the man who had spoken to him. However, all that he could think of was the dreamy joy of his match-winning goal and drifted back to sleep with a wry smile on his face.

✝

Cardinal Paul Billingham was a man of few vices. He didn't drink (apart from the altar wine during mass), he didn't smoke, and he lived a relatively scandal-free life. He did, however, have a keen interest in motor racing and was considered a car nut. His pride and joy was a Jaguar XK gifted to him by a London real estate agent who had assisted him with the sale of several church properties.

At busy and stressful times such as these, a sprint though the countryside in his beloved Jaguar would always help clear his head see things in a different perspective. But his Jag was in London and he was stuck in Rome at least until the end of the Conclave, which wasn't due to start for another eight days!

Whenever he was in Rome he stayed at the Hotel Alimandi, which was located just outside the Vatican walls. So as his tired legs brought him to his home away from home, he thought how nice it would be to spend a day driving through the hills surrounding Rome in his Jaguar. These thoughts stayed in his mind as he drifted off to sleep.

He was driving through the countryside at a rapid but controlled pace. The car he was driving was not his beloved Jaguar coupe but what seemed to be a fairly ordinary family sedan.

The road was unfamiliar as well. He appeared to be in the middle of an airport as he could see large jets parked nearby. The road itself was like a runway, a wide expanse of bitumen and concrete flanked by landing lights. Then it hit him: he was on a test track associated with one of his favourite television motoring programmes. He was aiming to be the fastest around the track and on this occasion, the fastest driver was not just going to receive a trophy. This was a race to decide the papacy!

He was driving the little car flat out and didn't even lift off for tight bends. Instead, he put the struggling car into a massive power slide and rocketed out of the turn in a cloud of tyre smoke.

As he came around the last corner on two wheels he knew he had it in the bag. He shot over the line at what he was certain would be a record time.

Now he was in the television studio with a presenter asking him, 'So how do you think you went?'

'Well, I know I did the best I could. I just wish I could have been driving my Jaguar out there instead of that jalopy.'

'Now-now Your Eminence, you know the saying, it's a poor workman …'

'Yes, I know, I know,' he retorted, inciting laughter in the audience.

'Still, you certainly were quick. But was it quick enough? Let's have a look at how some of your competition went,' the presenter said as he gestured towards a board where the times of the cardinals who had done a lap of the circuit before him were posted.

The cardinal sat forward in anticipation of his result.

'Now there's the French cardinal Prost, who did a one minute forty-five point three second lap. But Cardinal Montoya of Spain beat him with a one minute forty-four point eight. At the top of the board, we have Cardinal Schumacher of Germany with a one forty-three point five. Do you think that you could beat that?'

He tried to respond couldn't speak. Beads of sweat were now collecting on his forehead and his hands were shaking uncontrollably.

The presenter pulled out a piece of paper he had in his pocket. 'Well, I have your time here…'

The pause seemed like an eternity.

'You did it in …'

This pause was longer than the first. He clutched the crucifix around his neck and sweat was pouring down his face.

'… one …' the announcer repeated.

He was sitting so far forward on his chair that he slipped off and landed on his knees.

'… forty-three …'

He let go of the crucifix and buried his face in his hands. The audience was completely silent.

'… point …'

He moved his hands from his face to the top of his head. He was hoping against hope that the next number announced would be less than five.

'… three!'

He raised his hands in praise of the Almighty as the audience applauded and cheered.

The announcer helped him to get back on his feet and said, 'You go to the top of the leader board!'

He made the victory symbol with both hands as he was bathed in cheers and wolf whistles from the audience. Then he heard the announcer's voice again.

'But are you fast enough to take the big prize?'

Dismayed, he slumped back into the guest-chair as the announcer continued.

'You see … someone else did a lap of our track today.' The audience gasped in astonishment. 'And you'll have to admit that it would be very unusual for an Englishman to become head of the Roman Catholic Church.'

He raised his hands and nodded in agreement.

'However, if you were Irish that would be a different story.'

This puzzled him. Irish? He knew all the Irish cardinals. Only one of them could even drive a car and he drove a Fiat Panda!

The announcer rose to his feet. 'I'm afraid to say that this other driver actually did do a quicker lap than you. In fact, this driver has run the fastest lap of the contest!' The announcer then turned to the audience and asked, 'Do you want to meet him?'

He rose to his feet amidst the cheers from the audience, who he now saw had cleared a path to a door at the rear of the studio. Then he heard the announcer continue.

'Some say he can genuflect without bending his knees … and when he cries, nuns collect his tears and use them to cure sick babies.'

The door opened and he saw a figure dressed in a white racing suit and white helmet with a dark visor. The figure was now walking towards him and removing his helmet as the announcer added.

'All we know is … ladies and gentlemen … Habemus Papam!'

With those words the figure removed his helmet, and the new Pope was now standing before him. Strangely however, he didn't look like anyone that he knew. He was much younger than any of the other cardinals and couldn't be much over forty. His most striking features where his jet-black hair and bright blue eyes.

Billingham woke up with the image of this Irishman embedded in his mind.

An evening at 'The Dan'

Peter always looked forward to Sunday evenings because this was the time he got together with some of his mates at their local pub, the Dan O'Connell. These gatherings had been going on for several years now and although they were all locals, he hadn't really gotten to know this particular group of men until their children started going to school together.

They began regular meetings at the pub when one of the fathers noticed that children were, more often than not, picked up and dropped off at school by their mothers. This meant that fathers rarely had the opportunity to meet. The Dan O'Connell was a convenient meeting place for everyone, and no one could begrudge the hard-working fathers from imbibing in a few refreshing ales while discussing the wellbeing of their children.

The number of men attending the 'dads group meeting', as it was known, varied from week to week but there was always a core group of six men (including Peter) who had become great friends over the years.

Peter greatly looked forward to these gatherings. On this particular Sunday, he was more in need of a few relaxing ales than usual, as tomorrow was the day he was to have his vasectomy operation and he was more than a little nervous about it.

Peter's decision to have a vasectomy had tested his religious loyalties, but vasectomies were a big business in twenty-first century Ireland. In fact, despite the Vatican's position on contraceptives, the use of birth control pills had been accepted wholeheartedly by Irish women as soon as they were introduced in the 1960s and the days of the typical Irish family sporting ten to twelve children were long gone. Most families now settled for a pair or a trio at most. Peter and Mary's brood of six children was considered extremely large for the times and most of their friends and acquaintances would have expected them to have put a lid on things some time ago.

Peter and Mary loved all their children dearly and couldn't imagine their lives without any one of them. But they had simply decided they were getting too old for more babies. As it was, Peter would be sixty when his youngest came of age.

There were also the practical considerations. The largest mini vans available on the market could only seat eight, and although the family house was relatively large by suburban Dublin standards, the three boys already shared one room, the two younger girls took up another and their fourteen-year-old had the smallest fourth bedroom to herself. There simply wasn't enough room for any more.

'The Dan' was typical of most suburban Irish pubs and had a loyal following. Its decor was little changed from when it was constructed in the 1920s. The red brick facade consisted of two picture windows and a simple wooden door. The door opened to a small foyer, and a pair of swinging doors then led directly into the main bar. The timber panelled dado wall matched the bar which sat directly opposite the entry. Above the dado walls at each side of the bar was an eclectic assortment of advertisements for various ales and liquors. Some dated back to when the pub was first opened but others were quite contemporary. An area to the left of the bar was reserved for playing darts.

Peter arrived at 7.15 pm to find Niall Brodie, Paul Tyson and Rob Kennedy sitting at their usual table and most of the way through their first pints.

'Hey Macca,' Rob called out as he arrived.

'Your round mate,' added Niall immediately after.

'Hang on Niall,' said Paul, 'shouldn't we be buying a pint for the condemned man?'

'Right you are,' replied Niall. 'A man shouldn't have to pay for his last pint.'

Paul stood up and pulled an empty chair out for Peter. Supporting his arm as he sat, he said, 'You just sit yourself down there Macca, and I'll go and get you a pint. The good Lord knows you need one tonight.'

Peter looked suspiciously at Paul as he walked to the bar. He then turned to face Rob and Niall who were seated opposite him at the table. 'What are you fecking idiots on about?'

'Aye, we know you're in for the snip tomorrow,' answered Rob.

'Who told you?'

'It's all around the school,' Niall added, 'all the mothers are talking about it. My missus heard it from Rob's missus.'

'Well, so much for keeping secrets,' said Peter despondently.

'I must say,' continued Niall, 'I wouldn't have thought that a good Catholic boy like you would go for such a thing.'

'Yeah,' added Rob, 'you and Mary were putting us all to shame. Thought you'd keep going at least until you had an even dozen.'

Peter sat forward and raised his finger to respond to Rob's remark when Niall added, 'And it's a good thing that you finally worked out you don't need to make a baby every time you do the business,' said Niall.

Peter now turned his attention to Niall. A smirk appeared on his face. 'I don't think that. But once you've had six of the little beggars, it certainly does seem like it.'

'I can relate to that,' laughed Niall, 'and I've only got three. But seriously, you being on the parish council and all that. Aren't you worried you could get excommunicated or something?'

'Firstly,' responded Peter, 'it was meant to be a secret, and secondly, if the Church was going to excommunicate every Irish Catholic who practiced birth control, there wouldn't be any of us left, would there?'

'Right you are,' affirmed Niall.

Paul returned with a couple of pints just as Ian Brown walked in the door. 'Hey Macca,' he said, 'having a few to calm yourself for the big snip, I see.'

'Is there anyone who doesn't know about my personal business?' grumbled Peter.

'Aye, not many,' responded Niall.

Ian patted Peter on the shoulder and then continued to the bar to order his drink, while the others continued to quiz Peter on his decision.

When Ian returned a short time later, he took his seat at the end of the table between Paul and Rob and said to Peter, 'Don't worry yourself about it, Macca. Most of us have had it done, you know. It's not such a big deal.' The others all nodded in agreement and Peter started to look a bit more relieved. Then Ian added, 'Mind you, I've heard some horror stories though.'

'Yeah,' said Rob as he leant forward, 'a mate of mine had it done a couple of years ago. The day after the op he starts to feel a dull throbbing pain in his goolies. He doesn't think much about it because he just assumes that it's a normal side effect. Until he gets up to have a wee and finds himself waddling to the toilet to minimise the pain. He gets in there and sees that his goolies have swelled to the size of mangoes. And if that wasn't a big enough shock for him, he ends up peeing blood and puss.'

The others just sat there with their mouths agape. To put them at ease Rob added, 'His missus rushed him straight back to the doctor, of course. Turned out he'd developed an infection and was admitted to hospital for IV antibiotics. Was touch and go there for a while but he's doing okay now.'

Rob's additional remarks did little to relieve the concern of his audience. But after a short silence, Ian spoke up. 'I heard an absolute beauty the other week. This fella got through the op okay. Went home to bed and woke up in the middle of the night in a pool of blood.'

'Perhaps we shouldn't be telling these kinds of stories in front of Macca right now,' said Paul.

'Rubbish, you're okay with it aren't you mate?' assured Niall. 'I mean, you have to know what you could be in for, don't you?'

Peter nodded with a nervous smile on his face as he nursed his pint. He knew he wasn't going to get out of it whatever he said. This sort of banter was one of the main things he enjoyed about meeting with his mates at the Dan, and now that it was clear his secret was out, he fully expected a roasting.

'Anyhow,' continued Ian, 'this fella wakes up in a pool of blood and gets up to find one of his stiches has come undone. What's more, as he's standing there, one of his goolies pops out of his ball sack, unfurls itself, and is dangling near his ankles.'

At this remark, both Niall and Paul, who had just taken swigs from their pints, spat out their beer across the table. But this didn't deter Ian, who continued with his tale. 'He then faints and bangs his head on the side table. His missus wakes up screaming thinking he's dead, but eventually calls the ambulance. He's good as gold now apparently.'

Peter, who was using a handkerchief to wipe off the beer that Niall had spat over him, then said sarcastically, 'Thank you Ian. That has really put my mind at ease.'

Niall decided that it was time to change the subject. 'So, Macca! Who's your tip for next Pope?' he said.

'I don't know,' Peter replied, 'probably some fecking idiot who wants to bring back the Latin Mass.'

'That's not a nice way to talk about the future Holy Father.'

'I'd love it if we could get another Pope Anthony, but the College of Cardinals is still stacked with conservative idiots. They only elected him in the first place so that he could diffuse some of the scandals that were plaguing the Church. Now that he's gone they'll be champing at the bit to take control again.'

'I don't understand why they ever said mass in Latin anyway. If Christianity originated in the Middle East, how is it that they settled on Latin for the language of the Church? I mean, Jesus was a Jew so he would have spoken Hebrew or something like that, and weren't the Jews in Jesus' time being persecuted by the Romans?'

'Jesus actually spoke Aramaic,' Peter replied.

'Aramaic? I've never heard of it. What made them change?'

Peter leant back in his chair and took a large swig from his pint. He had built up a thorough, albeit rudimentary, knowledge of church history over the years and always relished the opportunity to pass some of it on. 'Well, as the story goes,' Peter said, 'the Roman Emperor Constantine followed the example of his wife and daughter and converted to Christianity.'

'That would have been a brave move at the time, wouldn't it?' Niall replied.

'Well actually I think it was more like, if you can't beat them, join them. And these Roman Emperors weren't stupid. They worked out that if you controlled the religion, you controlled the hearts and minds of people. So, the emperor became the Pope and set the rules that everyone followed. With legions of Roman troops to back him up, he didn't have much trouble convincing people that it was the right thing to do. And that, in a nutshell, is how Latin became the language of the Church.'

'So, when did they stop saying the mass in Latin then?'

'That would be a few years before you and I were born, back in the early 1960s, because of Vatican II.'

Niall, who was about to have a sip of beer, put his pint back down on the table and gave Peter a puzzled look. 'Vatican II! What the feck is that? I thought there was only one Vatican.'

'Honestly, Niall, don't you know anything about the Catholic Church?'

'I know all I need to know. Heaven and hell, prophets, and saints and all that shite. But I don't remember learning anything about a Vatican II at school.'

'Arr … you're just where the Church wants you to be then, one of the ignorant masses.' Peter knew Niall wouldn't take offence at this remark.

Niall leant across the table so that his face was only few centimetres from Peter's face. 'Who are you calling fecking ignorant?' he said. 'Just because I don't hobnob with bishops and cardinals like you do.'

Peter gently pushed Niall back into his seat. 'Hey, take it easy, big fella. I meant no offence. If it makes you feel any better, attending a diocesan meeting with Cardinal Doherty is about as enjoyable as getting a tooth pulled.'

Niall grinned as Peter took the opportunity to take another swig from his pint. 'That's not a nice way to talk about our spiritual leader! The cardinals are appointed by the Pope himself, aren't they? So they should know what's best for us. I mean, these fellas are the closer to God than you or I will ever be.'

Now it was Peter's turn to lean across the table. He had well and truly taken the bait. 'They miss the point!' Peter said, banging his fist on the table. 'Firstly, no one is closer to God than anyone else, and they well know that. Secondly, the Church – and any church for that matter – is first and foremost a community of the faithful. These idiots in Rome think that they are God's appointed leaders, but they've forgotten that a leader cannot function without the support and confidence of those being led.'

Paul, who had until then been having his own conversation with Rob and Ian, put his arm around Peter and said, 'Whoa there Macca,

Niall's not winding you up about the Church again, is he? You should know better, Niall! You know that Macca is in a fragile state at the moment.'

'Now Paul, you know I would never stir Macca up,' a grinning Niall replied, 'Macca was just explaining Vatican II.'

'Vatican II?' Paul took his arm back from Peter's shoulder. 'There's only one Vatican isn't there?'

'Oh, for feck's sake,' Peter retorted in frustration. 'Vatican II was the Second Vatican Council. It was called Vatican II because it was only the second time in the history of the Church that a gathering of Church representatives from around the world was called to discuss the future direction of the Church.'

'Only the second time?' Paul asked. 'When was the first?'

Despite his exasperation, Peter provided a brief explanation of the first Vatican Council, and by the time he was finished, he and his friends were all due for a refill. Niall got up and made his way to the bar.

'Okay Macca,' said Niall when he returned, 'if things were starting to change for the better after Vatican II, why do cardinals like Doherty want to go back to the way it was before?'

'Because they're fecking idiots.'

'That they may be, but what do you think is going through their heads?'

'These idiots look back at Vatican II and see that since that time, there have been fewer and fewer people going to mass, and no one wants to be a priest or nun anymore. So, they think that it is all Vatican II's fault.'

'Simple cause and effect argument.'

'Exactly, but the real reason Vatican II didn't work was that it didn't go far enough. It started off well enough but then the Curia in Rome began to think that they were losing control.'

'Who the feck is the Curia?' Niall asked.

'The Curia is the Vatican … executive committee, if you like. They're the cardinals who head the various committees and tell the Pope what he needs to know.'

'So why would the Vatican want to stop something that it started?'

'Because it wasn't their idea in the first place. Unlike Vatican I, which mainly consisted of bishops and cardinals, Vatican II actually included contributions from priests, nuns, brothers, monks and laypeople. They even had some non-Catholic observers!'

'Sounds surprisingly democratic.'

'It was, and out of the two thousand or so delegates that attended the council, over nineteen hundred voted for the changes.'

'A landslide result!'

'You would think so, wouldn't you? But unfortunately the one hundred delegates who voted against it where the ones that were meant to put it into place.'

'The fecking Curia.'

'Exactly, the fecking Curia; they were happy to go along with the initial changes and it helped them to grow the Church through Africa and Asia. But once individual dioceses started talking about things like married clergy and giving women more responsible positions in the Church they decided to put the brakes on.'

'But surely the horse had well and truly bolted.'

'In a way, yes; because most of the priests appointed just prior or immediately after Vatican II were the main drivers for the changes.'

'Priests like Fr Mick.'

'Yes, Fr Mick is a good example of the priests from that era. He believes that it is the community who makes the Church and that is the very same position emphasised at Vatican II. We are the body of Christ, for Christ's sake! The basis of Christianity is that all people are the living embodiment of Jesus on Earth. I'm sure that if the real Jesus was here today he'd be kicking some arses in Rome and telling them to get back with the program.'

'So, I can see that you haven't been thinking much about this much then?' said Niall sarcastically.

'Sorry mate, I know I can go on a bit. I've still got a chip on my shoulder from when they forced Fr Mick into retirement.'

'Didn't Father Mick retire because of his brush with the Big C?'

'He did have a bowel cancer scare at the time, but he expected to make a full recovery. He was never in the mind to throw it all in. Cardinal Doherty just used his sickness as an excuse to move him on. They didn't even give him a choice.'

'So, the cardinal had it in for him then?'

'Yeah, but if you ask him he'll say that he was only thinking of Fr Mick's health. But when we pointed out that Fr Mick had recovered and wanted to return to work, he started going on about how people in the parish had complained about the way the parish was being run.'

'Who would complain against Fr Mick?'

'I don't know for sure, but I suspect that the real antagonists were from outside of the parish. I found out that there are people who make it their business to go to parishes and take notes on all of the things that are not being done in accordance with accepted Vatican doctrine.'

'What sort of things did they pick on?'

'Oh, these fecking idiots, who people in the know refer to as 'the Temple Police', look for anything they think that the Vatican will disapprove of. Apparently, we were picked on because we weren't following the mass rituals in every detail and occasionally we had people who were not priests deliver the homily.'

'Like you did on Father's Day? That was a great sermon, I really enjoyed it.'

'Why thank you Niall, I did my best. But anyhow, someone other than a priest speaking at the homily is very naughty, no matter how relevant it is to the occasion.'

'These Temple Police sound like fecking troublemakers. Why do they have so much influence with the authorities?'

'Well, they go about their business in such a way that the bishops and cardinals can't afford to ignore them. They don't just send their report to the local bishop, they also send a copy straight to the Vatican.'

'Bastards!'

'That they may be, but although a bishop may be inclined to ignore or suppress their concerns, the Vatican officials cannot be seen to be turning a blind eye, even though they probably couldn't give a newt's testicle about it anyway. The same sort of thing must be going on throughout Europe, but they haven't got the goolies to pick on someone close to their home.'

'But our bishops think that this is all okay.'

'I know for a fact that some of the older ones don't like it one bit. But over time, they've been replaced with people like Doherty who cannot contemplate being out of step with the Vatican. So, when he receives a letter saying that things are out of shape in his diocese, he can't or won't let it slide.'

'So, what happened in our parish?'

'Doherty knew getting rid of Fr Mick wouldn't be easy because he was so popular. He started suggesting early retirement to Mick at least four years ago, but he wouldn't have a bar of it. But then he took ill. So not knowing whether he was going to pull through or not, he gave in to Doherty, who then landed us with Fr Damian O'Tool.'

'Fr Damian seems a nice enough fellow,' said Niall. 'Last time I met him we had a grand old chat about football and horse-racing. He loves the ponies.'

'I don't know many priests who don't,' Peter replied.

'Aye, the decline in priest numbers has certainly hit hard at the betting shops.'

Peter laughed. 'Yes, Damian is an okay fellow but he's not overly clever. He claims that Fr Mick was a mate of his but then goes on to sell the line spun by the diocese that we've all been led astray. Damian needs to show that he is a team player, so on the cardinal's orders, he shuts down some of the perceived liberties that Fr Mick had given us. This pisses everyone off and halves the number of people who regularly attend mass.'

Niall sat back and raised his eyebrows. 'I never realised that there was so much politics going on in the Church.'

'It's all politics at the top. I've come to the conclusion that the Vatican doesn't have a problem with putting the preservation of the Holy Roman Empire ahead of promoting Christian values.'

Paul decided to take him up on this point: 'So are you suggesting that the blokes running the show don't care about Christianity?'

'I don't know what they care about! It's just that to my mind, Jesus' whole message was that living your life according to the good book was not just about pleasing the big man upstairs. I mean, if you think about it, that's such a pagan concept.'

'Hold on there,' said Paul, 'are you now saying that the bishops and cardinals are pagan?'

'No!' answered Peter. 'All I'm saying is that it's pagan how some people think that being a Christian is all about appeasing the gods or "The God". Jesus' message was that we should stop looking for God up in heaven and focus on the God on Earth.'

Paul scrunched up his face and scratched his head. 'I didn't know there was a God on Earth!'

Peter let out a huge sigh and took another swig from his pint before answering, 'Why do I feel like I'm giving a lecture on Christianity 101?' He took yet another swig before continuing. 'We are God on Earth.'

'What – you, me and Niall?'

'No, not just the three of us! Everyone and everything! That was Jesus' main message to mankind. If we're not looking after each other then we're not doing God's work!'

Paul brought his hand to his mouth, rested his chin on his thumb and thought for a moment. He then looked up at Peter and said, 'But Jesus was God … and God is God … and the Holy Spirit is God … but now you're saying that we are God. I'm more fecking confused than I've ever been.'

This was one of the few occasions that Peter had a chance to sell his views on Christianity. But these views had been developed through years of active involvement in the Church. He now realised that it was asking a bit much for his friends to fully comprehend them in one evening over a few ales. So, he put his arm around Paul and said, 'All you need to know is that we were always God and that is what Jesus was trying to tell us all. So, in that respect, his resurrection was not about how one man conquered death. It is about how the things that man stood for live on in us two thousand years later.'

Paul just stared blankly back at Peter, looking more confused than ever.

Niall shook his head. 'You amaze me Macca. How do you come up with all this stuff? Are you studying theology part time or something?'

'No,' said Peter smiling, 'it's just that you don't spend the best part of your adult life working in the Church without picking up a thing or two.'

'Ok but tell me this: why do your views seem to be so different from those of Cardinal Doherty?'

'Quite simply, I think that Doherty, and most of the Vatican hierarchy have lost the plot.'

'That's a big call for a layman to make!'

'Well, put it this way: Everything I've learnt about Christianity and the Catholic Church has come from priests like Fr Mick and other people trained in Catholic theology. So, I think I've had a pretty good grounding in what it truly means to be a Catholic Christian.'

'And the hierarchy?'

'They're mainly politicians. All they care about is power and control. They want a Church where everyone believes what they're told to believe, and the Roman Curia controls the hearts and minds of all the Catholics in the world.'

'You've really got this sorted, haven't you Macca? If I had anything to do with it I'd make you the next Pope,' said Niall.

'Hang on Niall,' said Paul, 'Macca can't be Pope. He's not a cardinal!'

'No, I heard the other day on the radio,' Niall insisted, 'the Pope does not have to be a cardinal, so that means that any Catholic male can become Pope.'

'Even if that is true,' replied Paul sceptically, 'it's only the cardinals who can elect a Pope. So, what are the odds that they'd elect someone from outside their own circle?'

'I'd say about ten billion to one,' responded Niall before rising to his feet and clearing his throat to get the attention of the others at the table. 'Raise your glasses, boys, and have a drink to our next Pope, Macca the first. He may be about to lose his goolies, but he's still got the balls to stick it up the Vatican.'

How not to discuss Papal succession

It was the Sunday after the papal funeral and only four days until the start of the Conclave. All the cardinals were now in Rome but the Conclave was put off until Thursday to allow one of the preferred contenders, Cardinal Enzo Mangiafuoco from Messina, a couple more days to recover from surgery for gall stones.

Many of the cardinals had gathered in the various colleges that had a presence in Rome. In the lounge of the Jesuit College, Cardinal Luigi Pancetti of Milan was sharing a brandy with one of his good friends, Irish cardinal Patrick O'Faherty. 'You would not believe it Paddy; I dream the other night that the new Papa was Irish!' Pancetti said.

'Is that so, Louie,' responded O'Faherty. 'I had a similar dream myself, you know. But alas, it wasn't me.'

'I thought that the man in my dream could have been a younger version of you. He had bright blue eyes like you, but his hair was not white but dark.'

This intrigued O'Faherty, who had also dreamt of a young Pope with similar characteristics. His mind wandered to his dream of only two nights before. He was not one to vividly remember dreams normally, but this one was hard to forget.

He was playing golf, but not at his usual golf course. He was at the home of golf, St Andrews in Scotland, and he was competing in the British Open! His opponents were the best in the business: Tiger Woods, Nick Ogilvy and Greg Norman.

To his amazement, he actually won the tournament! This was despite playing the whole course with a seven iron and a putter! He was a bit perturbed when he first noticed that these were the only clubs that his caddy had brought to the match, but after winning hole after hole with only those two clubs, he stopped questioning his caddy and thought him to be a golf-angel whom the Lord had sent to lead him to victory.

It was at the end of his dream that he knew for certain that the Lord was on his side, as his caddy turned out to be the new Holy Father!

When he woke from his dream, the initial surprise at this revelation was quickly replaced with puzzlement. He knew immediately that this young Pope, with an Irish accent, dark hair and deep blue eyes, was not a cardinal, but he had a vague recollection that he had met this man before. He was not a bishop – he knew all the Irish bishops. A priest perhaps? With the declining number of ordinations over the past few decades, there were only a couple of dozen Irish priests at most in their early forties and he couldn't place him among them either.

He pondered this for the best part of a day before deciding to take an evening stroll to clear his head. He always enjoyed his walks through Rome and his hotel was only a short distance from many of the city's famous sites. On this particular evening he found himself wandering along the Via dei Due Macelli towards the Piazza di Spagna. Although it was only early spring, the weather was much more pleasant than in

Limerick, where he was based. There was no need for an overcoat, and he was more than comfortable walking around in his basic robes.

The evening was when this part of Rome really came alive. The boutique stores had just re-opened following the afternoon siesta, so local shoppers mingled with the throngs of tourists heading towards the famous Trinità Dei Monti which climbed away from the piazza.

Papal election time was a very exciting time in Rome; locals and tourists alike were honoured to make contact with so many cardinals. As he walked along many people greeted him cheerfully. 'Buona Sera Eminence,' they would say. 'Bon Fortuna,' some would add, referring to his chances in the papal election. Some of the cheekier ones called out in jest as he walked past, 'Viva il nuovo Papa.'

He was spotted by one such group of boisterous young people as he walked in front of a popular fast food restaurant. 'Habemus Papam!' they called out as he approached. Then one of them knelt as the side of the path, put his hands together as if in prayer, looked up to him and said, 'Benedice me Santa Papa.'

O'Faherty was more than happy to oblige. He stopped in front of the youth, placed his left hand on his head and gave him a slight but sharp slap on the face, as bishops do during the sacrament of confirmation. 'Bless you my son,' he said with a wry smile, before continuing on his way. The youth's companions laughed and cheered as the cardinal walked away. Without looking back, he raised his hand to acknowledge their cheers.

The youth he had blessed then called out, 'Gratzie Santa Papa! Addesso voulio diventare un Prete. I now want to be a priest,' he repeated in English.

O'Faherty always enjoyed positive encounters with young people and was never a stickler for protocol. It was nice to be treated like a normal human being for a change as well. But this encounter triggered something else in him … something to do with the man in his dream.

He turned to look back to the fast food restaurant where the youths were gathered. He smiled and gave a gracious wave as the youths called out to him again, 'Viva il nuovo Papa!'

But his eyes were drawn to the golden arches sign above their heads. What could McDonald's have to do with his dream?

He pondered the question a little longer … McDonald's … McDonald's … he repeated the name to himself over and over until it struck him. MacDonald … that was the name of the man in his dream! But how did he know this MacDonald? He racked his brain again … Yes, he remembered a diocesan meeting in Dublin a couple of years ago. This MacDonald was a member of the diocesan pastoral council for the Dublin archdiocese.

He'd been particularly vocal on the topic of retaining the Third Rite of Reconciliation, where Catholics could confess their sins in a communal service, as a valid alternative to individual confessions. His argument was that people didn't need absolution from a priest alone but needed to present themselves as a sinner (albeit quietly) and gain absolution from the wider faith community.

This was a position Cardinal O'Faherty heartily agreed with. He was one of the main champions of Vatican II in his day and it was his fervent belief that the true Church was represented by the community of the faithful and not the clergy and hierarchy.

He also remembered that he had corresponded with this MacDonald fellow more recently. Yes … he now recalled that his first name was Peter. It was Peter MacDonald who had written to him to report on his dismay on the way his parish had been treated in the wake of the sudden, and somewhat forced, retirement of his parish priest Mick Finlay.

Mick had been in the seminary with him and was still a very good friend. O'Faherty wished he could have done more for him at the time, but all that he could do was provide a few meagre words of support in his reply to Peter's letter. How strange was it that this man would appear to him as Pope in his dream?

His thoughts were broken by Cardinal Pancetti nudging him out of his daydream. 'Dark hair and blue eyes y'say,' said O'Faherty. 'That's very peculiar. Because the man in my dream had similar features. And he was definitely Irish?'

'Most definitely!'

'How old do you think he was?'

Pancetti pondered the question before answering, 'Bo! Non l'so. Quaranta-tre, quatro, about forty-three or forty-four.'

'Did you recognise this man? Did he seem familiar to you?'

'I've met a lot of men in my years, so I couldn't tell for certain that I hadn't seen him before. But he didn't seem to be someone I knew. Infactamente, when the dream led me to think about an Irish Pope, all I could think about was you, my friend.'

'Well, that's very flattering,' O'Faherty replied, laughing. 'But you and I know that is never going to happen. But getting back to the man in your dream. When you say his hair was dark, was it dark brown or more black?'

'Oh, no no no, nero come l'notte, as black as coal as you would say.'

'Extremely peculiar,' said O'Faherty, more intrigued than ever.

'You seem very puzzled by this, Paddy. What are you thinking?'

O'Faherty thought a bit more before responding. 'Well, you see the man in your dream seems very similar to the man in my dream. The only difference is that I think I know who the man in my dream is.'

Strange coincidences

Cardinal Enrico Curiosa from the USA was born into an Italian immigrant family and raised in the state of New Jersey. He was always good for a joke and often added one to the end of his sermons. Had life taken him on a different path, he could easily have fit into the role of a late night show host, such was his personality and charisma. But Curiosa had instead used his charm and personality to further the word of God. The combination of his knowledge of the scriptures and his ability to communicate this knowledge to people at all levels made him one of the USA's most respected theologians.

Curiosa was only a young man at the start of the Second Vatican Council, but his academic prowess and superior communication skills proved invaluable, and he served as a chief advisor throughout the proceedings. As with many young priests of his era, he believed that Vatican II signified a positive renaissance for the Church – he still considered his contribution to the council as one of his major life achievements.

In recognition of his contribution to Vatican II, in the late 1970s, when he was still in his 30s, he was ordained a bishop and it was only seven years later that he was promoted to cardinal.

Now he was seventy-nine years of age, and this would be his last opportunity to attend a Conclave. He was determined to make the most of it.

The gradual and persistent winding back of some of the Vatican II reforms in the last couple of decades had been depressing for him. As a respected theologian and essentially one of the authors of the finished document, he took it upon himself to inform the Roman Curia on the error of their ways. His mistake of publicly voicing his concerns resulted in him being ostracised from having any real authority within the American branch of the Church.

However, following the election of his good friend Federico Bontempi as Pope nine years ago, he had returned to the fold and was slowly making some headway in promoting true reforms. But now Frederico was gone, and the conservatives were positioning themselves to have a stranglehold on the Church once again.

When in Rome, Curiosa frequently visited the Jesuit College. On this occasion, with the Conclave about to commence, he was certain that some of his old colleagues would be there.

When he arrived at the college, he was not surprised to find his old friends Luigi Pancetti and Patrick O'Faherty conversing in the lounge room. Noticing that O'Faherty and Pancetti were both hunched over and talking in whispers, he considered standing back so as not to intrude on their conversation, but his curiosity got the better of him. *They must know something pretty interesting,* he thought. He had to find out what it was.

He sat down heavily in a vacant armchair next to Pancetti, 'What's news, fellas?' he asked.

Startled, Pancetti sat upright in his chair, but smiled with relief when he saw that it was Curiosa who had intruded on them. 'Buona sera Ricky,' he said, 'I was just telling Paddy that I dream the next Pope is Irish.'

'You don't say!' replied Curiosa. 'You could be on to something there Louie. I had a dream where I met the new Pope, and guess what! In my dream he was Irish as well!'

Pancetti and O'Faherty were staring at him with their mouths agape. He thought this to be a little odd but resolved to interpret their slack-jawed silence as an invitation to describe his dream. He thought it was a great dream, so he had no qualms about sharing it with them.

'I was at the Comedy Club in New York doing a stand-up routine,' he said, 'the audience roaring with laughter. Everyone who was anyone in New York was there. But towards the back of the room I could see a fellow in white robes. It was totally unbelievable! The Pope himself had come to see my act!'

Curiosa loved the opportunity to tell funny stories, and the way that both Pancetti and O'Faherty were staring at him made him think that they were lapping it up.

'I launched into my grand finale, which was the story of when I was a young priest in Jersey and I had to say morning mass. Outside the church there was this fellow named Dominic. This poor fellow was a homeless bum, but he hated to take charity and if you offered him anything, he always insisted on doing something in return. On this particular morning I thought I'd beat him to the punch. "Good Morning Dominic," I said, "Morning, Father," he replied.

'Then I said, "Dominic, I really need your help today. I'm about to say Mass this morning but I don't have anyone who can take up a collection. Can you come in and do it for me?"

'"I don't know Father,' he replied. 'You know I don't go into mass that often. I wouldn't know when to pass the plate around."

'"Don't worry!" I assured him, "I'll give you a signal when it's time."

'So, Dominic comes into the Church with me and takes a seat at the back with the collection plate at the ready. Mass starts and we're just getting into the Gospel reading, but this is back when we were still saying mass in Latin of course. So, I put my arms in the air and say, "Dominus vobiscum." Shortly after I notice that Dominic is taking up the collection when I hadn't yet given him the signal.

'After mass, Dominic hands me the plate and I thank him, saying, "You did a great job Dominic, but why did you start the collection before I gave the signal?"

'"I thought you did!" replied Dominic.

'"No, I didn't!" said I.

'"Yes you did!" insisted Dominic. "You put your arms in the air and said: Dominic, go frisk em! So I did."'

Having delivered what he thought was a brilliant punch-line, Curiosa expected that his friends would be rolling around in laughter. But instead, all he got was more blank stares.

Pancetti broke the silence, 'Ricky my friend,' he said nervously, 'you say before, in your dream you meet the Papa!'

'Oh yeah!' replied Curiosa.

Pancetti was almost too afraid to ask. '… And what did he look like?'

'Well, I couldn't make out his face at first. But after I finished my joke, everyone stood up … clapping and laughing!' He paused to emphasise how he expected his friends to react to his joke. 'I then saw that the Holy Father was walking towards me. He had his hand outstretched, so I immediately went down on my knees in order to kiss the papal ring. Then he says to me,' Curiosa put on his best Irish accent, '"Well done Ricky, I'm sure even the angels in Heaven had a good chuckle at that one." The Irish accent took me by surprise to so I look up to find out who this fella is, and I must say the face I saw was certainly not a face that I was expecting to see in papal robes.'

Curiosa was totally taken aback when Pancetti then shook his arms in the air and shouted: 'Yes Ricky, but what did he look like? Did you recognise him?'

The volume of Pancetti's cries caught the attention of a pair of young priests who were sitting at the other end of the lounge. They were both now looking at the cardinals to see what the fuss was about. Curiosa gave them a nervous wave and then tried to calm Pancetti. 'Easy there Louie,' he whispered, 'it was only a dream. What does it matter what he looked like?'

Pancetti's face was red with embarrassment after his outburst and he took a handkerchief from his pocket to wipe the sweat from his brow before responding in a much softer voice, 'Maybe it not matter, but I just want to know.'

'Well okay then,' Curiosa replied, 'for starters, he was really young. I mean he couldn't have been much over forty!'

O'Faherty and Pancetti looked at each other before returning their attention to Curiosa. O'Faherty then asked him, 'Now, think very carefully Ricky, did he have any distinguishing features?'

'Well, come to think of it. A couple of his features did stand out to me, but they shouldn't matter, it was only a dream!'

'It may not matter at all,' O'Faherty replied, 'but we would really like to know.'

'Okay, but you're both starting to freak me out a bit here.'

'Just humour us, please.'

'Well, he certainly didn't have any grey hairs because I distinctly remember noticing his thick jet black hair … and then there were his eyes. They were the brightest of …'

'… Bright blue!' O'Faherty and Pancetti said in unison.

'How … did you know that?' Curiosa stammered.

Pancetti then put his hand on Curiosa's. 'Well Ricky,' he said, 'you know I also dream of the new Papa. Well, in my dream he also is young, he also is Irish, and he also has black hair and blue eyes!'

Curiosa sat back in his chair, 'Wow!' he said. 'How curious.'

'It gets even more curious,' added O'Faherty. 'You see I also had a dream where I met the new Pope and guess what?'

'Was he Irish?'

'Yes.'

'Was he young?'

'Yes.'

'Did he have black hair and blue eyes?'

'Yes and yes.'

Curiosa was almost speechless. 'That is ab-sol-utely incredible!' he stammered. 'It's not possible! Could we have seen the same person in our dreams?'

'Well it is more curiosa, Curiosa,' said a now grinning Pancetti. 'You see, me and you, we cannot say we know the man in our dream. But Paddy …' Pancetti turned to place his hand on O'Faherty's shoulder, '… he say that he know the man in his dream.'

'Well, we're still not sure it is the same person,' O'Faherty cautioned, 'but I am ninety-nine percent sure that the man in my dream is a Dubliner named Peter MacDonald.'

'McDonald! Like the burger place? Isn't that a Scottish name?' asks Curiosa.

'No not like the burger place! It's the Irish MacDonald with an A in the Mac bit!'

'Like in Big Mac?'

'No! … Okay yes, like in Big Mac. Anyway, I've met this fellow Peter MacDonald on a couple of occasions. His former parish priest Mick Finlay is a good friend of mine.'

'Sensational!' Curiosa exclaimed. After a short pause he says, 'Hang on, you said his former parish priest is a friend of yours.'

'That's right,' O'Faherty assured.

'But this MacDonald fella is a bishop or something, right?'

'Well no. He's not even a priest. I'm pretty sure he's married with a family.'

This fact stunned both Pancetti and Curiosa. Pancetti turned back to O'Faherty and cried out, 'He is no a priest!' Pancetti's voice was again loud enough to attract the attention of the young priests on the other side of the room. He ignored their attention and moderated his voice to almost a whisper. 'You say the pope in your dream is a layman!'

'Yes,' O'Faherty replied.

'Santa Madonna!' Pancetti crossed himself.

Curiosa couldn't believe what he was hearing. Not only did they all dream of a pope with remarkably similar features, but it was also now possible that the man they all envisioned was in fact a lay Catholic. The ramifications of this were phenomenal. A lay Pope! His initial curiosity soon turned to fear. 'Now Paddy,' he said, 'before we go any further, can you tell me if this MacDonald fella is a white hat or a black hat?'

This question confused Pancetti. 'What difference make the colour of his hat?'

'It's a reference to the old cowboy movies Louie. In those movies, the good guys always wore white hats, and the bad guys always wore black hats.'

O'Faherty said, 'Oh, most definitely a white hat. In fact, he even had the guts to stand up to Doherty on the issue of maintaining the Third Rite of Reconciliation as a valid form of the Sacrament of Confession. He didn't get anywhere but I was impressed by his efforts.'

'Fantastic! Have you got a picture of him?'

'No, we only just discovered this coincidence a few minutes ago! But I guess I could call Mick in Dublin and he could post me one.'

'Too slow!' Curiosa thought about it a bit. 'Tell you what, why don't you Google him.'

'Do what to him?' was O'Faherty's stunned reply.

'You know, look him up on the internet. You've got a cell phone haven't you?'

'I have a phone,' O'Faherty said as he pulled a ten-year-old Nokia handset out of his cassock pocket. 'But I have never come to grips with this Internet nonsense! It takes all my technical knowhow to remember how to make a call with it.'

'No matter, we'll use my iPad.' Curiosa reached into his briefcase and extracted a leather folder which to O'Faherty's surprise opened to reveal a computer screen. He spoke out loud as his fingers tapped the screen. 'Let's see what we have here. Peter MacDonald. Seems to be a very common name. Let me add "Dublin Diocese" to the search and BINGO! Here we go, there's a link to the Diocesan Pastoral Council. There are photos … Oh my God!'

'What is it Ricky?' a nervous Pancetti asked. 'Show me what you found.'

Curiosa still could not speak. Slowly he turned the screen to face O'Faherty and Pancetti.

'Santa Maria!' gasped Pancetti, 'e lui, e lui! it's him! He is the one in my dream!'

Yet again Pancetti's outburst caught the attention of the young priests at the other end of the room, who now got up to leave.

A still shocked Curiosa finally managed to splutter out the words, 'He's the man in my dream as well. I'm sure of it!'

As the young priests left the room, they politely acknowledged another cardinal who was entering the lounge. The other three cardinals were still staring at the screen in stunned silence. They didn't notice that Cardinal Paul Billingham had entered the room until he was standing right behind them.

'What are we looking at, gents?' Billingham asked, startling his colleagues in the process. Not waiting for a response, Billingham looked at the screen himself: 'Hey, that looks just like a fellow I saw in a dream I had the other night. Funny thing is, in my dream, he was the new Pope.' His smile quickly faded when he noticed the stunned expression on each of his three friends' faces. 'Something is obviously up … you're all looking at me like stunned mullets! Anyone care to let me in on what's going on?'

Without changing his expression, Curiosa addressed Billingham in a subdued tone. 'Take a seat Paul … you may be in for a little shock.'

Curiosa passed the iPad to Billingham for him to have a closer look. 'Okay Paul, when you say you saw a fellow who looked like this in your dream, how close do you think the resemblance is?'

Billingham moved towards the remaining free armchair between Curiosa and O'Faherty, and looked closely at the photograph of Peter MacDonald. 'I'm not normally good at remembering dreams but I'd have to say in this case, those blue eyes and black hair look strangely familiar. I can't say for sure … it was only a dream, after all. But if this is not the man in my dream then I dreamt of someone who looked very similar to him. Who is he?'

'We'll get to that in a minute, but first you should know that the three of us have also had dreams where the new Pope has appeared to us. I knew it would be impossible for us to have all dreamt of the same person, but we decided to see if we could find a photo of him on the internet anyway. The picture you're looking at is the result of our web search.' Curiosa tapped the tablet screen. 'This man is the man that Paddy saw as Pope in his dream. Furthermore, I am certain, and Louie is also certain, that this same man appeared to us the new pope in our dreams.'

'Oh my God!' Billingham exclaimed. 'This is a miracle! An honest to God miracle!'

He lifted his head to look at O'Faherty. 'Who is he, Paddy?'

'His name is Peter MacDonald.'

'He's Irish then?'

'Yes.'

'He's not a bishop, I think I know all of the Irish bishops. Is he a priest?'

'No, he's not a priest. In fact, I'm pretty sure he's married with children.'

'What? Married … a layman!'

O'Faherty nodded to each of Billingham's remarks.

Billingham put his hands on his head and leant back in his chair. 'I'm flabbergasted,' he said, 'what could this mean? What do you think we should do, Ricky?'

'I'm just as stunned as you. I always say that God works in mysterious ways, but I never expected anything like this.'

Pancetti took the iPad from Billingham to have another look at Peter's face. 'All four of us dreamt of this man as pope. Who else could have had this dream?'

All four sat in stunned silence for a while. Curiosa's mind was spinning. Surely this man was not destined to be pope! Canon law allowed for any Catholic male to become pope with the proviso that they be in communion with the Holy See. So, it wasn't impossible. Infinitely improbable perhaps, but not impossible. But the world wasn't ready for a lay Pope and the Church would never accept a lay Pope. Furthermore, this particular layman is a religious progressive. *Great way to rock the apple cart,* he thought. To put a layman forward for the papacy was one thing, but a progressive layman? No way Jose! So, if he was to be presented to the Curia they would have to hide his politics and present him as a traditional and loyal Catholic …

Wait! What was he thinking? Present him to the Curia? Present him as … what? He could imagine the way the conversation would go: *Well chaps, we've had this dream where this fellow appeared to us as Pope. So, we think you should all give him the job. Oh, and by the way, he's only in his forties, is married with children and will most likely change the whole fabric of our existence …* Surely the Curia would respond saying: *Oh well, if you card-carrying progressives had this dream then we've got to go along with you. When can he start? …* Not bloody likely!

But what was God trying to tell them? If it is not that we should have a lay pope, it could be that this layman has been sent to influence their decision. So, they certainly couldn't go into the Conclave without at least meeting him.

Billingham broke the silence. 'Paddy, you said that this fellow's parish priest was a friend of yours.'

'Former parish priest,' O'Faherty responded.

'Whatever, but can you get in touch with him? I think we should bring him to Rome.'

'Surely you're not suggesting that we put him forward as Pope?'

'Don't be ridiculous! We'll be laughed out of the Vatican. I just think that the fact that all four of us saw him in our dream must mean something. So, I think we should at least meet with him before we go into the Conclave.'

'I agree wholeheartedly,' Curiosa added, 'We can't let this amazing revelation pass and do nothing. We must act in some way and meeting with him seems the least we can do.'

Pancetti chimed in. 'Da cordo, I also agree, let's meet with him.'

'Okay, I'll call my secretary in the morning,' said O'Faherty, 'but what exactly are we going to tell him? I mean, Mick Finlay is a very good friend of mine, but even he will think that I am finally losing my mind if I tell him that we need Peter MacDonald here because we dreamt that he was the next Pope!'

'Yes that could present a problem,' Billingham agreed. 'He will require some sort of explanation. It is a highly unusual request.'

'We could say he could come see the inauguratzione papale,' Pancetti volunteered.

'That might work,' Curiosa replied, 'but we need him here tomorrow, not next week!' Curiosa thought a little longer. 'Paddy, you said he was on the diocesan council?'

'Yes, but he's in Doherty's diocese, not mine.'

'No matter, we could tell him that all the cardinals have been asked to select a layperson from their country to present their views on the Church before the start of the Conclave.'

'But why would I choose him ahead of someone from my own diocese?'

'Just tell him what you told us. That you were impressed at how he represented his community when you met him last.'

'That might just work,' added Billingham, 'but what happens if he tells his family and friends, and word gets out to the media? The Curia will suppress the story within seconds!'

'We'll tell him that it is highly secretive, and the Curia doesn't want to let on that it needs to consult with the laity.'

'Fantastico,' said Pancetti, 'he should not suspect if he think the Curia not want anyone to know about it. Infactamente, it would make him more interested in coming.'

'Okay, I'll give it a go,' O'Faherty replied, 'but I'm not making any promises.'

'Just tell your friend that we need him here by Tuesday morning. Tomorrow would be better.'

The following morning, O'Faherty woke at 6 am as usual. He thought of calling his secretary right away but stopped himself when he realised that it was only 5 am in Ireland.

He had breakfast delivered to his room and then spent some time reading up on the biographies of all eligible cardinals that had been provided by the Vatican prior to the Conclave. He noted that his own official Vatican biography included explicit detail of his role in reforming the Church after Vatican II. Although his biographers did not criticise him in any way, their phrasing was such that anyone who wanted to return a conservative balance to the Church would be left in no doubt that he was a potential troublemaker. But he'd gotten off lightly compared with his friend Curiosa, whose biographers described as modern, innovative, and courageous. These were definitely not the qualities that the conservative majority of cardinals wanted their next pope to have. In contrast, the cardinals favoured to take out the papacy were described as pious, traditional, and trustworthy.

O'Faherty kept checking his watch to see if it was late enough in the morning to call his secretary and as soon as he saw it was 9 am he made the call. She was able to provide him with Michael Finlay's phone number. He noted it down and then proceeded to explain that she may need to organise flights for someone to join him in Rome ASAP. As she frequently booked flights between Dublin and Rome, she was able to provide him with some indicative flight times before he ended the call.

Fr Mick had just sat down to breakfast in his small council flat when the phone rang. He pushed his chair away from the table in frustration so that he could stand and walk over to the kitchen bench where the phone was located. 'Hello?' he said as he picked up the receiver.

'Would that be you Mick?' said the voice on the other end of the phone.

Fr Mick was a bit perturbed by the frankness of his caller, 'Yes this is Father Michael Finlay here, who are you?'

'It's Paddy O'Faherty here.'

Fr Mick's mood lifted. 'Paddy,' he said enthusiastically, 'what are you doing calling me at this hour? Haven't you got a Conclave to attend or something?'

'I need you to do something for me, Mick. But before I get to that, how are you going? Still keeping that cancer at bay?'

'The situation is desperate but not serious, so I'm okay. How are you keeping? What's your handicap nowadays?'

'Oh, I still can't get much under fifteen and you know how it is, it's hard to improve as age gets the better of us.'

'Speak for yourself! I'm playing off nine at the moment. I have to thank Cardinal Doherty for making me retire. It's done wonders for my golf game.'

'Perhaps that's something I can look forward to in the near future.'

'Not confident in getting the top job then?'

'Very funny Mick! The day they make me Pope is the day hell will freeze over. But listen, as I said, I have a favour to ask.'

'What will it cost me?' a suspicious Fr Mick asked.

'It's nothing like that,' O'Faherty replied. 'You know that fellow from your parish who spoke for you at that Diocesan meeting a couple of years ago, the one who was on the Diocesan Council?'

'Peter MacDonald!' a surprised Fr Mick exclaimed. 'What about him?'

'Well, this is going to sound a little unusual but … I need him to come to Rome.'

O'Faherty went on to explain his request to an incredulous Fr Mick before ending the call with a request that Peter take an 8.00 pm flight to Rome that very evening. Fr Mick was very suspicious of O'Faherty's motives. The Roman Curia consulting with the laity in the days before a Papal Conclave was inconceivable. But he and O'Faherty had been great friends since their days in the seminary. O'Faherty was not one to take risks where offending the Curia was concerned, so what he was asking must be above board – however unusual.

As it was just after 8.30 am Fr Mick knew that Peter, as manager of his local council's planning department, should already be at his council office. He dialled Peter's personal line, but the call was automatically diverted and answered by one of the council's customer service officers. 'County Kildare Council, Bridget speaking.'

'Err hello Bridget,' said Fr Mick hesitantly, 'I was wanting to speak to Peter MacDonald please.'

'I'm sorry sir, but Mr MacDonald will be out of the office for the next couple of days. Can someone else in the Town Planning Department be of assistance?'

'No, I need to speak with him personally. I have his cell phone number; I'll try to catch him on that.'

He ended the call and dialled Peter's cell phone, but the call was immediately diverted to messagebank. He hung up and dialled Peter and Mary's home number. He heard the phone ring a few times before the answering service cut in. It seemed that Peter didn't want to be contacted today. He hung up without leaving a message.

He called Peter's cell phone once again and left a message: 'Peter, when you get this message can you give me a call please. It's Fr Mick here. You know the number.' Hopefully, Peter would get his message and call him back that afternoon.

Just a small snip for mankind

The day for Peter's vasectomy had arrived and Peter was more than a little nervous. He had been blessed with good health all his life and had never spent a day in hospital. Not that his vasectomy would result in a hospital stay; he wasn't even going to have a general anaesthetic. The procedure would be done under local anaesthetic in the specialist's surgery and he would be in and out within a few hours.

Mary, on the way to taking the children to school, dropped him off at Dr Wallace's vasectomy clinic promptly at 8 am. She and Suzanne would be back in a couple of hours to pick him up.

'Why is Daddy going to the doctor?' a curious Patrick asked.

'Daddy is just going to the dentist for a couple of fillings. He'll be home when you get back from school,' Mary advised them.

It was convenient that the medical complex where Dr Wallace had his surgery also housed many other practitioners including their family dentist.

'Oh,' said an excited Connor, 'then you can play football with us.'

This caught Peter off-guard; he knew the vasectomy operation was not overly debilitating but a game of football would be out of the question for the rest of the week. 'Um … Daddy often doesn't feel well after going to the dentist, so I don't think I'll be able to play today. Maybe on Friday?'

'Friday, that's ages away!' protested Patrick.

Mary brought the argument to an abrupt end. 'Daddy will let you know when he is feeling better, and you can play then. Okay boys?'

Peter kissed Mary goodbye and walked into the medical centre on his own.

The medical centre consisted of a large open foyer with a small general reception desk directly opposite the entry doors. A pharmacy was sited immediately to the left of the entrance and a cafe to the right. Beyond the desk were the general practitioners' rooms, and the entrances to separate medical wings – dental on the right, specialist rooms on the left.

To access the specialist rooms Peter had to walk diagonally across the foyer, which was already about one third full with patients. Although the word about his vasectomy was definitely out, he was pleased that he managed to get to the specialists' wing without being seen by anyone he knew.

Alas, any pretext of anonymity was lost once he entered Dr Wallace's rooms to be greeted by the familiar face of Denise O'Malley. Denise was one of his fellow members on the Parish Pastoral Council. 'Hello Peter, I thought it was you on the appointment list today.'

'Hi Denise, I didn't know you worked here,' Peter nervously replied.

'Yes, I normally work in the afternoons but Bridget Flanagan, who works mornings, is on holidays this week, so I've taken on her morning shift.' Sensing that Peter was more than a little nervous, she added, 'Now there's no need to worry, I've seen plenty of men from the parish come through Dr Wallace's rooms. I'm not one to gossip about the coming and goings at the doctor's surgery, so you just sit yourself down and the nurse will be with you shortly.'

Denise's words did little to settle his nerves, but he sat himself down as requested and picked up a magazine at random from one of the side tables. He was almost halfway through reading an article when he realised that he was in fact reading a two-year-old copy of *Cosmopolitan*! He quickly threw the magazine back on the table and rummaged through the pile for a magazine that was more appropriate reading for a middle-aged man about to have a vasectomy. He settled on a recent copy of *Time* magazine.

He soon lost himself in an article on the Greek economy and was up to the last paragraph when he noticed a young man dressed in white approaching him. 'Ah, Mr MacDonald, I thought it was you!' Peter was perplexed by the young man's familiarity; the young man sensed Peter's dilemma and added, 'I'm Brendan O'Connor, you work with my dad David at the council.'

'Young Brendan!' he exclaimed. 'Well you certainly have changed since I last saw you. What are you doing with yourself?'

'I've been at university studying nursing. I'm doing a six-week placement with Dr Wallace, and I'll be assisting him with your procedure today.'

'Great …' was Peter's subdued reply.

'Now, no need to worry Mr MacDonald, patient-doctor confidentiality extends to nurses as well and I won't even tell my dad that I saw you here. Now come with me and I'll get you prepped up.'

Brendan took Peter across the hall and into the surgery theatre. They went through a separate door out of the surgery into a small examination room, where Brendan handed Peter a plastic laundry basket. 'Now I need you to get your kit off and put your clothes into this basket.'

'Everything … or just the bottom half?' Peter enquired.

'Everything I'm afraid,' Brendan replied as he pulled a surgical gown out from a drawer beneath the examination bed, 'and when you're done you can put on this gown. I'll be in to check on you in a few minutes.'

Peter was in the process of removing one jean leg when he noticed Brendan looking back at him with a concerned expression on his face.

'You haven't brought a change of underwear with you by any chance?' Brendan asked.

'No, I didn't think that it was necessary,'

'Well, it normally isn't but you may find you need something a bit more supportive than those boxers after the procedure.'

'I thought that it would be better having something loose-fitting.'

'Well I can't speak from experience but I'm reliably informed that it is best to wear something that keeps things firmly in place immediately after the vasectomy, if you know what I mean. Never mind, I'll see if I can dig something up for you.'

With that remark Brendan left a worried Peter to remove the rest of his clothes and put on the hospital gown. He was fiddling with the ties at the back of the gown when there was a knock at the door and a different man's voice enquired, 'Are you decent?' Without waiting for a response this man entered the room. 'Peter MacDonald!' he exclaimed, 'fancy seeing you here.'

Peter was dismayed to see the face of Dermott O'Grady looking directly at him. Dermott was the husband of Peter's first cousin Bernadette. 'Hello Dermott,' was Peter's worried reply. 'What are you doing here?'

'I'm going to administer your anaesthetic today.'

'Great …' sighed Peter as he extended his hand.

Dermott grabbed Peter's hand and shook it enthusiastically while squeezing Peter's right shoulder with his left hand. 'Must be years since we caught up with you! How are Mary and the children doing?' he asked.

Peter was definitely not in the mood for conversation but knew that it would be impolite not to reply. 'Just fine thanks,' he said. Then after a short pause he asked, 'How's Bernie and your brood?'

'They're just grand,' replied Dermott, who hadn't yet released his grip from the handshake. Instead, he drew Peter towards him and added in a softer voice. 'Now I know this must be a bit awkward for you Peter, but you needn't worry about a thing. I'll not even tell Bernie that I saw you here.'

'I'd appreciate that Dermott, thank you,' Peter replied.

'No problem,' said Dermott as he released his grip and slapped Peter on the back. 'Mind you, if I did say something to Bernie she'd be saying it was about time you and Mary put a lid on things. We have trouble managing a pair of children, I don't know how you manage with … how many is it exactly?'

'Six … and we manage quite well thank you,' was Peter's terse reply.

'Well, good on you Peter,' said Dermott as he shook Peter by the shoulder again. Dermott then released his grip and slapped his hands together. 'Now, I'd better let you in on what you'll be going through this morning. Take a seat,' he said.

The only thing available for Peter to sit on was the examination bed. So, he sat himself up on that.

'I'll be injecting a local anaesthetic into your groin area which will prevent you from feeling any pain when Dr Wallace makes his incisions,' said Dermott before again putting his hand on Peter's shoulder. 'Now don't you worry, before the surgeon does anything, I'll check to make sure that the drugs have kicked in.' He released his grip and added, 'The anaesthetic should only last a couple of hours or so. After that you may feel some discomfort. Dr Wallace will prescribe some painkillers that will get you through the next couple of days. Any problems, just give Dr Wallace a call and he'll sort you out. Any questions?'

'No, I think I've got the gist of it, thanks Dermott.'

'Anytime,' said Dermott as he shook Peter's hand again. 'Say hello to Mary for me and I'll see you in the room across the way in a few minutes.'

Dermott left the room and a relieved Peter was on his own again. He began to wonder how many more acquaintances would intrude on what was a very private and personal event.

Thankfully, the next person to enter the room was young Brendan. 'How did you get on?' he asked. Not waiting for a reply, he handed him a pair of disposable underpants. 'I've brought you these to put on afterwards – they should be a bit more supportive than your boxers.'

Peter couldn't see how this paper-thin garment could provide any support whatsoever, but he thanked Brendan and put it into the basket with the rest of his clothes.

'Dr Wallace will be ready for you shortly. Now have you had a shave this morning?'

Peter felt his face. 'Yes I shave every morning.'

'No, not your face,' said Brendan as he stifled a laugh, 'I meant your nether regions!'

'No one said anything to me about having to shave down there!' an indignant Peter replied.

'It's no big deal, most lads get away without it, just so long as you're not overly hairy. Do you mind if I have a look?'

Peter recoiled at the thought of exposing himself to the young son of a work colleague and friend. But reconciled by the fact that young Brendan would be observing the procedure anyway, he begrudgingly consented. Peter was still sitting up on the examination bed, so Brendan asked him to lift his hospital gown and proceeded to examine his scrotum.

'Yes, I think you'll get away with it,' he remarked, 'if any pubic hairs get in the way, Dr Wallace should be able to remove them before he makes his incision.'

✝

A couple of blocks away, Fr Michael Finlay was rushing into the grounds of the parish primary. He'd decided that rather than waiting for Peter to call him back, he would see if one of his children might know of his whereabouts. He entered the school grounds just as morning assembly had finished and the children were walking into their individual classrooms. He had missed Mary, but while scanning the moving lines of a group of first graders, two identical heads of thick black hair stood out in the group of twenty to thirty odd students, most of whom were blond or ginger. *That must be the twins*, he thought as he quickly set off after them. He managed to reach them just as they were entering their classroom.

Their teacher was Lorna O'Day and she knew Fr Mick quite well. 'Good morning Father,' Lorna said as he approached. 'How are you today?'

Not used to vigorous exercise, he was panting heavily by the time he got there. Fr Mick paused to catch his breath before responding. 'Good morning Lorna,' he said between breaths, 'I was wondering if I could have a quick word with the MacDonald boys?'

'Sure you can,' she said as she led Fr Mick into the classroom. 'Good morning class,' she said.

'Good morning Mrs O'Day and God bless you,' they all replied in unison.

'We have a special visitor with us today. Some of you will know Fr Mick Finlay, who was parish priest before Fr Damian. Say good morning to Fr Mick please?'

'Good morning Fr Mick, God bless you,' they all chimed.

Fr Mick did not intend to generate quite a fuss but didn't want to disappoint the children either. 'Good morning everyone and may God's blessing be on all of you too,' he announced.

Lorna then asked Patrick and Connor to come forward and Fr Mick led them out into the hallway and crouched down in front of one of the boys. 'Hello Patrick my boy, how are you?'

'I'm Connor!'

'Of course you are.'

'I'm Patrick!' the other boy announced.

'That you are,' he said. 'Now boys, I need to get an important message to your father this morning, do you know where I could find him?'

'Mammy took him to the dentist this morning,' Connor volunteered. 'The one on High Street,' Patrick added.

'I think I know the one, thank you very much boys. I'll let you get back to your class now.'

With that he left the school and walked at a frantic pace to the medical complex.

By the time he arrived at the complex he was almost completely out of breath. Not knowing where exactly Peter would be, he headed straight towards the central reception desk. Fortunately for him, Denise O'Malley chose just that moment to go out for a coffee break.

'Hello Fr Mick, you off to see your specialist today are you?' she enquired.

'Denise, glad I bumped into you.' He paused to catch his breath. 'You haven't by any chance seen Peter MacDonald here today?'

'Well as a matter of fact I have,' said a surprised Denise.

Fr Mick has expected her to elaborate on her response. So, after a short silence he said, 'Oh that's grand because it is extremely urgent that I see him as soon as possible. Do you know where I can find him?'

Denise hesitated, 'Well, err … it's urgent, you say?'

'Yes, I need to tell him something right away,' insisted Fr Mick.

'Oh, I can get a message to him if you like?' she responded.

'No, sorry Denise, this message has to come from me personally.'

'It's that important?'

'Yes, terribly important!'

After another short pause Denise replied, 'Well … he's with Dr Wallace actually but …'

'Brilliant! Where can I find him?' Fr Mick interjected.

She pointed to a corridor to the left of the reception desk. 'He's in his surgery with Peter at the moment actually but …'

Before she could finish, Fr Mick ran off. Denise called out after him, 'Stop Father, you can't go in there!'

But Fr Mick was deaf to her pleas, frantically scanning the name plaques on the doors until he came to one that had the words 'Dr Wallace' and 'Surgery' written on them. Without so much as a tap on the door, he pushed the door open.

The second he burst into the room, Fr Mick realised that he had made an unforgiveable intrusion. He saw a man, whom he presumed was a surgeon, sitting on a backless swivel chair wearing magnifying glasses and holding a scalpel. This man had swivelled his chair around when Fr Mick burst into the room and was now staring at him. Two other men in surgical gowns were also staring back at him. Between these two men and the surgeon was a patient in a reclined position, with his legs held up in stirrups either side of the surgeon.

He didn't know what to do so he nervously called out, 'I'm sorry, I was looking for Peter MacDonald.'

Peter recognised Fr Mick's voice immediately and craned his neck to the side so that he could see around Dr Wallace, who had been blocking his view of the door. 'Fr Mick!' he exclaimed, 'What in feck's name are you doing here!'

'I need to speak to you,' was the sheepish response.

'Well, I'm sort of busy now!' said a clearly irritated Peter.

By this stage, Denise O'Malley had caught up with Fr Mick and was trying to lead him out of the door. However, as she turned him around, Fr Mick noticed what was written on the door opposite the surgery: 'Dr Wallace's Vasectomy Clinic'. He quickly realised that this was why Peter was in such a compromising position. He turned to face Peter again and exclaimed, 'A vasectomy! Peter, what about your marriage vows?'

Peter, who counted Fr Mick as one of his closest friends as well as his pastor, always treated him with the upmost respect, but on this occasion he was not able to contain his anger, 'What fecking vows?' he yelled.

'To accept children lovingly from God,' Fr Mick responded.

'Well, I've accepted six of the little beggars so I think I've done my bit, thank you very much!'

At this point Dr Wallace intervened. 'I'm sure that Peter will be happy to talk with you when we're done here, I'll only be another ten minutes or so. Denise will show you where you can wait.'

A humbled Fr Mick turned around and let Denise show him to the waiting room across the hall.

Once the door had closed, Dr Wallace tried to get back to the task at hand. 'Now, where was I?' he said.

'Oh, for feck's sake!' said an exasperated Peter.

Denise dutifully escorted Fr Mick into Dr Wallace's waiting room. Three other men were in the room at the time. Two of them Fr Mick recognised as parents of children at the school, and it was clear from the nervous look on their faces that they recognised him as well. They certainly would not have expected to see their former parish priest at a vasectomy clinic.

'Good morning … Father,' one of them mumbled.

Fr Mick didn't recognise the third man in the room, but he was obviously bemused about the situation and was chuckling to himself.

Mary dutifully arrived at ten to pick Peter up after his surgery and walked into the waiting room with young Suzanne in her arms. 'Fr Mick, what on earth are you doing here?'

'I had to come to see Peter.'

'How did you know he was here?' a worried Mary asked.

'I saw your boys at the school. They told me he'd gone to the dentist!'

'Ah yes, we didn't want to have to explain the finer points of their father's surgery to the younger children. Why did you have to see him so urgently? Couldn't it have waited until we were at home this evening?'

'Well, it's a bit hard to explain and I'd rather not have to go through it twice. So perhaps it's best to wait until Peter joins us.'

Fr Mick and Mary then took a seat in the waiting room. Young Suzanne immediately went up to Fr Mick with a picture book about zoo animals that she always carried around with her. Fr Mick dutifully picked her up onto his knee and started reading the book to her. He was pleased to have something to distract him from the awkward glances of the other men in the room. Fr Mick had just started going through the book for the third time when Peter joined them.

'How are you feeling, darling?' Mary enquired.

Noticing that her father had entered the room, Suzanne jumped off Fr Mick's lap and ran towards him. 'Daddy!' she shouted as she went to hug him.

Peter immediately bent down to pick her up but as he did her little legs swung forward, hitting him fair and square in the groin. Fortunately, the anaesthetic had not yet worn off. 'I'm still a bit numb thankfully.' He then turned his attention to Fr Mick. 'Hello Mick,' he said coldly.

Still embarrassed, Fr Mick responded, 'Hello Peter, sorry about the intrusion but I really needed to see you urgently.'

'Well, all I can say is that it better be something very important. It was a not very pleasant experience to have my surgeon startled like that when he was holding a scalpel less than an inch away from my manhood!'

'Well, it was a bit of a shock for me too!' responded Fr Mick, who was now very anxious to get out of the waiting room before someone else from the parish saw him. 'Is there somewhere we can go to talk that is more private?'

'There's a coffee shop out the front, we could get a table there,' Mary volunteered.

'Grand, let's go there.'

Just then Brendan O'Connor entered the room. 'Mr MacDonald, there are a few things we have to go through before you leave us today.

Firstly, I wouldn't do any heavy lifting or strenuous activity for the next couple of days.'

Peter, who was still carrying Suzanne, went to put her down before Brendan stopped him.

'I think that the baby is okay but nothing heavier. Also, the doctor has prescribed you some painkillers. The anaesthetic should wear off in a couple of hours so you should take two before then. You also need to come back in a week to have your stitches removed. Oh, and you may still have viable sperm within your system, so if you want to avoid pregnancy you should not have unprotected sex for the next few weeks. Ideally you should have a sperm test done before resuming normal activities.'

Now both Mary and Peter were blushing. To receive direction on marital activities from someone they had known since he was a boy was bad enough, but to have it spelt out in front of their priest was just too much.

Peter thanked Brendan for his assistance, took the prescription from him and made his way towards the coffee shop. Mary composed herself enough to ask Brendan to pass on their regards to his parents as they left.

Once at the coffee shop, Fr Mick made sure that they sat at a table at the rear of the premises which was out of earshot of the other patrons. A waitress promptly came to take their order. Peter, who had been fasting prior to the surgery, ordered a ham and cheese sandwich, chips and an orange juice, while Fr Mick and Mary just ordered a pot of tea.

Peter spoke first: 'Well Mick, out with it, what is so urgent?'

Fr Mick decided not to beat around the bush. 'Cardinal O'Faherty wants you to go to Rome.'

'What?' responded Peter and Mary in unison.

'Well you know that Cardinal O'Faherty is a good friend of mine.'

'Yes, you were in the seminary together, weren't you?' Peter replied.

'Well, he called me out of the blue this morning and asked me if I could get in touch with you. He said it was all a bit hush-hush, but the cardinals had decided that they needed to consult with some of the laity before the papal election.'

'Cardinals consulting with the laity! That's unheard of!'

'That's just what I said to him. In fact, I thought he must be joking! Listen, I know it sounds odd and I still suspect that there is something else behind this, but he said that I should trust him.'

'But why me? Why not someone from his own diocese?'

'You made a good impression on him when he met you a couple of years ago and he feels like he owes you one because he did feck all when you asked for his help regarding my forced retirement.'

'When does he want me to be there?'

'As soon as possible, apparently. There's an 8 pm flight from Dublin tonight. He's already worded up his secretary to arrange a ticket for you.'

'Well, I just can't drop everything and go to Rome! I should be convalescing, for Christ's sake! What do you make of all this, Mary?'

'Well, I admit it sounds highly irregular,' said Mary as she gathered her thoughts. 'But if the cardinal says he needs you there, who are we to question him? You weren't going back to work until Thursday anyway and you should be able to rest up well enough in Rome as you can at home.'

'So, you think I should go.'

'I can't see how you can refuse. I doubt if you'll be able to seriously influence the papal election but I'm as intrigued as you to find out what this is really about.'

'But will you be alright on your own for a couple of days?'

'It's not like I haven't done it before. You were away for a week last year when you attended that planning conference in Birmingham. Frankly I'd be better off not having you under my feet for a couple of days. You know what a pain you can be when you're convalescing.'

'Okay, but I'm not going alone. You'll have to come with me, Mick.'

'I don't know if the cardinal will cover my fare as well!'

'If he was desperate enough to send for me, he'll cover your costs as well. You ring his secretary and make the arrangements.'

'Will you be okay to leave tonight?'

'I may as well. It will get me out of having to explain to the boys why I can't kick the football around with them.'

The waitress then arrived with their order. Peter hastily started eating his sandwich while Fr Mick and Mary sipped their tea. Once Peter had finished eating, Fr Mick nervously asked, 'So, how are you feeling down there?'

'Well, it's starting to feel a bit tender at the moment, best I pick up these painkillers on our way out. What time did you say the flight to Rome was tonight?'

'Eight pm.'

'Can you then meet me at our place about five? We'll have a quick bite to eat then catch a taxi to the airport.'

'Okay, I'll see you then.'

With that Fr Mick got up, kissed Mary and Suzanne goodbye, and turned to leave. He was still a bit flustered by the circumstances in which he had found Peter, so he turned to him intending to make an apology for intruding on his surgery, but he couldn't find the right words so he just raised his hand to wave and walked out.

When he was out of earshot, Mary cast a stern look at Peter, 'Where do you get off barking orders at Fr Mick like that? He's our friend but he's also our priest – and as I've told you thousands of times before, you need to treat him with the proper respect.'

Peter couldn't see what the issue was. He had known Fr Mick all of his life and thought he treated Mick as well as he would treat his own father. 'What are you on about? I'm sure Mick wouldn't have taken offence. Anyhow, after what I've been through this morning, I felt that I was entitled to a few liberties. Mick's the one who knows O'Faherty's secretary, so it makes sense for him to contact her and make the arrangements.'

With that he got up to leave and immediately felt a sharp pain in his groin.

✝

Back at his home later that afternoon, the painkillers that the surgeon had prescribed managed to take a slight edge off the pain in Peter's groin, but he also found some comfort in a strategically applied ice pack. The pills also made him somewhat drowsy. He managed to grab a couple of hours of sleep on the sofa, but his slumber was disturbed by the arrival of the children from school.

Patrick and Connor saw their father lying on the sofa and made a beeline for it. Luckily, Mary managed to stop them before they jumped on him. 'Daddy is a bit sore after being at the dentist today boys,' Mary chided.

Peter then took the opportunity to sit up so as to avoid a second assault. But as he did so the ice pack fell off his groin, leaving a distinct wet patch on his jeans.

Lauren stated to laugh and cried out to the others, 'Look, Daddy's wet his pants!'

At that remark the four other children all burst into spontaneous laughter. Mary had to chuckle as well.

Peter, who was used to being the butt of the family's jokes, looked down and calmly said, 'Indeed I have!' before making his way upstairs to run himself a salt bath, the sounds of his family's delight echoing behind him.

Despite an initial sting when he first immersed himself, Peter found the bath to be very soothing. He took the opportunity to check out the surgeon's handiwork while he was in the bath. He noticed that everything seemed to be in order and all he could see was a couple of stiches where the surgeon had made his incision. One thing he did notice however was that a pubic hair had been caught up in the stitches. This had been what was causing him the most pain and there didn't seem to be anything he could do about it.

Peter got out of the bath, carefully dried himself, dressed and packed his overnight bag with his medications and toiletries, as well as a couple changes of underwear, a spare pair of trousers and a spare shirt. He then made his way gingerly back down the stairs to find that Fr Mick had already arrived and was sitting at the kitchen table chatting with the children over a cup of tea.

'Hello, Mick,' he said, 'everything okay then?'

'Yes it's all arranged.' Fr Mick answered. 'O'Faherty's secretary was a bit reluctant to book the extra ticket so she had to call him first to get the okay. But she quickly called be back to say it was alright.'

'Are you really going to Rome?' Michael asked.

Before Peter could answer Fr Mick stepped in, 'Now remember, it's a big secret boys, so don't tell anyone.'

'Thank you Fr Mick,' Peter said sarcastically. He knew quite well that his children were never good at keeping secrets. 'Yes, but it will only be for a couple of days, and we really don't want anyone to know about it.'

'Will you be meeting the Holy Father there?' Connor asked innocently.

'Don't be silly!' Lauren called out, 'the Pope is dead!'

'Well, I didn't know that!' an indignant Connor replied.

'You should know, we've said prayers for him at school and everything.'

'Oh yeah, I forgot.'

'You may get to see the new Holy Father then!' said Michael.

'I don't think so. We'll be home before the start of the Conclave,' Peter replied.

'Well, you'll probably see Cardinal Doherty there, and he might be the next Pope.'

Unfortunately, Michael made this remark just as Fr Mick was having a sip of his tea. The concept of Patrick Doherty as Pope caused him to spit most of it over the table. 'God help us!' he said under his breath once he had composed himself.

'You right there Mick?' an amused Peter asked.

'I'm okay thanks.' Then he turned to address Michael. 'I'm sure Cardinal Doherty would make a fine Pope,' he said with a wry smile.

Mary called everyone to the table and served dinner. Throughout the meal, Peter and Fr Mick fielded seemingly endless questions about the trip to Rome. They answered as best they could, constantly reminding the children not to tell anyone where Peter was going.

At about 6 pm the taxi arrived, and Peter and Fr Mick got up to say their goodbyes. Brydie looked up from her smartphone-induced daze and asked, 'Where's Dad going?'

'He's going to Rome!' Lauren called out.

'Since when!'

'We've been talking about it all during dinner!' Mary replied, 'Seriously Brydie, I wish you'd take those ear pods out and join the rest of the world sometimes.'

Peter collected his things and walked gingerly towards the taxi. He had taken another dose of painkillers at the end of his meal, but they were yet to take effect. He certainly hoped that he didn't have to move around too much when he was in Rome.

Peter's entry to Rome

It was 11.30 pm in Rome and Cardinal O'Faherty was struggling to keep himself awake. Cardinal Pancetti had given in and was peacefully snoring in his armchair. Cardinal Curiosa, on the other hand, had no trouble staying awake. He was excited to finally meet the man who had so intrigued them over the past twenty-four hours. 'What time did you say the plane landed Paddy?'

The question roused O'Faherty from his doze. 'Ten pm,' he replied with a yawn. O'Faherty would have been content to leave the meeting to the next morning, but as he was the one to invite Peter to come to Rome he felt obliged to stay up and welcome them.

'So, they should be here any minute now.'

'I think you'll have to wait a little longer, Ricky. When I flew in the other week it took well over an hour to pass through customs.'

'Shouldn't take very long this time of night, surely.'

'I wouldn't bet on it. This is a busy time in Rome, remember.'

'Well, at least the drive from the airport should be quicker.'

As it was, it took another hour before Peter and Fr Mick finally arrived at the Jesuit College in Rome. Curiosa had arranged for one of the college staff to meet them and at the airport and bring them directly to the college, where a room had been set aside for them.

O'Faherty had given in to the urge to sleep and was now dead to the world so it was only Curiosa who was up to greet them when they arrived.

The college staffer led Peter and Fr Mick into the lounge where the cardinals were waiting. The second that they entered the room, Curiosa got to his feet and ran towards them. 'Peter MacDonald!' he called out. 'How good it is to finally meet you!' Curiosa was prepared to embrace him but the stunned look on Peter's face made him settle for a hearty handshake. 'Welcome, welcome! O'Faherty has told me all about you.' Then without letting go of Peter's hand he briefly glanced over to Fr Mick before returning his gaze to Peter. 'And you must be Fr Finlay. Thank you very much for accompanying our man here to Rome. O'Faherty would have wanted to welcome you himself but unfortunately he didn't last the distance.'

Peter was wondering what he had gotten himself into now and gently tried to prise himself out of Curiosa's handshake; Curiosa just kept holding on, all the time smiling inanely. Fr Mick's was equally surprised. Peter's hand was starting to ache now, so he had to resort to using his other hand to release himself before cautiously responding to Curiosa's greeting. 'Err, good to meet you too Your Eminence …'

Curiosa interrupted him before he could say anything else. 'Oh! How foolish of me, I haven't introduced myself have I?' Grabbing Peter's hand again he said, 'I'm Cardinal Enrico Curiosa from New Jersey. O'Faherty and I go way back. The other cardinal sleeping in the chair next to O'Faherty is Cardinal Luigi Pancetti of Milan. We've all been greatly looking forward to your arrival.'

For a second time, Peter had to prise his hand from Curiosa's grip; 'Thank you Your Eminence, but I have to say, I'm puzzled as to why I was summoned here in the first place. I understood that there would be other laypeople here for discussions. Is someone not coming from your diocese?'

This caught Curiosa a little off-guard. 'Ah, others … yes, there will be others … they just haven't arrived yet.'

Curiosa's hesitant answer intrigued Peter. 'I can't help thinking that I haven't been told something. Can you tell me what the real story is?'

'No!' was Curiosa's curt reply. 'Perhaps it's best that you settle into your room, and we talk more about this tomorrow.' He addressed to the college staffer who had picked them up from the airport in Italian. Then he said to Peter, 'Giorgio will show you to your room. I'm afraid that accommodation is a bit tight in Rome at the moment, so you'll have to share, I hope that this is not a problem.'

Peter turned to Fr Mick. 'It's okay with me if it's okay with you, Mick!'

'No problem,' Fr Mick replied, then turning to Curiosa added, 'say hello to Paddy for me when he gets up.'

'Will do,' Curiosa replied.

With that they wished each other a good night and Georgio, who didn't speak a word of English and had not spoken a word to them during the whole drive from the airport, led them to their room. Peter was still suffering from the after-effects of the surgery and his painkillers were wearing off again. So, the trip upstairs to where their bedroom was located was a fairly painful one.

Once upstairs they walked along a short corridor to their room. It was small and simply furnished with two single beds separated by a single bedside table. The only other things in the room were a timber wardrobe and a strange plastic-looking box in one corner that was about the size of a portable toilet. Georgio opened the door to this box, turned to the men and said, 'Banio,' while simultaneously rubbing his hands together as if to wash them. Peter and Fr Mick peered past him and were surprised to find that the box actually housed an en-suite bathroom. A shower, basin and toilet were all contained in an area that couldn't be bigger than one square metre. This was a bit of a setback for Peter, as he was hoping to continue his salt baths over the next couple of days and had brought a container of salt with him expressly for that purpose.

Georgio then opened the wardrobe doors and showed them where the towels and extra blankets were kept. His job done, he said, 'Buona notte,' and left them alone in the room.

'I've got a bad feeling about this, Mick.'

'I know, this whole bathroom is smaller than the toilet on the plane.'

'I wasn't talking about the bathroom, Mick! I was referring to the cardinal. Have you met him before?' Peter asked.

'No, never, but he greeted you like you were an old friend!'

'I know! And what do you think he meant when he referred to me as our man? Surely they'll have their own representatives coming!'

'It's like I told you back in Dublin. I think there's more to this than old Paddy was able to say over the phone. Hopefully they'll let us in on it in the morning.' Then gesturing to Peter's nether regions he asked, 'And how are you coping?'

'Them painkillers have been pretty good, but I'm certainly ready for another dose. Walking up those stairs was excruciating.'

'Best get on to it then. I'm ready to hit the sack,' said Fr Mick as he pulled out his pyjamas and toothbrush from his travel bag. He then squeezed himself into the bathroom and started to brush his teeth.

Peter gingerly changed into his pyjamas, checking to see that nothing untoward had happened to his groin while in transit. The horror stories that he heard in the pub the previous evening were still preying on his mind, so he was relieved to see that everything was intact. When Fr Mick had finished with the bathroom, Peter went in to wash his hands and face, brush his teeth and take his medication. By the time he'd finished, Fr Mick was already in bed, so Peter turned off the light and got into bed himself. After a few uncomfortable minutes, the painkillers started to take effect and he fell into a deep sleep.

Despite his natural body clock's preference for more sleep, the return of the pain in his groin woke Peter up at about 6 am. He got out of bed to go to the toilet and take another dose of painkillers. He was meant to have salt baths over the next few days to prevent the sutures becoming infected, but the miniscule bathroom didn't have a bath. He eventually worked out that if he filled the basin with salty water, he could position himself over the basin and soak his testicles in the water for a few minutes, which hopefully should provide adequate disinfection.

Checking to see that Fr Mick was still asleep, he took the container of salt from his travel bag, filled the basin with water and mixed in the salt. It was a bit uncomfortable, but it worked okay and he managed to support himself over the basin for at least five minutes before a sleepy Fr Mick, who had assumed that Peter was still in bed, opened the bathroom door to find Peter leaning over the basin with his underpants around his ankles and his dangly bits in the water.

'What in heaven's name are you doing man!' he yelled.

'I thought you were sleeping!' a shocked Peter replied as he quickly dried himself and pulled on his underpants.

'I wish I was!'

Blushing profusely, Peter muttered, 'My doctor said that I needed to have salt baths twice a day.' Then as he gathered up his things and brushed past Fr Mick to vacate the bathroom for him he added, 'This was the best that I could arrange under the circumstances!'

'Well, next time lock the door or something!' Fr Mick replied, locking the door behind him to press the point.

Neither of them went back to sleep after that encounter. Peter got dressed and composed a text message to send back to Mary and the children to let them know he was okay.

> Good morning family. Slept well did u? Staying at Jesuit College in Rome sharing a room with Mick. He says hi. Pain bad but drugs good. Love to all ☺

He had just sent the message when Georgio knocked on the door to call them down for breakfast. Or that was what he presumed Georgio was doing when he made the gesture of bringing his hand to his mouth and rubbing his tummy. Peter thanked him and said they would be down shortly.

He waited for Fr Mick to finish shaving before they both made their way downstairs. Georgio was waiting for them and directed them to a dining room where cardinals Curiosa and O'Faherty were seated with two other cardinals. One was the Italian cardinal they saw sleeping in the chair next to O'Faherty the night before but the other they had not seen before.

'Good morning gentlemen,' Curiosa called out as they walked into the room, 'please come and take a seat.' He gestured to the two empty seats beside him.

O'Faherty, who was seated at the other side of the table, also stood up to greet them as they walked in. 'Mick Finlay my old friend, how are you? And Peter MacDonald, how good to see you. Thank you for coming to meet us at such short notice.' As he spoke, he walked around to their side of the table and gave them each a firm handshake.

The other two cardinals didn't say a word. Instead, they just sat in their chairs with their mouths agape staring at Peter. Peter found these silent stares to be somewhat unnerving. 'Err, good morning Your Eminences,' he said nervously.

Curiosa then remembered that Peter and Fr Mick had not met the other two cardinals. 'Oh, I should introduce you to my colleagues, shouldn't I?' He introduced him first to Cardinal Pancetti, who was seated directly opposite Peter. Despite Curiosa addressing him directly,

Pancetti did not break out of his stare. The other cardinal was seated opposite Curiosa. 'Peter MacDonald, this is Cardinal Billingham.'

Billingham at least realised that he had been staring and managed to snap out of it enough to loosely shake Peter's hand, but he was still speechless.

Breakfast, which was prepared by the multitalented Georgio, consisted of a large bowl of scrambled eggs, a bowl of sautéed mushrooms, some grilled tomatoes, a platter of fried bacon and sausages, toast, coffee, tea, and orange juice. All the platters were placed in the centre of the table for people to serve themselves. Peter was very impressed by the spread. *That Georgio can't speak a word of English, but he certainly knows his way around an English breakfast,* he thought.

In deference to the importance of their hosts, Peter and Fr Mick waited for the cardinals to start before making a plate for themselves. However, at least two minutes passed without anyone touching the food – and with cardinals Pancetti and Billingham still staring at Peter inanely, Curiosa gestured for him and Fr Mick to start.

Fr Mick didn't hesitate and started filling his plate with something from each dish. He had been keeping house for himself for over a year now and normally couldn't be bothered with the effort involved with preparing a cooked breakfast. So, this was a real treat for him. Peter was a bit more reserved but nevertheless served himself a decent helping of eggs, bacon, and sausages.

Curiosa and O'Faherty then started to serve themselves, but Pancetti and Billingham were still too entranced by Peter's presence to do anything. Curiosa called out to them. 'Paul, Luigi, aren't you eating this morning?' That was enough to stir them into some form of action and the two cardinals slowly started to put some food on their plates, all the time still staring across the table to where Peter was sitting.

Peter eventually broke the silence and addressed Curiosa: 'Thank you for your hospitality, Your Eminence, but I am still a bit in the dark.

Is every cardinal consulting with lay Catholics before entering the Conclave or is it just a select few?'

Curiosa didn't quite know how to answer him. Frankly, he and the other cardinals hadn't discussed what they were going to do with Peter once he arrived. All they knew was that the vision of him in their respective dreams must mean something and meeting him might help them to sort out what. 'Well, I have to be honest with you Mr MacDonald, bringing you to Rome was a spur of the moment decision. Suffice to say that the events that led to this decision are … a mystery even to us, but were significant enough to justify the decision itself.'

This response made him even more confused. 'When we met last night, Eminence, you suggested that you would be consulting with other laypeople as well. Is this still the case?'

'Well frankly, no!' was Curiosa's hesitant reply,

'No one else? You mean to say that out of the billion lay Catholics in the whole world, you chose to consult with me about …' now Peter was hesitating. '… What exactly do you need to consult with me about?'

O'Faherty tried to diffuse Peter's line of enquiry. 'Well Peter, we were talking about the future of the Church … and my friend Ricky here,' he gestured to Curiosa as he spoke, 'mentioned how many Catholics in the States who are active in church ministry were disappointed that the Church is losing relevance in modern societies. I said to him that the same thing was happening in Ireland. Then I brought you up as an example of someone who had good ideas about where the Church should be going but was being frustrated by the system. Ireland being a damn sight closer to Rome than New Jersey, we decided that we should bring someone like you in for a chat before entering the Conclave.' O'Faherty surprised himself with the fluency of his response – and from the relieved look on Curiosa's face, he could see that he may have gotten away with it.

'Well, that helps clear things up a bit. But do you mean to say that you want my opinion as to where the Church is heading?'

'Yes,' O'Faherty replied.

'Really?' Peter enquired incredulously.

'Yes really!'

'Honestly?'

'Yes, honestly.'

Peter was still worried about revealing his opinions on the Catholic Church to men so high up in the Church hierarchy, but he figured that if they had gone to the trouble of summoning him to Rome, he owed it to them to give them the full Peter MacDonald experience. 'Well, if you want the honest truth … despite the good intentions of the late Pope Anthony, I fear that regressive conservatives still have a stranglehold on the way the Church is run. With the result that the Church is quickly going to Hell in a handbasket!'

Peter looked around the table expecting shocked expressions from the cardinals, but instead they were still just smiling at him. Curiosa gave him an encouraging look and said, 'Please, tell us more.'

Still very nervous, Peter continued, 'Well … The Church could deal with the shortage of priests by empowering the laity. But instead, they are persisting with centralised control which is placing more and more stress on an aging clergy. They want the laity to be involved but don't want them to have any real responsibility.

'The Church's views on human sexuality is delusional, and is and always has been out of step with cultural views and norms.

'The church steadfastly refuses to consider the possibility of women clergy, which is an insult to the hordes of women who actually keep the Church functioning at the grassroots level.

'Senior clergy seem to have forgotten that the Church is first and foremost a community of the faithful, and the celebration and preservation of these communities is more important than making sure that each community is conducting its services in a Vatican-approved manner.

'The way that priests are appointed to parishes for short periods and then moved around from parish to parish prevents them from bonding with the community that they are meant to lead.

'The requirement for priests to be celibate is unnatural and unnecessary. It forces them to deny their sexuality and makes it harder for them to relate convincingly to issues surrounding marriage and family.

'The Church's views on birth control and abortion cannot be taken seriously if the clergy can't openly discuss human sexuality.

'The Church's authority to speak on such issues is also undermined by the fact that it keeps philandering priests and those accused of sexual abuse in service, while at the same time requiring priests who fall in love and want to marry to resign!'

Peter could have gone further but thought that he had probably said enough for now. He looked around the table again, expecting angry glares from the four cardinals seated there – but instead their smiles had grown even wider.

Curiosa was ecstatic. In his mind it was clear that the appearance of Peter in their dreams was God's way of telling them to push for a more liberal leadership once the Conclave was convened. 'Is that all?' he asked Peter.

'Oh, did I mention that I think that the Vatican Curia are, in reality, the last bastions of the Roman Empire and are more concerned with maintaining authority and control than spreading the word of God?'

'No, but that is quite perceptive of you,' Curiosa replied. 'I reached a similar conclusion myself a few decades ago but after the Second Vatican Council, I began to hope that we'd seen the end of those bad old days. However, I didn't count on the strength of the conservative forces within the Curia. Slowly but surely, many of the freedoms and opportunities that we gained with Vatican II were wound back.

'Pope Anthony was a good friend of mine and I know he had plans to push forward with many reforms. But these good intentions were blocked at every turn by the conservative forces that are entrenched in the Curia. Given more time he may have overcome these but sadly, it seems that his untimely demise has provided an opportunity for the old guard to re-assert their dominance.

'Still, they say that hope springs eternal … and hearing what you have to say certainly gives us hope. Isn't that right fellas?'

'How so Ricky?' Pancetti enquired.

'I'm saying that Peter MacDonald's presence here has given us a clear sign of the direction we should take in the Conclave.'

'And what direction might that be?' Billingham asked incredulously.

'Well, I'm not suggesting we discuss it now,' Curiosa answered, 'that would be highly inappropriate. We all know that we are not permitted to discuss the succession with anyone not directly involved with the selection process. We must let the Holy Spirit guide us towards the right choice. But I believe that the Holy Spirit has launched an advanced assault in the form of Peter MacDonald here, and it is our obligation to allow the Spirit do his work both inside and outside of the Conclave.'

Peter was now even more perplexed by the behaviour of his hosts. They summon him to Rome only a couple of days before a papal election, then they fawn all over him and now they're suggesting that he was sent to them by none other than the Holy Spirit! What were these guys on? He looked over to Fr Mick, whose expression indicated that he thought these cardinals were off with the pixies as well.

O'Faherty smiled at him and said, 'I think, Ricky, we need to introduce Peter to a few more of our colleagues while he is here.'

'My thoughts exactly Paddy. How can we arrange it?'

'Well, I know that the Vatican correspondents from *Time* magazine are hosting a function at the Hilton Hotel this evening. I imagine that there will be a few more of our likeminded colleagues there as well as a few other moderates.'

'Excellent, we'll bring him there. Where else can we take him?'

'Well, we could invite some more cardinals to meet us here tomorrow,' O'Faherty said. 'When are you meant to be back in Dublin, Peter?'

Peter hesitated; he was starting to feel like a pawn in a game that the cardinals were playing. 'I'm meant to be back at work on Thursday morning, actually.'

Curiosa looked concerned, 'You couldn't stay another day, could you? The Conclave is meant to start on Thursday, and it will be good for you to be in Rome until then. If you could stay until the end of the week that would be even better. I doubt that we'll have a result by then but at least you'll have a day to yourselves to explore the sights of Rome.'

'Well, I suppose that if I stay till Thursday, there will be no point in going to work for just one day. But I'll have to make some phone calls and let you know?'

'That will be fantastic. We'll make the arrangements. Paddy, are you able to keep our guests entertained until this evening?'

'I had a couple of diocesan issues to attend to this morning but that shouldn't take me too long. There's the General Congregation as well but I don't think I'll be missed there.'

Pancetti, who was a bit embarrassed about his initial stunned reaction to seeing Peter in the flesh, was keen to really get to know this man they were putting their faith in. 'Do you mind if I come along with you Paddy?' he asked.

'No, not at all, the more the merrier,' O'Faherty replied.

'I want to come too!' interjected Billingham. Realising that he sounded like a petulant child he added. 'I mean to say, I have some time free today and I could take Peter and Fr …'

'Finlay, Michael Finlay. Pleased to meet you,' said Fr Mick patronisingly.

'Of course you are,' an embarrassed Billingham replied. 'I could take Peter and Fr Finlay through the Vatican Museum.'

'Excellent,' said Curiosa, 'we'll meet back here for dinner at 6 pm before heading out to the *Time* magazine function.'

While they were waiting for the cardinals to re-arrange their affairs, Peter returned to his room to telephone Mary. He'd sent her a quick text when he arrived in Rome the night before, and another in the morning, but he knew she'd be anxious to find out what was going on. It was still only 7.30 am in Dublin so the family should be finishing breakfast, ready for the school run.

'Hello, MacDonald residence, Lauren speaking.'

'Hello Lauren speaking, it's Daddy speaking here.'

'Hello Daddy! How are things in Rome? Are you staying in a nice hotel?'

'No, it's not a hotel darling. I'm staying at the Jesuit College.'

'You're staying in a school!'

'No darling, the college is just the name they give to the place where the priests and religious live when they visit Rome.'

'Oh! But you're not a priest!'

'Yes darling I know, but they're letting me stay here anyway.'

'Well, that's nice of them.'

'That it is Lauren, now can I speak to Mammy please?'

Peter had to pull the phone away from his ear as Lauren screamed for her mother without putting the phone down at her end. After a short while Mary picked up the phone.

'Hello Peter, how did you get on?'

'Good morning darling. I'm getting on fine but things here are weirder than I could have imagined.'

Peter then proceeded to describe to Mary his curious experiences with the cardinals.

'This is sounding very strange indeed, Peter. I don't know how I feel about it actually.'

'I still have no bloody idea what this is all about. I'd only met O'Faherty a couple of times before, but he greets me like I'm an old mate as well, and barely acknowledges his actual old mate standing next to me. The other two cardinals don't say a word and just stare at me like I'm … I don't know what! I tell you, I was pretty freaked out.'

'I hope that you didn't offend them?'

'On the contrary, I think I spurred them on. They now want to introduce me to as many cardinals as they can, and they want me to stay the whole week!'

'The whole week! Have you called work about that yet?'

'No not yet, but I was going to once I got off the phone with you. They only want me to stay until the start of the Conclave on Thursday, but I thought there was no point in only going to work on Friday so Mick and I will spend the extra day sightseeing. Will you be okay with that?'

'Yes, but I really have a bad feeling about where this stuff with the cardinals is heading. You just watch yourself. But whatever happens, I definitely need you home on Saturday because the twins have a party to go to which is on at the same time as Brydie and Lauren's ballet classes.'

'Not a problem, we'll see if we can get a flight on Friday afternoon.' Peter could hear Brydie in the background yelling at everyone to hurry up because they were making her late for school. 'I'd better let you go before the Brydie monster attacks.'

'Ok, let me know what you decide. Send our love to Fr Mick.'

'Will do, Bye.'

'Bye.'

Mary hung up the phone and hurried the children along to get them into the car. Brydie, who despite her teenage recalcitrance took her responsibilities as eldest child quite seriously, noticed her mother's pained expression. 'Was that Dad?' she asked. 'Is everything okay?'

'Oh, everything is just fine,' she replied, 'just a bit strange is all.'

'What do you mean?'

'Well, when Cardinal O'Faherty asked him to go to Rome he said that all the cardinals were bringing someone from their diocese to consult with, but now your father has found out that he was the only one.'

'You mean that out of all of the Catholics in the world, they chose my dad to talk with before they elect a new Pope?'

'I know, that's why I'm worried.'

'Wow, our dad has been asked to help choose the new Pope. That's really freaky!'

'He hasn't been asked to help choose the new Pope, they just want to talk to him is all. And remember, no one is meant to know that he is in Rome, okay?'

'Don't worry, I'm not talking to my friends about church stuff.'

'Very well.'

However, what Brydie and Mary didn't know was that nine-year-old Lauren had been listening intently to their every word. Her daddy was the only Catholic in the whole wide world who had been asked to help the cardinals choose a new Pope! She knew full well that it was meant to be a secret, but this was too big a secret for her to keep to herself. Surely she could confide with her best friend Ebony. Besides, Ebony was always going on about how her dad met famous people every day in his job at the newspaper. *My dad met Bono yesterday, or my dad is going to interview the President today,* she would say. Well, her daddy was going to choose the next Pope Ebony should know about it.

How really not to discuss Papal succession

While Peter and Fr Mick were being shown around Rome and the Vatican by no fewer than three cardinals, Curiosa was busy working the phone to see which of the other cardinals would be attending the *Time* magazine function that evening. He still had no idea of how Peter's presence could influence the Conclave, but he was anxious to see what the reaction of the other cardinals to Peter would be.

So far, he knew of at least three other liberal-minded cardinals who would be there: the French cardinal Pierre Soutier, the South African cardinal Eric Mobutu, and the Indonesian cardinal Phillip Suryani. There were also some other not-so-liberal-minded cardinals attending. These were Stewart Johnson from California, Peter Quinn from Australia, Jessie Marcos from the Philippines, and Cardinal Francesco DiMattina from Brazil.

He was curious to see the reaction of these cardinals to Peter's presence. If they reacted in a similar way to Pancetti and Billingham then it was almost certain that Peter had appeared in their dreams as well. But before they expose him to just any cardinal, perhaps it would be better to test the Peter dream theory against some of their liberal colleagues first. So, Curiosa arranged for Soutier, Mobutu and Suryani to join O'Faherty, Pancetti, Billingham and himself for dinner that evening prior to the *Time* magazine function.

Peter was appreciative of the cardinals spending their valuable time with him but was also mentally and physically tired. They had done the whole tour on foot and all the time he was being hounded with questions on his views on the Church and information on his family and work. He was also still in terrible pain and would have preferred to spend the day resting in bed. Of course, the cardinals were not aware that he'd had surgery only twenty-four hours earlier and Peter didn't really want them to know the nature of the operation. So, he just had to grin and bear it.

Despite this pain and discomfort, Peter was genuinely enthralled by seeing the sights of Rome first-hand. He expected the Colosseum to be big but he was not prepared for the intricacy of the structure. The Roman forum also caught him completely off-guard. For some reason he thought that the only thing left of ancient Rome was the Colosseum, but the forum opened his eyes to the sophistication and complexity of Roman civilisation. He wished he'd paid more attention in history classes so that he could better appreciate the wonders he was seeing.

The biggest surprise of the day, however, was the Trevi Fountain. He'd imagined that it would be in a prominent location but was amazed to see it appear seemingly out of nowhere while negotiating narrow lanes in what appeared to be a shopping district.

The cardinals were doing a great job of describing what he was seeing but would always take the opportunity to steer the conversation back to questions of his personal life and his opinions on the Church. They started with the obvious ones: How long had he been married? How many children did he have? What did he do for a living? But then they started hitting him with questions on issues facing the Church today, including married clergy, women clergy, the form of the mass, administration of parishes, abortion, and sex abuse scandals. This was not unexpected, as it was the premise they had used to summon him to Rome in the first place. But it was still very unnerving all the same.

It was strange that, no matter what he said, they didn't challenge any of his views but just seemed to be enthused by them. It was also strange that apart from small talk, they practically ignored Fr Mick.

It was about 3 pm when the party returned to the Jesuit College. Peter was relieved, for now he was both physically and mentally drained. He went up to his room, took some painkillers and promptly fell asleep.

He was not permitted to sleep long, as less than two hours later he was woken and summoned downstairs to the lounge. When he entered the lounge, he saw that Fr Mick was sitting comfortably on his own at one end of the room drinking whisky. The cardinals Pancetti, Billingham, O'Faherty were sitting at the other end of the room and were chatting with a cardinal of Asian appearance.

Curiosa welcomed Peter with his now customary enthusiasm. 'Ah Mr MacDonald, how good to see you again. Let me introduce you to another of our colleagues.' Curiosa led Peter to where Cardinal Phillip Suryani was seated and made the introductions. Suryani shook hands with Peter and gave him a polite smile.

The other four cardinals were looking at Suryani, intently expecting his reaction to be more pronounced, but the subdued response disappointed them.

Suryani looked back at Peter; Curiosa got the reaction he was looking for. Suryani's jaw dropped as he raised his shaking hand to point at Peter. He then dropped his head and brought both hands to his face before turning to his colleagues with a look of utter disbelief, only to find them all smiling back at him and nodding their heads.

If Peter didn't already think that all the cardinals in Rome were off their rockers, he was certainly starting to believe so now. He looked around him to see if there was something else that may have resulted in Cardinal Suryani reacting in the way he did and why the other cardinals took so much delight in that reaction. But he couldn't for the life of him see anything.

Then, Curiosa took Peter aside and said, 'We have some important business to discuss with Cardinal Suryani at the moment. Would you mind sitting with Fr Finlay for a while? Georgio will get you a drink, Irish whisky okay?'

Curiosa called out to Georgio to prepare the drink and Peter joined Fr Mick. As Peter sat down in an armchair across from him, Fr Mick raised his glass and said, 'They've banished you too I see. Secret cardinals' business, I believe.'

'Weird cardinals' business more like,' Peter answered, 'it's no wonder the Vatican is going to pot if they all behave as strangely as this lot.'

Georgio then arrived with Peter's drink and dutifully took Fr Mick's glass for a refill.

Cardinal Suryani was now sitting back in his chair but still had a stunned look on his face. 'What's the matter Phillip?' Billingham asked innocently.

'That man seems familiar to me,' a nervous Suryani replied.

'Does he really? Where do you think you've seen him before?'

'Well, it took me a while to work it out but I think it was in a dream I had the other night.'

'Really? Tell us more.'

'In my dream I was in a Venice concert hall playing Rachmaninoff on a Steinway Grand and when I took my curtain call, the Holy Father himself walked on to the stage to congratulate me ...'

Before he could finish, Curiosa stepped in: 'And the man who appeared as the Holy Father in your dream looked remarkably like Mr Peter MacDonald, who is the man you just met.'

'Yes … Yes …' a surprised Suryani answered. 'He looked exactly like him, I believe. How did you know?'

'We've all had similar dreams.'

'No, it's not possible!'

'I'm afraid it's true. In fact, it is very interesting that in your dream you were doing something you loved because in my dream I was performing at the Comedy Club, which is something I always wanted to do. What were you doing in your dream, Paddy?'

'I was competing in the British Open and won the Cup after scoring an albatross on the eighteenth hole.'

'And Louie, what where you doing?'

Pancetti hesitated before answering, as he couldn't reveal the true nature of his dream to his colleagues. He finally said, 'I was conducting the wedding of my favourite god-daughter.'

'And Paul?'

'I was driving a car on a racetrack,' Billingham replied.

Cardinal Suryani could not believe what he was hearing. 'You mean to say that you all have had dreams where you met the new Pope and in all of your dreams the Pope looked like this Irish man with a Scottish name?'

'It's an Irish name too!' an annoyed O'Faherty interjected.

'Yes Paddy, we know that now,' Curiosa said.

Curiosa prompted O'Faherty to explain to Suryani the series of events which led to them identifying Peter as the man in each of their dreams.

'That's amazing!' Suryani responded. 'How many more cardinals do you think have had this dream?'

'Well, so far it's five out of five!' Curiosa answered. 'We're expecting Soutier and Mobutu to arrive any minute now, so we'll see how they react.'

Right on cue, Cardinal Eric Mobutu of South Africa arrived. Mobutu's slender physique and height betrayed his Zulu heritage. Mobutu waved to colleagues seated at the other end of the room and started to walk towards them. He also acknowledged the presence of Peter and Fr Mick in the room and gave them a polite nod as he walked past. He'd only walked a few steps towards his friends when he turned to have another look at Peter.

He kept staring back at Peter while he was still walking towards the other cardinals and didn't notice that an armchair, where Cardinal Pancetti was seated, was immediately in front of him. He took one step too many and fell face first across Pancetti's lap.

Peter and Fr Mick, who witnessed the tumble, were immediately concerned for the wellbeing of the two cardinals. However, the cardinals not involved in the incident issued screams of delight – even Pancetti was smiling and laughing. Perplexed, Peter and Fr Mick settled back into their chairs and had another swig of whisky.

Billingham and O'Faherty got the African cardinal back to his feet, which was not an easy task because he was a good head taller than Billingham and was almost twice the size of the diminutive O'Faherty. Nevertheless, they managed to seat Mobutu next to Cardinal Suryani.

Peter and Fr Mick barely managed to take a couple more swigs of whiskey when they were startled by a tremendous crash. A third cardinal had entered the room and walked straight into the drink trolley that Georgio had left in the passageway, knocking it against the wall. An empty gin bottle and a few glasses fell from the trolley, smashing on the tiled floor. Thankfully he managed to stay on his feet and thus avoided falling onto the many shards of broken glass.

Peter and Fr Mick instinctively rose to assist the elderly cardinal but were again distracted by the cheers from the other side of the room. Cardinals Curiosa, O'Faherty, Billingham and Pancetti were all jumping up and down, punching fists into the air and clumsily attempting to high-five each other. Only the Asian cardinal that Peter had just met and the African cardinal who had walked in not fifteen minutes earlier were still seated. Their stunned expressions at least provided Peter and Fr Mick some assurance that not all the cardinals were totally insane.

By this time, the dutiful Georgio had gone to the aid of the cardinal and, after checking that he was alright, proceeded to clear the broken glass off the floor.

Fr Mick got up and casually walked up to the drinks trolley to commandeer the bottle of Irish whisky. He and Peter were definitely ready for another drink.

This new cardinal, French cardinal Pierre Soutier, proceeded to walk towards his colleagues but kept looking back at Peter as he did so.

The other cardinals had left an empty chair for him. Their reaction to his mishap had not gone unnoticed and he looked suspiciously at their smiling faces as he sat himself down. 'Can anyone please tell me what is going on, and who is that man sitting over there?'

Curiosa proceeded to question Soutier in the same manner as he had questioned the others, but these questions had become rhetorical to him because he was now certain what the answers would be.

Flabbergasted by this revelation, Soutier asked. 'How do you know all this? Do you have the means to infiltrate my mind?'

'No, we don't, but apparently someone else does because we have all had similar dreams,' Curiosa informed him.

'Mon dieu!'

'Exactly!'

Curiosa proceeded to inform Soutier on what they knew about Peter and why they thought it was important to bring him to Rome. Then Mobutu asked, 'If this same man appeared in all of our dreams as the new Holy Father, what can that mean? Surely we can't seriously promote the idea of electing a layman to the papacy!'

'I don't really know what it means,' Curiosa replied, 'we have lived our lives telling others that God works in mysterious ways, not expecting that we will be directly implicated in his mysteries. But now we know that there are seven of us that have dreamt of Mr MacDonald over there as the new Pope and although we are only seven, we haven't yet found a cardinal who has not had the dream!'

'Do you think that each and every cardinal has had this dream?' Soutier enquired.

'I don't see how we can think otherwise. At this stage the score is seven–zip. You're a betting man, Pierre – with that run would you bet on no other cardinals having the dream?'

'Non, I suppose I would not. But surely we can't seriously put this man forward as a candidate!'

'Well, canon law does allow for it!' Billingham volunteered.

'I know it does,' said O'Faherty, 'but I still don't see how we could make it happen. Even if we can convince the rest of the cardinals that they have experienced a miracle, they will still be reluctant to vote for him once they realise how progressive his views are. In fact, they are so sure that they are currently on the right path that they may take the revelation as a warning against supporting a liberal candidate.'

'So, he is not one to support conservative views?' Suryani asked.

'No, he is very much to the left of the left as far as the Curia is concerned. He regards them at being totally out of step with the needs of the Catholic faithful in the Western world at least, and he supports all of the progressive issues that the Curia refuses to discuss.'

'Such as?'

'The ordination of married priests, greater involvement of the laity in the administration of parishes and expanding the role of women in the Church.'

'Excellent!' Soutier exclaimed. 'So electing him would really be … how you say … putting the cat among the pigeons.'

At this point Curiosa thought that he needed to take control of the conversation again. 'I think that we're getting ahead of ourselves a bit, fellas. Just because he appears as Pope in our dreams does not necessarily mean that we should make him Pope. I mean, that wouldn't be fair to him. He's a married man with children, isn't he Paddy?'

'Yes I believe so,' O'Faherty responded, prompting Billingham to recount to the others everything he and Pancetti had gleaned from Peter during their day in Rome. O'Faherty then added, 'He's picked up on the fact that the Vatican has singled out the Church in Western societies for special attention, accusing them of not following the proper Catholic rites and rituals while churches in developing countries are free to integrate their indigenous culture with their religious celebrations.'

Mobutu countered, 'I don't know about that, Patrick. I too have received several letters from the Congregation for the Doctrine of the Faith, stating that parishioners have complained about parts of the mass being sung when they should be spoken, and priests dancing in the Sanctuary.'

'… And what have you done about them?' O'Faherty asked.

'I just file them under "R" for rubbish!'

'You're a braver man than I,' O'Faherty replied.

'Well, they're fools if they think that the Church in Africa can grow without singing and dancing. I go to my churches, and I see people filled with the Holy Spirit celebrating their love for God in the best way they know how. If I even suggested that they should change their ways they'd all run off and join the Methodists in an instant!'

A frustrated Suryani spoke up. 'Gentlemen, surely what we have experienced here is a true miracle. I am still in shock about what I have learned this evening. If it is true that every cardinal has dreamt of this man as Pope, then what we have received is a clear and unequivocal message from God. We must therefore forget about what we think is the best way to move forward and think of what God wants of us.'

Suryani had succeeded in getting the attention of his colleagues so he continued, 'It appears that all our dreams have involved us doing something we enjoy – therefore, the dreams themselves must be viewed in a positive light. That the man who appeared to us as Pope is someone who is not happy with the way the Church is being run at the present time suggests that God wants the Church to change. However, we can only come to this conclusion because we have recognised that we have all dreamt of the same man as the new Pope.

'I agree that to make an unsuspecting layman Pope will not be in his best interests, but it seems that the only way that we can do what is required of us is to get all of the other cardinals to meet with him and make the same connection that we have.'

'That's exactly what we had in mind Phillip,' said Curiosa. 'We're planning to take him with us when we go to the *Time* magazine function tonight and then invite some more cardinals here tomorrow to see what their reaction is.'

'Seeing him in the flesh is one thing Ricky,' said Soutier, 'but if the miracle is to mean something, they also need to know who he is and that there are other cardinals who have dreamt of this man as Pope.'

'That's what I was worried about,' said O'Faherty. 'If they have had the dream, they will no doubt react the same way as Phillip, Eric and Pierre have this evening. We can then reveal to them that we know why this man intrigues them so much and let them know that we have all had similar dreams. However, if we claim that the significance of the dreams is to elect a liberal as Pope, they will be immediately suspicious and will accuse us of using this magnificent revelation to promote our personal agenda. If we are not too careful, some of the more conservative cardinals will sanction us for discussing the succession with the laity and could have us barred or worse!'

'What do you suggest we do, Paddy?' Curiosa asked.

'I don't know, Ricky, I just know that we can't go into this with all guns blazing for fear of being shot down ourselves.'

Pancetti then spoke, 'I agree with Paddy, we cannot risk the accusation that we try to manipulate the Conclave. So, the only place we can talk about it is during the Conclave.'

'How do you propose that we raise the issue, Louie?' asked Billingham.

'Well, as you know when we vote first time it is very late and there is only time for one vote on that day. Because there is no time to discuss properly, we always put our own name on the vote so the Conclave must continue next day. What we can do this time is write "Peter MacDonald" on our first vote. To vote for someone who is not a cardinal will have to be discussed. When we discuss we can find out if everyone had had the dream. Then we can say what we know about Peter MacDonald.'

'Well,' said Curiosa, 'it's taking a bit of a risk to wait for the start of the Conclave, but it seems like we have no other choice.'

'I think that there is still no harm in letting the other cardinals see or meet this man before the Conclave,' said Suryani, 'but I agree with Louie that the proper place to discuss the issue is within the Conclave. Yes, there are risks, but I think that now more than ever, we need to trust the Holy Spirit to guide us.'

'I think that the Spirit has done a pretty good job getting us this far,' agreed Billingham, 'and this will surely be the most fun I've ever had at a Conclave.'

Georgio then arrived to call them into the dining room for dinner. The cardinals started to move towards the dining room. Mobutu and Soutier in particular were very eager to get there, as they had not yet been formally introduced to Peter and were keen find out more about him. However, they were disappointed to find Peter fast asleep. The combination of his painkillers with three healthy serves of Irish whisky had made him dead to the world. Fr Mick's attempts to wake him were in vain so they resigned themselves to dining with Fr Mick alone.

A secret revealed

Earlier that same day, an excited Lauren MacDonald arrived at school eager to find her best friend Ebony O'Shea so that she could share her special secret with her. But Ebony had arrived at school late that day and it was not until morning recess that Lauren had the chance to talk to her friend in private.

'I've got a very special secret, but you have to promise that you won't tell anyone,' Lauren whispered.

'I promise, I promise,' Ebony, who loved secrets, eagerly replied.

'Well, yesterday my daddy had to go to Rome.'

'That's not such a big secret; my daddy is always going to different places to write stories for the newspaper.'

'I haven't told you why he is going yet!'

'Okay, why is he going to Rome?'

'He's going to help choose the new Pope.'

'He can't choose the new Pope! They have those special priests who do that.'

'The cardigans.'

'Yes, the cardigans.'

'No, it's true! I swear! Fr Mick came and picked him up and they went to the airport last night. Fr Mick said that the cardigans wanted to speak to some ordinary people about who should be the Pope and one of the cardigans asked especially for our daddy. Then Daddy called from Rome this morning and I heard Mammy tell Brydie that Daddy told her that there were no other ordinary people there and of all the people in the whole world, our daddy was the only one asked to help choose the new Pope.'

'The only one out of all the people in the whole world!'

'Yes, isn't it amazing!'

Ebony was more than a little sceptical about Lauren's claim. She knew how jealous Lauren was when she told her about her dad meeting famous people, whereas Lauren's dad only worked for the local council. But her friend seemed genuinely excited about something, so she didn't want to disappoint her.

That night, Ebony was waiting in bed for her father to come home. Ebony's father, Rory O'Shea was a senior journalist with *The Irish Times*. He often worked back late at the newspaper office putting his finishing touches to the articles for the morning edition. However, he always tried to be home before his daughter's bedtime so he could have a short chat about her day and kiss her good night. She was about to doze off when her father walked into her bedroom.

'Hello, my darling, sorry I'm late today.'

'That's okay Daddy,' Ebony replied, yawning.

'How was your day?'

'Oh, just grand daddy, how was yours?'

'Oh, mine was grand too.'

Ebony was struggling to stay awake, but she had to tell her father what was on her mind. 'Daddy?' she asked.

'Yes Dear?'

'You know how the Pope died …'

'Yes, that he did.'

'And you know how they need to choose a new one …'

'Yes.'

'Well, is it just the cardigans who choose the Pope or can ordinary people help?'

'No, only the cardinals are allowed to choose a new Pope.'

'That's what I thought, but Lauren MacDonald told me today that her daddy had gone to Rome to choose the new Pope.'

'Did she now?'

'Yes, she said that the cardigans …'

'Cardinals.'

'Yes, the cardigans had asked for him especially and out of all the people in the whole world, he was the only one who could choose the new Pope.'

'Is that so? Well, he'll have to be a very special person then.'

'Do you think that he is really choosing the new Pope?'

'If Lauren seems to think so, who are we to argue?'

'I just thought she was fibbing, is all.'

'Well, Lauren is your best friend, she may be confused about what her father is doing but I don't think she would tell you fibs.'

'Oh, I suppose so,' said Ebony as she let out another huge yawn.

'You better go to sleep now darling, and I'll see you in the morning.'

'Okay, good night daddy.'

'Good night my darling,' said Rory as he kissed his daughter on the forehead.

Rory knew that children had very active imaginations, but nevertheless was intrigued by what his daughter had told him. It was extremely unlikely to be true, but wouldn't it make a fantastic headline for tomorrow's paper: 'Our man the Pope-maker'.

Ebony and Lauren had been friends since kindergarten, so Rory and his wife Rachael knew Lauren's parents Peter and Mary quite well. He knew that Peter was involved with the Church at a diocesan level so it wasn't impossible that Cardinal Doherty may have called him to Rome for some reason – highly *improbable*, but not impossible. He figured it wouldn't hurt to make a quick call to the MacDonald house before dinner to see if there was any truth what Lauren had told Ebony.

'Hello, MacDonald residence, Michael speaking.'

'Hello Michael, it's Rory O'Shea here, would your father be home?'

'No sorry, he's gone away for a few days.'

This mildly intrigued Rory. He knew Peter's work at the council was all Dublin-based so it would be extremely unusual for him to travel for business – and with six children at home he was unlikely to have gone on holidays on his own. 'Oh, he's gone away has he? He's a lucky man to be away from this miserable Dublin weather. Where has he gone, somewhere nice I hope?'

Michael knew that his father's whereabouts were meant to be a secret, but the direct question from an adult took him off his guard. 'Yes, he went to Rome with Fr Mick last night.'

That was interesting. Perhaps they had tickets for the papal inauguration. But surely it was a bit early for that? 'Well, he's a lucky man indeed to be in Rome during a papal election. Is he meeting with other people there?'

Michael had now realised that he had probably said too much. 'My mammy is here, do you want to speak to her?'

'Oh yes please.'

Although Rory had introduced himself at the start of the conversation, Michael had forgotten his name already. He thought it was best to own up to it. 'Whom shall I say is calling again?'

'It's Rory O'Shea, I'm Lauren's friend Ebony's dad.'

'Okay, I'll get her for you.'

Michael took the phone upstairs to Mary, who was just saying goodnight to Patrick and Connor. He handed the phone to her. 'Telephone Mammy.'

'Who is it?'

'It's Lauren's friend's dad, Rory O'Shea.'

'Oh alright.'

It was unusual for Rory to call their house, as most of the communication regarding Ebony and Lauren's activities were between Ebony's mother and herself. But she assumed that the call would have something to do with the girls. She put the phone to her ear. 'Hello Rory, how are you?'

'Hello Mary, I'm just grand thanks. I was just calling to see how Peter was doing in Rome.'

'How did you know that Peter was in Rome?'

'Oh, I have my sources. It was very lucky for him to be summoned to Rome during such an important time.'

'How did you know he was summoned there?'

Rory felt a bit guilty about manipulating the conversation in this way, but Mary's reaction now gave him a clear indication that there was more to this story than met the eye. So, he decided to spin a few more white lies to see if he could get more information out of her. 'Oh, the cardinal's office called the newspaper this afternoon.'

'That's nice, they tell us it's a big secret then they go and alert the media themselves, that's rich.'

Rory the journalist was smelling blood now. So, it was a secret? Interesting. 'It certainly is a big deal for a layman to be asked to help choose the new Pope.'

'Is that what they've told you? He's doing nothing of the sort; you can't expect a layman to have any influence over a papal election, can you?'

'So why do you think he was summoned?'

'I have no idea and Peter is pretty much in the dark as well! He was initially told that all the cardinals were consulting with lay members of their diocese, but then this morning he finds out that he is the only one.'

Rory couldn't believe his luck. 'Out of the one billion Catholics in the whole world they're only talking to him! That's amazing.'

Mary realised that she'd said too much. 'Now Rory, don't make too much out of this, it's just a few cardinals who are interested in his opinion.'

'Still, it was very special that Cardinal Doherty's office would send for him.'

'Cardinal Doherty! What makes you think that Cardinal Doherty's office had anything to do with it?'

'Um, err … I just assumed that it would be Doherty because we're in his diocese.'

'I thought you said before that you were notified by the cardinal's office this afternoon. Was it Cardinal Doherty's office that contacted you?'

'Oh, did I say that? I was actually acting on another lead.'

'You mean you didn't hear anything from the cardinal's office today?'

'No, I'm afraid not.'

'So, all you really know about it is what I've told you now! Rory, promise me that you're not going to put this in the paper tomorrow. It could cause a lot of trouble,' she said.

'I'm sorry Mary, but this is too good a story to pass up. I think that Ireland has to know that we have a Pope-maker in our midst.'

'Rory, that is a gross exaggeration, you can't go ahead and print that! All Peter has done is accept a free trip to Rome.'

'Well, it's going to make a fantastic headline, but rest assured that we will clarify the situation in the body of the article.'

'Rory, I'm begging you. Please don't do this. Peter and Cardinal O'Faherty could get into a lot of trouble and for no good reason. How could Peter possibly influence a papal election?'

'Ah, so O'Faherty is involved!'

'Rory!' Mary screamed, 'you can't mention his name!'

'Don't worry Mary, I'll make sure that we don't do anything that will result in anyone getting into trouble.'

'If they do Rory, I'll be holding you responsible and I'll make sure the whole school community knows about it.'

'Sorry Mary, but I've got to do what I've got to do!'

With that Rory hung up the phone, leaving a shaking Mary at the other end.

Mary was totally flummoxed. How the hell was this happening? Her husband accepts a free trip to Rome, admittedly under weird circumstances, and now the newspaper thinks he is going to help choose the Pope? No one in their right mind could believe that story, surely. But of course, no one has to believe it; the headline alone is enough to sell papers, and that is all that matters to the media nowadays. She would have to call Peter to tell him what had happened.

The sound and vibration of his cell phone ringing woke Peter from his sleep. He was surprised to find that he was still sitting in the Jesuit College lounge. Everyone else including Fr Mick had gone and the lights in the room had been turned off. He took the phone out of his pocket and saw that someone from home was calling him. He also noticed that the time was 8.45 pm. He must have slept through dinner … and wasn't there some sort of function that he was meant to go to tonight?

He answered the call to find Mary at the other end. 'Hello Mary,' he said in a tired voice.

'Were you sleeping already?' a surprised Mary asked.

'I must have dozed off this afternoon. Last thing I remember I was having a few whiskies with Fr Mick.'

'Exactly how many whiskies did you have?'

'Oh, only two or three.'

'And when was the last time you took painkillers?'

'Sometime this afternoon.'

'And had you eaten anything?'

'No, I've slept through dinner apparently because everyone's gone and left me on my own.'

'Well, it's no wonder if you're drinking on an empty stomach and when you're taking painkillers to boot. Honestly Peter, you should be more careful.'

'Sorry darling, how is everything at home?'

'Oh, just grand, I've just got off the phone with Rory O'Shea. He's got a fantastic story to put in the paper tomorrow, about how a local Dublin layman has been called to Rome to help choose the new Pope.'

'Oh no! How did he find out about that?'

Mary relayed the recent conversation, and Peter exclaimed, 'Oh my God! So, he's going to go ahead and publish then?'

'I'm afraid so. I begged him not to and that it was a total beat up, but he was not going to let the truth get in the way of a good story. I suppose you'll have to tell O'Faherty what happened.'

'He won't be happy about it.'

'Sorry darling, I hope that it doesn't cause problems.'

'I hope so too. Anyway, what's done is done.'

'What are you going to do now?'

'Well, I was meant to go out to a function with the cardinals tonight so that I can meet with some of their colleagues, but I think I've slept through that as well. So, I'll see if I can find something to eat then I'll take some more painkillers and go to bed.'

'Okay. I'd better go, I think Lauren is still up and I need to get her into bed. Did you call work to let them know that you won't be in at all this week?'

'No, I forgot. I'll get on to it first thing tomorrow morning.'

'Don't forget. Tell Fr Mick and Cardinal O'Faherty that I'm sorry about what's happened.'

'Will do, give my love to the children.'

'Bye.'

'Bye my love.'

Peter ended the call and thought about how he was going to let the cardinals know about his presence in Rome being published in *The Irish Times*. However, in the meantime he needed to find something to eat. He needed some more painkillers and he couldn't bear to have another dose on an empty stomach.

He wandered into the dining room where he found a door leading to the kitchen. In the kitchen he found Georgio watching what appeared to be a dubbed version of *The Bachelor* on the TV. Georgio had anticipated his guest's hunger and still had a pot of hot water simmering on the stove. He threw a couple of handfuls of freshly made pasta into the pot and within a matter of minutes was able to serve Peter the best pasta bolognaise that he had ever tasted, complete with shaved parmesan, crusty bread, and a glass of red wine. Peter thought of refusing the wine because of the medication he was on, but he got the distinct impression from Georgio that the drinking of wine with dinner was not optional.

He finished his meal, thanked Georgio, wished him good night and went upstairs to bed. He took the opportunity to shower while Fr Mick was not in the room, took another dose of painkillers and quickly fell asleep.

Soon after his call with Mary, Rory O'Shea placed a call to his editor. They both agreed that there could be no substance to it, but a local man being invited to Rome for consultation during the papal election was newsworthy enough. They decided to run with the story in the morning edition and Rory set to work drafting the article.

Luckily for Peter, Rory and Rachael O'Shea were not close enough with the MacDonalds to know about Peter's recent surgery; Rory's work commitments meant that he was often unable to join some of the other school dads for Sunday night drinks at the Dan, even though Peter had invited him to come along on several occasions. Had he known of Peter's vasectomy, he certainly would have made mention of it in the article, as it was just the sort of juicy titbit that his editor always thought sold more papers.

Rory managed to extract the photo of Peter that was on the diocesan website and sent it to the night editor with his article:

Our Man the Pope Maker

A Dublin father of six has been summoned to Rome to assist with the selection of the next Pope. Unconfirmed reports indicate that Mr Peter MacDonald, who currently works as Town Planning Manager at Dublin City Council, was summoned to Rome for the purpose of consulting with some of the cardinals on the state of the Catholic Church. Mr MacDonald is a prominent lay member within the Dublin Archdiocese and is also a member of the Diocesan Pastoral Council. The Times has not yet been able to confirm this story with Cardinal Doherty's office.

There is, however, considerable doubt over the veracity of these reports, as lay involvement in Papal elections is both unprecedented and forbidden by canon law. However, provided the selection of specific candidates is not discussed, there is nothing to prevent cardinals to consult with anyone on the state of the Church.

For the past twelve hundred years the selection of the Pope has been the sole responsibility of the cardinals, and this is unlikely to have changed.

Never let the truth get in the way of a good story

Fr Mick and the cardinals were enjoying their evening at the *Time* magazine function in Rome. Well, Fr Mick was anyway. He was having a grand old time sipping Irish whisky and telling anyone who'd listen what he thought was wrong with the Catholic Church today. The cardinals, on the other hand, were still troubled with just what to do with their revelation. Had Peter been there with them, they had hoped that his presence would have caused a stir among the other cardinals. But with him missing, they were still a bit wary about raising the subject of Peter with others.

It was almost 11 pm, which was the time that Curiosa had planned to leave the function and many of the other guests had already left. Curiosa was chatting with Mobutu and Suryani. Fr Mick had found himself a comfortable chair and was having a snooze. Having had a very full day for men in their seventies, Billingham, O'Faherty and Pancetti had decided to leave the function an hour earlier.

Before leaving, the trio came across cardinals Peter Quinn from Australia and Stewart Johnson from California. Both were well known to Curiosa and although they couldn't be described as ardent conservatives, they had not done much for the liberal cause and had largely coalesced with the whims of the Vatican over the past decade.

They struck up a conversation which led to Quinn enquiring on the whereabouts of Cardinal O'Faherty. This in turn provided Curiosa with the opportunity of mentioning his dream of the next Pope being Irish.

'You wouldn't believe it,' Quinn exclaimed. 'I had a dream the other night with an Irish Pope in it as well. It was a rippa dream, I was competing in a triathlon at Bondi Beach.'

Quinn went on to describe the dream in detail further validating the premise that all cardinals had had similar dreams.

Curiosa then looked over to his countryman, Johnson, who had turned quite pale. He soon uncovered, not unexpectedly, that Johnson had had a similar dream. Curiosa sat them both down and proceeded to show them the image of Peter was now saved on his phone.

Suitably stunned by the revelation before them, Quinn and Johnson were enthralled to find out that Peter was in Rome and jumped at the opportunity to meet with him at the Jesuit College the following morning.

The early night had done Peter a world of good. He awoke from a peaceful sleep relatively pain-free but thought that he would need another dose of painkillers to get through the morning. As he reached over to the side table to pick up his wristwatch, he was pleased to see that Fr Mick was happily snoring away in his bed. He looked at his watch: 7.30 am. He did indeed have a good sleep.

He got out of bed and went into the closet-like bathroom to go to the toilet and shave. He was about to attempt another mini salt bath for his sutures (this time with the door locked) when he heard his cell phone ringing. He quickly ran out to answer the call, lest the ringing would wake Fr Mick.

He had assumed that the call would be from Mary but was surprised to see Niall Brodie's name on the screen. 'Hey Niall, what are you doing calling me at this hour?'

'Macca! How are you lad? I just wanted to see how you were getting on in Rome.'

'How did you know I was in Rome?'

'It's on the front page of *The Irish Times*!'

'*The Irish Times*!' Peter then remembered the conversation he'd had with Mary the previous night. 'Oh! That's fecking Rory O'Shea's doing. I still don't know how he worked it out.'

'It's a grand story Macca. "Our Man the Pope-Maker" is the headline. So was having the snip just a cover for this?'

'I tell you Niall, I knew nothing of this until mid-morning on Monday. In fact, I was in the surgeon's chair having the snip done when Fr Mick burst in to tell me that Cardinal O'Faherty wanted me in Rome.'

'Did he really? That must have been a shock for the poor old fellow?'

'Not as big as a shock as it was for me and the surgeon!'

'So, what's the real story Macca?'

'I still don't really know! Somehow O'Faherty and a few of his cardinal mates got it in their heads that it would be good to talk to someone like me before they go into the Conclave.'

'Do they know what you think of the people running the show at the moment?'

'Yeah, I told them exactly what I think, and they just lapped it up! It seems to me like they want to push a liberal agenda at the Conclave but it's ludicrous to think that the opinions of one layman could change the conservative bias of the Curia.'

'Oh well, me and the lads will be cheering for you back here. When are you coming back?'

'Mary wants me back Friday night so that I can be there to do the run around with the kids on the weekend.'

'We'll have to catch up for a pint on Sunday then.'

'Looking forward to it.'

He had no sooner got off the phone when it rang again. This time it was Ian Brown calling. 'Macca!' he called out when Peter answered the call, 'I always knew you had greatness within you. So, who are you going to anoint as Anthony's successor?'

'Shut the feck up Ian,' Peter replied jokingly. 'It's nothing like that. I'm simply here to offer my opinion on the state of the Church.'

'If it's anything like the opinion that you delivered to us the other night I'd say you were setting yourself up for rapid excommunication.'

Peter had to laugh at this comment. 'You'd be surprised Brownie. It certainly surprised me that there were still a few fellas at the top who want things to change as much as I do. Still, they are definitely in the minority so I don't see how my opinions could make more than a gnat's willy's difference in who becomes the next Pope.'

'Don't sell yourself short Macca, I'm sure you'll have them all on your side by the time that the day is out. But anyway, what happened with the snip? Did you still go ahead with it?'

'Sure did, and I'll tell you I've been popping those painkillers like they're Tic Tacs. I was definitely not a very comfortable boy yesterday, but things seem to have settled down a bit today.'

'Oh well, that's God's way of punishing you for breaking your marriage vows. You didn't expect him to make it easy for you now, did you?'

'No, I suppose not.'

'Okay, well you look after yourself and I'll catch up when you get back. Enjoy the rest of your holiday and make sure you pick a good one out for us this time.'

'It's not a holiday, I'm convalescing,' Peter protested. 'And yes, I'll see you at The Dan on Sunday night if you're interested and I'll tell you all about it.'

When Peter got off the phone with Ian he noticed that he already had three voicemail messages. But before he could check who they were from, the phone rang again. This time it was Callan Dyson, the planning director at the council and Peter's manager. He picked up the phone immediately. 'Hello Callan, how are you? I suppose you're wanting to find out what I'm doing in Rome.'

'Rome? What are you doing in Rome?' was the confused reply. 'I thought that you were convalescing after your little operation.'

'Oh!' said an embarrassed Peter, 'I thought that you'd maybe seen my picture in the paper. Otherwise, what are you doing calling me at this hour when I am supposed to be on leave?'

'What hour? Oh, it's just gone 7 am. I suppose it is a tad early, but I've been up for hours trying to sort out the information we need for this planning appeal that we have to attend on Friday. I just called to make sure that you were coming back tomorrow to help me with it. But what's this thing about having your picture in the paper and why in feck's name are you in Rome?'

'Well, it's a long story but you know how I've been involved with the Church for some years now. On Monday, my old parish priest, Fr Mick contacted me and said that one of the cardinals wanted to see me in Rome because they were interested in my views. I'd already planned to take a couple of days off after my surgery so I thought I could rest up just as easily in Rome as I could in Dublin.'

'So, you'll be coming back tonight, right!' the statement was more of a command than a request.

Peter had forgotten totally about the planning appeal hearing this Friday. It wasn't imperative that he attend but it would certainly make it difficult for his colleagues if he didn't. 'Um, err … I've been meaning to call you about that. You see, the thing is that the cardinals want me to stay here at least until the start of the Conclave.'

'Christ! When is that going to be?'

'Actually, it's tomorrow but I figured there was no point coming into the office for just one day so I was planning to stay until Friday. Do you think you could handle the hearing without me?'

'Well, I don't think so! You're the one with the most knowledge of the case so it's best that you be there.'

Peter knew that they certainly could handle the hearing without him, but Callan's guilt trip had worked a treat. 'Okay, I'll try to get a flight tomorrow evening so I'll be able to make it in on Friday.'

'Oh, that's grand Peter. And you can tell those cardinals from me that they've got their job to do, and you've got yours.'

With that Callan ended the call. But the moment he hung up, several more voicemail messages appeared on Peter's phone and almost immediately the phone began to ring again. This time it was Mary. 'Good morning darling, thank Christ it's you. I've been fielding calls about the *Times* article all morning,' said Peter.

'The phone hasn't been exactly quiet here either!' was Mary's disgruntled reply.

'I'm sorry dear, this thing is getting out of hand isn't it?'

'That's an understatement, I've even had Fr Damian call me this morning.'

'What did you tell him?'

'The same thing that I've told everyone else, that the newspaper has made a mountain out of a molehill.'

'Did he buy it?'

'It's hard to say. But I think he was more worried about you stirring up trouble with Cardinal Doherty again. You know how the cardinal expects him to keep you under control.'

'Poor Damian, I can see how getting myself into the paper would trouble him. Anyway, I'd better go and think up how I am going to explain all this to the cardinals … if I can ever get off the phone.'

'Just switch the thing off. There's nothing more you can tell them. You can fill them all in once this is all over.'

'Sounds like a good idea. Say good morning to the children for me and I'll try to call you back later on.'

'Okay Peter, look after yourself and try not to get into trouble.'

Meeting the man
of your dreams

Once he had switched off his phone, Peter was finally able to get himself ready for breakfast. He would have to give the pseudo salt bath a miss as the incessant telephone rings had wakened Fr Mick and he was presently in the bathroom. Peter got dressed and waited for Fr Mick.

Fr Mick had overheard parts of Peter's conversations, so he knew that something was up. As soon as he got out of the bathroom he said to Peter, 'I suppose that the cat is well and truly out of the bag.'

Peter was holding his head in his hands. 'Well and truly.' He looked up at Fr Mick. 'Apparently I've made the front page of *The Irish Times*.'

'The front page, that's very impressive,' Fr Mick replied. 'How did that happen?'

Peter then gave Fr Mick a brief account of how he believed Rory O'Shea may have come across the story and Rory's subsequent phone call to Mary.

'Sneaky bugger!' Fr Mick replied when Peter finished his account. 'Anyway, what's done is done and there's nothing we can do about it now. But in the meantime, let's go and get some breakfast, I'm famished.'

'Me too, let's go.'

With that they made their way downstairs; it was almost 9 am. Peter walked straight into the kitchen with Fr Mick to find Georgio waiting for them. Without asking what they would like, Georgio set about preparing a full cooked breakfast for each of them similar to the one he prepared yesterday. He also had a coffee pot ready to put on the boil, and so within ten minutes a sumptuous breakfast was served complete with toast and freshly squeezed orange juice.

After breakfast, Peter and Fr Mick retired to the lounge to wait and see what the cardinals had in store for them today. Peter was worried about the morning's events, so he voiced his concerns with Fr Mick. 'How do you think the cardinals will handle *The Irish Times* business?'

'Given their response to anything to do with you so far, I'd expect them to be ecstatic.'

'But they're not meant to discuss the succession of the papacy even among themselves before the Conclave. I imagine that the Curia would not think highly of them discussing the papacy with a layperson.'

'Yes that would be a very serious thing … if that is what they are doing.'

'Well, isn't it?'

'Well firstly, I don't think there is a problem with the cardinals discussing the succession among themselves in the lead up to a Conclave – it's only an issue when the Pope is still alive. But secondly, has anyone actually asked you who you think should be the next pope?'

'No, not really.'

'And have you heard the cardinals discussing who should be Pope among themselves?'

'No, I don't recall that I have.'

'There you go then, there is no question of them discussing the papacy outside of the Conclave. Admittedly, the Curia may have difficulty with the concept of cardinals actually discussing the state of the Church with a layperson, but that in itself is not an offence.'

Their conversation was interrupted by the sounds of a scuffle coming from the hallway. Peter heard what sounded like Georgio's voice calling out: 'Vietato, e vietato entrare,'

At the same time he heard a second voice that was definitely not Italian, calling back: 'Va bene … tutto bene!'

He looked over to the door connecting the lounge to the hallway to see a man in a pale grey suit burst through, with Georgio in hot pursuit trying to pull him back out.

'Ah, Mr MacDonald,' the man said in a broad Irish accent, 'I thought I'd find you here.'

Georgio, who was obviously flustered by the intrusion, was clutching on to the man's arm, restricting him from approaching Peter and Fr Mick. 'Mi scusi Padre, mi scusi Signore, Gli ho detto di non entrare.'

Fr Mick signalled to Georgio that it was okay and Georgio reluctantly let go.

The man pulled his left arm away from Georgio's grasp and walked towards Peter with his right arm outstretched. 'Mr MacDonald, it's grand to meet you. I'm Declan O'Reilly, the Vatican correspondent for *The Irish Times*.'

Peter accepted his handshake. 'Good morning Mr O'Reilly.' He then gestured where Fr Mick was standing. 'This is Fr Michael Finlay, what can we do for you?'

'Good morning Father,' Declan said to Fr Mick before turning back to Peter. 'Well, Mr MacDonald, I was wondering if I could ask you a few questions about your visit to Rome?'

'I thought that Rory O'Shea already knew all about it. Or at least he made out he did in his article in the paper,' Peter replied.

'I'd like to confirm the story with you if I may. Rory's sources said that you were summoned to Rome be consulted on the succession of the papacy.'

'That's a ludicrous assertion for a start. Cardinals don't even discuss the succession among themselves! Why in heaven's name will they discuss it with a layman? That Rory O'Shea better check his sources!'

'I was led to believe that Rory's source was none other than your wife Mary MacDonald.'

'Aye, is that what he told you? I think our Rory is bending the truth a bit there. If you press him further, I think you'll find that Rory's source was likely his nine-year-old daughter, who is my daughter's best friend.' This was a bit of a guess on Peter's part, but it emphasised his case that the story was not credible. 'We're simply here as guests of Cardinal O'Faherty, who was in the seminary with Fr Finlay here,' he added.

Poor Declan looked terribly confused and embarrassed. Being invited to Rome during a Conclave was a much more logical explanation than the story that ended up in the paper. Declan had even accused Cardinal Doherty over the phone of trying to cover up Peter's visit. It would not be easy to apologise to the cardinal. 'I'm sorry Mr MacDonald, there must have been some misunderstanding. I will contact the newspaper to issue a correction.'

'That would be a very good idea.' Peter had barely finished this sentence when two cardinals whom he had not met before burst into the lounge.

Cardinals Peter Quinn and Stewart Johnson had taken Cardinal Curiosa up on his invitation to come to the Jesuit College to meet with Peter. As they were familiar with the college, they didn't bother to make an appointment. Seeing the two cardinals approaching him, Peter stood out of courtesy.

'Mr MacDonald,' Quinn said as he grabbed Peter's right hand and started shaking it, 'it's really great to meet you.'

Not waiting for Cardinal Quinn to release his handshake, Cardinal Johnson grabbed Peter's left hand, saying, 'Mr MacDonald, Cardinal Curiosa told us we'd find you here.'

Now Peter was trapped by two cardinals each smiling at him as they shook his hands and refusing to release their grip. He gave Fr Mick a worried look and then sheepishly looked over to Declan.

In his five years as a correspondent in the Vatican, Declan had never witnessed a cardinal going out of his way to greet a layperson. Cardinals were generally people you had to seek audiences with. Why would Cardinal Quinn greet someone he had obviously just met so enthusiastically? And Cardinal Johnson seemed just as enthusiastic to meet him as well. What was going on?

Johnson said that Cardinal Curiosa had told them where to find Peter MacDonald. Curiosa was not quite the last of the liberal cardinals, but he certainly was historically vocal against conservatism in the Curia. But even he had to moderate his views in the past, as it was obvious that the numbers were not on his side.

This was Curiosa's last Conclave – what was he up to? He knew that Cardinal O'Faherty was a closet liberal as well. If O'Faherty was involved, then that would explain the incredulity that Cardinal Doherty had displayed in their telephone conversation that morning. There was definitely something to this story and it was far bigger than O'Shea had considered.

Declan managed to compose himself and moved to stand next to Peter so that he could face the cardinals as their eyes remained fixed in Peter's direction. 'Good morning Your Eminences, I'm Declan O'Reilly. May I ask how you know Mr MacDonald here?'

Before the cardinals could respond, Peter quickly interjected saying: 'Declan is the Vatican's correspondent for *The Irish Times*.'

A worried look immediately came over the cardinals' faces, and they quickly released their grip and took a couple of steps away from Peter. 'Um … Err … Mr MacDonald is a good friend of Cardinal Curiosa,' Johnson blurted out.

'Yes … yes …' Quinn added, 'this is Mr MacDonald's first time in Rome and Cardinal Curiosa wanted us to make him feel welcome.'

These lame explanations only aroused Declan's curiosity even further. It was one day before a Conclave, for Christ's sake! Surely the cardinals had other things to get on with rather than seek out a layman from Dublin. 'Cardinal Curiosa, really?' Declan replied incredulously. 'Are you really good friends with Cardinal Curiosa, Mr MacDonald?'

Peter's face sank. Mouth agape, he looked over to Fr Mick, and then to the cardinals, hoping for some support. Reluctantly, he turned to face Declan, grimaced and nodded his head a couple of times.

Declan was certain he was on to something. 'Cardinal Curiosa is based in New Jersey, is he not? Does your work with the council in Dublin take you to New Jersey often?'

Peter was stuck on that one. He barely knew O'Faherty, and he was Irish! How could he explain being friends with a cardinal from New Jersey? He had never even been to the United States. In fact, this trip to Rome was the furthest away from Dublin that he'd ever been. A few moments passed as Peter struggled to respond, but his thoughts were interrupted by the entrance of cardinals Mobutu, Suryani and Soutier.

Mobutu spoke first. With his booming voice, he called out as he walked across the room to Peter, 'Mr MacDonald, how good it is to finally meet you.' He gave Peter a hardy handshake. 'I am Cardinal Eric Mobutu from Cape Town in South Africa. I believe you were introduced to Cardinal Phillip Suryani here last night.'

Suryani then stepped forward to shake his hand. 'Pleased to meet you Mr MacDonald, we will be very interested to hear your thoughts on the state of the Church.'

Mobutu then gestured to Soutier. 'And this is Cardinal Soutier from Paris.'

Soutier then came forward to shake his hand as well. 'Bonjour Monsieur MacDonald, I think perhaps that our colleagues wore you out yesterday. We will have time to talk today, yes?'

Peter just stood there stunned. He shuddered to think what Declan was making of all this. He wanted some answers himself now. Who did these cardinals think that he was?

Declan O'Reilly, for his part, was thinking the same thing. These cardinals all obviously see something special in Peter MacDonald, what could it be? This was certainly the story of the Conclave. He knew Quinn and Johnson to be political moderates who generally sided with the conservatives on contentious issues, as they would never want to be seen as ones to rock the boat. But Mobutu, Suryani and Soutier were three of the last surviving liberals. Curiosa was a card carrying liberal and it was widely known that O'Faherty had liberal leanings. All he needed now was for cardinals Billingham and Pancetti to enter the room and he had the makings of a full-blown liberal conspiracy.

But what would they hope to achieve? There was no way any one of them would have the numbers to have any impact on the papacy. And how could this Peter MacDonald promote their cause in any way?

Almost on cue, cardinals Billingham and O'Faherty entered the room. Billingham walked straight towards Peter, just as the others had done. However, O'Faherty recognised that there was another layperson in the room, and it was none other than the Vatican correspondent for *The Irish Times* Declan O'Reilly, whom he had spoken with on several occasions. 'Declan, my boy, what brings you to the college today?' O'Faherty said nervously as he walked towards Declan.

'Good morning Your Eminence,' Declan replied, 'I don't quite know where to begin. I have so many questions I'd like to ask you. But to kick things off: I was tipped off that I'd find Mr Peter MacDonald here at the college. We ran a story on him in this morning's edition.'

'Did you really?' O'Faherty replied. 'Now why would you run a story on this simple man then?'

'Well, one of our senior journalists in Dublin, Rory O'Shea, found out that he'd been sent to Rome to consult with the cardinals with regard to the succession of the papacy.'

'Now why would someone suggest something like that? I know you haven't been Vatican correspondent for very long, but you should know well enough that cardinals wouldn't discuss the succession of the papacy with an ordinary layman.'

'I thought so too, before I saw how your colleagues here were so excited to meet with him. I can't help thinking that there is something really odd going on here.'

O'Faherty saw by the nervous look on the faces of the other cardinals that they may have been unaware that a journalist was in the room, and that they may have been overenthusiastic in the way that they greeted Peter. 'Declan, you know that we're all a friendly lot, why should it surprise you that we are excited to meet someone new?'

'I'm sorry Your Eminence, but what I've just witnessed cannot be explained by ordinary friendliness. All these cardinals greeted Mr MacDonald as an old friend, although it was clear from their greeting that they hadn't actually met him before. I would like to know how exactly Mr MacDonald is going to help you with the choice that you have to make over the next few days.'

O'Faherty knew that one or two cardinals meeting with a layperson before the Conclave would not be seen as such a big deal. But that fact that Peter was discovered in the company of no less than seven cardinals would certainly raise eyebrows. He called Declan over. 'Declan my boy, can I have a word with you in private?'

'Certainly!' an excited Declan replied.

O'Faherty then spoke to Georgio, who was still standing in the doorway observing what was going on. No-one could hear what O'Faherty had said to him but at the end of their short conversation Georgio nodded, pulled his keys out from his pocket and walked back along the hallway.

O'Faherty gestured to Declan to come with him. 'Georgio will show you to a room where we can talk, I'll just consult with my colleagues beforehand if that is okay.'

'That's fine Your Eminence, I'll see you shortly then.'

Georgio led Declan to a door on the right-hand side of the central hall way, switched on the light and motioned for Declan to enter the room. 'Si accomodi prego signore,'

'Grazie,' Declan replied before noticing that Georgio was trying to remove his suit jacket from him. This was a problem because the jacket contained his voice recorder, notepad, and smartphone. He started to resist but was distracted by the sight of cardinals Curiosa and Pancetti entering the hallway from the front entrance. *Yes!* he thought. Now he had the full set of liberal cardinals and a couple of moderates to boot. This was really big! He was so excited that he didn't notice that Georgio had in fact managed to remove his jacket completely and was hanging it on a hall stand outside the room. He decided not to risk another confrontation with Georgio and let him do what he wanted. After all, he could always pop out to get his things if he needed them.

Declan entered the small prayer room and Georgio shut the door behind him. He was still so excited about what he had uncovered that he didn't hear the sound of the additional click as Georgio locked the door.

Strange revelations

Curiosa and Pancetti entered the lounge to find Peter surrounded by no less than seven cardinals with worried expressions and Fr Mick looking on in bemusement. 'Good morning gentlemen, glad that you all could make it,' said Curiosa. 'What are we looking so worried about?'

'Just had a bloody journalist sticking his head in where it didn't belong,' a clearly irritated Quinn announced.

O'Faherty elaborated, 'His name is Declan O'Reilly, he's the Vatican correspondent for *The Irish Times*. They wanted to know about our mate here.' He gestured to Peter.

Peter said, 'The paper must have tipped off their Vatican correspondent to get more information, so he came looking for me. Fr Mick and I had him almost convinced that the story was a big beat-up but then these two cardinals arrived.' He gestured to Quinn and Johnson. 'Then he knew something was up.'

'Where is he now?' Curiosa asked.

'He's locked in one of the prayer rooms,' O'Faherty responded.

'Locked!' said an alarmed Curiosa. 'We're taking prisoners now are we?'

'It's just temporary until we work out what to tell him.'

Johnson then entered the conversation. 'Wouldn't he still have a cell phone on him? He could be reporting back to Dublin as we speak.'

'I had Georgio take his coat from him before he went in the room,' said O'Faherty

'Good thinking,' said Johnson, 'so what are we going to tell him?'

'Excuse me Your Eminences!' Peter announced, 'Before you think about what to tell the newspapers, don't you think I need to know what is really going on here? I mean, before I arrived on Monday night, I barely knew one cardinal while today I have no less than nine treating me like I'm an old friend. I think I deserve some sort of explanation!'

'You mean they haven't told you?' Quinn enquired.

'Told me what?' an indignant Peter replied.

'Do you want to handle this Ricky?' O'Faherty asked of Curiosa.

'I guess I'll have to.' He turned to address Peter. 'Well, Mr MacDonald ...'

'Peter please.'

'Okay Peter, I think you'd better sit down for this.'

Peter sat back down on the armchair. Fr Mick hadn't bothered to get out of his chair but was now sitting forward, eager to hear what this all was about. Curiosa sat down on a sofa opposite and was joined by Quinn and Johnson. Soutier and Mobutu managed to balance themselves on the arms of the sofa while O'Faherty perched himself on the arm of his friend Fr Mick's armchair. Pancetti, Suryani and Billingham commandeered chairs from other parts of the room and positioned themselves around their colleagues.

Curiosa was still not sure what to say to Peter. It was true that he deserved to know the truth, but the truth was so incredible – would he accept it? He supposed it would explain the way they were acting so strangely around him. He waited for everyone to get settled then he began to speak. 'Well Peter, if we have been acting a bit strangely around you it is because we have been through quite a strange experience ourselves over the past few days. A totally incredible experience in fact.

'We all thought nothing of it to start with. Everyone has dreams after all. It so happened that on the evening of Pope Anthony's funeral I had a wonderful dream which culminated with me meeting the new Pope. I guess that that is not unusual in itself as the succession would have been at the top of my mind that night. But we have since discovered that we all had similar dreams and I believe that we all had them on the same night.' Curiosa looked around to his colleagues and received nods of agreement from each of them. 'It appears that each of us had our own very personal dreams with the only similarities being that in our dreams we were all doing something we enjoy – and at the end of the dream we all met the new Holy Father.

'Now I must stress that we didn't know about each other's dreams until a couple of nights ago, when Louie here,' Pancetti smiled as Curiosa gestured to him, 'was chatting to Paddy in this very room. Louie casually mentioned to Paddy that he had dreamt of the new Pope.' He looked at Pancetti again. 'You may want to fill in this bit Louie.'

Curiosa's request caught Pancetti by surprise, but he quickly managed to compose himself. 'Oh, okay Ricky. Well, Paddy and I were sitting over there.' He pointed to the arrangement of sofas and armchairs situated just opposite the hallway door. 'And I say to Paddy, you would not believe it, but I dream the new Papa was Irish, because in my dream I meet the Papa and he talks the same as Paddy.'

O'Faherty then took over the story. 'That sparked my curiosity because the Pope in my dream had the same features as the Pope in Louie's dream. Then Ricky here shows up – lo and behold, he goes on to tell us about a dream he had the other night where he met the Pope, and his Pope was a young Irishman as well. This all starts to look like a strange coincidence then I told them that I actually recognised the man who appeared as Pope in my dream.'

Curiosa then spoke again. 'So, when Paddy said he knew the person in his dream and gave us a name we had to check to see if it was the same person. I googled the name on my iPad and found a picture of him. Both Louie and I couldn't believe our eyes. The man in the picture we were looking at was identical to the man in each of our dreams.'

Peter still had a puzzled look on his face. 'What does this have to do with me?'

'More than you can imagine,' Curiosa replied. 'Would you like to see a picture of the man we all saw in our dreams?'

Peter gave a nervous nod as Curiosa pulled his iPhone out of his jacket pocket and brought up the same picture that he had shown to Quinn and Johnson the previous evening. He slowly turned the phone around so that Peter could see the image.

It took a while for Peter to come to terms with what he was looking at. He was looking at the photo of himself that was posted on the Diocesan website. His face went white, and he thought that he might bring up his breakfast. He looked up incredulously to find Curiosa smiling and nodding back at him.

'No … no … no!' he said repeatedly as he got out of his chair and walked to the other side of the room. 'No, this is impossible, you couldn't all have possibly dreamt of me as Pope! It's ludicrous, I'm not even a priest! I have a wife and six children, for Christ's sake!' He looked over to Fr Mick – who, having seen the image on Curiosa's phone, was now laughing uncontrollably. A look of fear now came over Peter. 'No, no way! There is no way you could think that I could be Pope, you can't possibly be suggesting that!'

'Well at least you understand why we couldn't tell you the truth about why we wanted you to come to Rome,' Curiosa said softly. 'And rest assured, although we're not sure what the meaning of these dreams are, we don't think they mean you should be Pope. Sit down and we'll talk about what we think we should do.'

Peter slowly walked back to his chair, passing a worried glance to Fr Mick who was still chuckling away. 'This is not funny Mick!' he said indignantly as he slumped back into his chair and put his face in is hands. He eventually lifted his head up to look back at Curiosa. 'Are you all sure it was me in your dreams?'

'If we weren't then, we certainly are now,' Curiosa replied. 'You see, when we summoned you to Rome there were only four of us who recognised you in their dreams. However, as of last night we have nine cardinals who are sure that you appeared in their dreams as the new Pope. We deliberately didn't say anything to Eric, Pierre, and Phillip before they came to the college yesterday evening. We just wanted to see what their reaction was when they saw you. Although none of them had heard about you or seen a photo of you, they all recognised you immediately because they'd had the dream as well.'

Curiosa continued, 'And yesterday we wanted you to come with us to the *Time* magazine function just to see how the cardinals who were there would react to your presence. We were a bit disappointed when you were indisposed but I had stored your photo in my iPhone. Towards the end of the night, we got talking to Quinnie and Stewie here,' he gestured to where Quinn and Johnson were sitting, 'and I casually mentioned that I had dreamt of an Irish Pope and they both replied that they had also dreamt of an Irish Pope. I showed them the picture of you and they both identified you as the Pope in their dream as well!'

Peter's head was spinning now. What could this possibly mean? Why him? How could he infiltrate the dreams of cardinals?

O'Faherty then spoke. 'You see Peter, so far there have been nine who we know have seen you in their dream. But the thing is, we are yet to find a cardinal who has not had a dream where you appeared to them as Pope. Although we're a fairly small sample, we have no reason to believe that every cardinal has not had a similar dream.'

Peter now thought that his brain was about to explode. He held his head in his hands and was rocking back and forwards in his chair. 'How can this be? How can I appear in the dreams of people I haven't met before? Why is this happening? This is completely crazy, completely crazy!'

'It's a bloody miracle,' said Quinn. 'I couldn't believe it myself when they first told me last night. But now that I've seen you in the flesh, I am certain that you were the one in my dream and I'll be buggered if I know how you got in there.'

'We all think the same way, n'est pa?' Soutier added. 'This can only be the work of God himself!'

'But why would God put the image of a particular layman in our minds just before a Conclave?' asked Johnson. 'It's totally against the rules for us to consider the opinion of any lay influence in our decision.'

'Perhaps God doesn't play by our rules,' Curiosa replied. 'And besides, I hate to be the one to break this to you Stewie, but God is not Catholic.'

'What do you mean, God is not Catholic? Of course he's Catholic!'

'Well, think about it Stewie. Jesus was born a Jew and our God is also the God of Abraham, Moses and Mohamed – and truth be told, is probably not far removed from Buddha as well.'

This statement tested Johnson's moderate views and raised his ire. 'Listen Ricky, if you think you're going to use this magnificent revelation to push a liberal agenda at the Conclave, you've got another thing coming. I'd want to hear what our man Mr MacDonald has to say before pushing for radical change!'

'I thought you just said that was against the rules?'

Curiosa's comment had stumped Johnson, so Quinn decided to give his friend a helping hand. 'Stewie, I think that you'll have to accept that this thing is so fantastic that we have to forget about the rules of the Conclave for the time being. God put this fellow in our minds for a reason, so you're right; we have to listen to what he has to say before we go into the Conclave.'

Peter felt that he wanted to scream. How could it have come to this? Could his opinions really guide the selection of the next Pope? He had freely spoken his mind the previous morning, but he knew that his views were diametrically opposed to the majority of cardinals and the Roman Curia itself. This would truly be a miracle if he could change their conservative views overnight.

The ensuing silence was interrupted by the sound of banging coming from the end of the hall.

'Oh, that will be poor Declan,' O'Faherty announced. 'He's probably worked out that he's locked in. I'd better go to him. Any ideas as to what I should tell him?'

'I'll come with you,' said Curiosa, 'together we'll work something out.'

Doherty's dream

The phone conversation that Cardinal Patrick Doherty had just had with *The Irish Times* Vatican correspondent, Declan O'Reilly, was disturbing. Young Declan, whom he had met on several occasions over the past few years, had made an incredible assertion that he personally had something to do with summoning a lay member of his Diocesan Pastoral Council to Rome for consultation about the papal succession. This was a ludicrous suggestion, and he couldn't imagine where the newspapers got such wild ideas. But what was really disturbed him was that the particular layman, named by Declan as Peter MacDonald, had recently appeared to him in a dream.

He hadn't thought much about that dream until Declan O'Reilly's phone call. No doubt about it, it was a strange dream, but he'd had strange dreams before. He was just recovering from a head cold and his dreams where often quite surreal when he was feverish.

But why would Peter MacDonald appear to him in a dream – and as the Pope, no less?

But Peter MacDonald it was, and it appeared that this very same Peter MacDonald was actually in Rome at the present time. Furthermore, *The Irish Times* was reporting that it was he who had summoned Peter MacDonald to Rome. This was a complete fabrication; he would never have contemplated doing such a thing. He knew the rules; no layperson was permitted to influence the choice of Pope for any reason.

Doherty's fervent view was that laypeople were far too involved with the function of the Church as it was, and Vatican II had a lot to answer for in that regard. In fact, he considered that the steady decline in mass attendances and the decline in religious vocations over the past few decades was a direct result of the Vatican II reforms going too far.

He firmly believed that had Church services remained true to their original Latin form, the churches would still be packed with believers and the seminaries would be full. He therefore was actively working with other 'right minded' cardinals and bishops to redress some of these changes. He only persisted with lay representatives on his Diocesan Pastoral Council because he wanted to maintain the impression that he consulted with the people. He only convened the Diocesan Council twice a year and always deferred to Vatican doctrine when questions were raised by the laity.

Striking a deal with Declan

O'Faherty and Curiosa walked up the hallway to where Declan O'Reilly was frantically banging on the door. 'Hello Declan, it's Cardinal O'Faherty here, can you please stop with the banging in there?'

'You can't keep me in here forever!' Declan called back to him.

'It's alright Declan. I have Cardinal Curiosa here with me and we would like to have a talk with you?'

'Okay Your Eminence, but you better have something good for me – don't think that I'm above pressing charges against a cardinal for imprisonment!'

O'Faherty motioned for Georgio, who had followed them down the hall, to open the door so that they could enter the room. 'Now what's this talk of imprisonment there Declan?' O'Faherty asked cagily.

'Your man out there locked me in here!' Declan angrily replied.

'Locked you in?' said Curiosa incredulously as he walked back to the door and rattled the handle a few times before opening the door. 'I think you'll find that this handle gets sticky at times. I've asked Georgio to have a look at it, but he hasn't got around to fixing it yet. Why would you think we'd want to lock you in?'

Declan's expression clearly showed that he hadn't had the wool pulled over his eyes, but he also knew that if he pressed the point no-one would believe him over the good cardinal. 'Well, I thought that you were trying to prevent me from reporting on what I had observed in the lounge this morning.'

'What exactly did you see that was worth reporting?' Curiosa asked innocently.

'With respect, Eminence, I think that a half dozen or so cardinals fawning over a layman who they had just met is certainly worth reporting! Especially when I was following up on a report from Dublin that this very same man had been sent to Rome to be consulted on the papal succession.'

'Now you don't want to be jumping to conclusions there,' said O'Faherty. 'Firstly, the rules of the Conclave expressly forbid any lay influence. Secondly, that is not why Mr MacDonald happens to be in Rome. He is here as my guest and came with my very good friend Fr Finlay who was also Mr MacDonald's parish priest.'

Declan smiled. 'You know Eminence, I almost bought that story from Mr MacDonald himself. But that was before cardinals Quinn and Johnson walked in and greeted Mr MacDonald as an old friend even though they obviously hadn't met him before. Then Suryani, Mobutu and Soutier arrived and did the same thing! You can't tell me there isn't something going on here!'

Curiosa looked despairingly back at O'Faherty. It was clear that they couldn't talk their way out of this one. He sighed before looking back at Declan. 'Well, Mr O'Reilly is it? How would you like to have an exclusive on one of the biggest stories in Vatican history, or Christian history for that matter?'

Declan's grin was as big as his face. 'So, there is a big story here.'

'But before we tell you,' Curiosa added, 'you'll have to agree to an embargo.'

'And if I don't?' Declan replied.

'Well then, let's just say that it may take Georgio a few days to get around to fixing this sticky doorknob.'

'So, if I agree to the embargo you'll let me walk out of here.'

'Yes we will.'

O'Faherty pulled Curiosa aside. 'Just a minute Ricky, what's to stop him telling his story once he gets out?'

Curiosa made sure that Declan could hear every word. 'Well Paddy, I think that when Mr O'Reilly hears what we've got to tell him, he'll fully understand the need for secrecy until after the Conclave begins.'

'So once the Conclave starts the embargo will be lifted?' An increasingly curious Declan enquired.

Curiosa gave the matter a little thought. They wouldn't want their secret known until they were making headway in the Conclave. If they got a quick result it would give them a chance to explain the result before the media got hold of the story. However, if it was a prolonged Conclave, which was very likely given the controversy that their revelation would generate, it wouldn't be fair to Declan to have to hold on to this information while everyone else was wondering what was going on.

'Tell you what,' he eventually replied, 'let's make it three days or the end of the Conclave, whichever comes first.'

'Two days!' Declan declared.

'Four days then!'

'… Okay, three days or the end of the Conclave.'

'So, it's agreed.' Curiosa extended his hand to Declan.

Declan accepted Curiosa's handshake. 'Yes, agreed.'

'Okay Mr O'Reilly, you'd better sit down for this. It's not going to be easy for you to fathom.'

Curiosa hardly knew where to start. Each time he re-told the story he had to remind himself that it was really happening. Curiosa and O'Faherty then proceeded to explain to Declan how they came to be aware that they had all dreamt of an Irish Pope and the miracle that the Pope in each of their dreams was Peter MacDonald.

'When you said this was going to be hard to believe, you weren't kidding were you? Are there any other cardinals who have seen Mr MacDonald apart from those here today?'

'Not that we know of, however one or two may have seen us when we were out and about yesterday,' O'Faherty replied.

'But all nine who have met him are sure that he was the man in their dreams.'

'Yes,' Curiosa replied emphatically.

'So, the odds are that other cardinals have had this dream. In fact, you'll have no reason to believe that all cardinals haven't had the dream. This is crazy stuff! I mean if this is true it is far more than a coincidence. It must be …' Declan hesitated before he said it out loud. 'It must be a bloody miracle!'

'Told you it was big,' Curiosa said smugly. 'So now you understand why you can't reveal this story before the Conclave. If this got out now, people would think it was a total fabrication or worse, they would think that those of us involved were trying to unduly influence the Conclave. And although we strongly suspect that others have had this dream, we can't be sure until we bring it up during the Conclave.'

'What exactly are you going to say in the Conclave? Are you going to nominate Peter MacDonald for Pope?'

'Of course not!' Curiosa snapped back. 'We can't possibly do that.'

'Why not? That's what your dreams are telling you, isn't it? I mean, this is the first time since … since I don't know when, that God shows you his hand and you're going to ignore it!'

'We're not going to ignore it. We just don't think the dreams mean that he should become Pope. The papacy is a life sentence; most of us don't want it for ourselves, why would we impose it on a layman? He has a wife and family to consider!'

'So, what are you going to do?'

'I'm not sure really. But the line I'm thinking is that the dreams are an obvious sign that a significant change is required in the Church.'

'How exactly do the dreams tell you that?'

'The dreams don't tell us anything, really. Each one of us has had a different dream with the only common threads being that in our dreams we were all doing something we enjoyed, such as playing golf and surfing, or in my case, performing at the comedy club in New York. The only commonality is that at the end of the dream, we meet the Pope who appears to us in the form of Mr MacDonald.'

'So how do you read into that that the Church needs to change?'

Curiosa was struggling a bit with giving Declan a credible response. 'Once we had met Mr MacDonald, we found out that he was unhappy with the direction the Church was taking. So, we resolved that this meant that we shouldn't shy away from pursuing for a more liberal Pope at the Conclave.'

'Well, having excluded the possibility that Mr MacDonald should be Pope, I can see how you would read that into your own dream. But isn't that just channelling your own viewpoint? How would you convince the likes of Cardinal Doherty or Cardinal Mangiafuoco that this is what their dreams mean? If, in fact, they had the dream. Given their views of the future of the Church, they might just interpret a dream of a lay Pope as a warning against increased liberalism.'

'That thought has crossed our minds and is one of the reasons why we thought we shouldn't say anything until the Conclave. I know that we will be up against some opposition – that's why I don't expect it to be over within a couple of days. It is also why I agreed to let you publish our story after three days, as if it is a prolonged Conclave, the faithful should know why it is taking so long.'

'Okay, but if that's your strategy, I don't see how you'll ever make your way out of the Sistine Chapel.'

Telling it like it is

While cardinals Curiosa and O'Faherty were busy with Declan, cardinals Suryani, Soutier, Mobutu, Quinn and Johnson took the opportunity to get to know the man of their dreams.

'So, Mr MacDonald, what are your thoughts on the state of the Church?' Cardinal Johnson asked.

Peter was in no mood for conversation. His head was still spinning from the revelation of why he was summoned to Rome, and he was reluctant to be as candid with his reply as he was the previous morning. The cardinals would be hanging off his every word and trying to use them to set the direction of the Conclave. This was a high-pressure situation.

When Peter hadn't responded after a few seconds, Cardinal Quinn decided to prompt him with a more specific question. 'What, Mr MacDonald, would your view be on the abortion issue?'

The question irritated Peter because he knew this was not a

clear-cut issue. 'Oh I don't know!' he replied. 'I don't approve of it, I guess.'

The cardinals nodded in approval. A pleased Cardinal Johnson then asked, 'So you would support the Church's push for the closure of abortion clinics?'

'Certainly not!'

'But how can you be against abortion but not for the closure of abortion clinics?' a shocked Johnson asked.

Peter was now at boiling point. Why was he in this situation? In his frustration he resolved that if they really wanted his opinion he would give them both barrels. 'Because you have to tackle the issues that lead women to have abortions if you really want to prevent them!' Peter blurted out.

The stunned silence of the cardinals forced Peter to reluctantly elaborate on his answer.

'You only have to look at history. Abortions have been a fact of life for many centuries and wherever medically supervised abortions have not been available, women have sought terminations wherever they can, often with tragic outcomes. So, unless we do something to prevent women finding themselves in such situations, we can't remove the option of a safe abortion from them.'

'What do you suggest we do then?' Johnson barked back at him.

'You can start by looking at the reasons why women have abortions. For many it is because they weren't prepared for a child, for others it is because they are in an abusive relationship, but there are also those who are simply ashamed to have a child out of wedlock because it is regarded as sinful. Have you ever considered that the Church's own stance on reproduction and sexuality could be contributing to a number of abortions?'

'But if people lived by the doctrines of the Catholic Church, these things wouldn't happen.'

'Perhaps, if anyone could in fact live by them! The best I can say about Church's doctrines on human sexuality is that they are delusional. They ignore the fact that sexuality is part of human nature and cannot be denied. You can't expect people to only have sex within marriage when the average marriage age in the Western world at least, is over thirty, and you cannot expect people to accept that the only alternative to sex outside of marriage is abstinence. That's not how society works!'

This was all too much for Johnson. 'What do you expect us to do? Tell everyone that the Bible is wrong?'

'No, the Bible is not wrong!' Peter replied, 'But where exactly in the Bible does it say that people cannot have sex outside of marriage? What the Bible *does* talk a lot about is fidelity and adultery, and these are the issues the Church should be running with. I'm not saying that it should be a free-for-all, what I'm saying is that instead of saying that sex can only occur within the confines of marriage we should be emphasising that couples should not engage in sexual activity without some form of commitment to each other.'

'But the sacrament of marriage is a commitment before God to share your life with another, is it not?' argued Soutier.

'Marriage is just one form of commitment. The Church is so focussed on the preservation of the institution of marriage that it gives society the impression that it supports people who remain in abusive, adulterous, or dysfunctional marriages, while it condemns those who live in harmonious and loyal relationships but have chosen not to formalise or sanctify their union. Is it no wonder then that society feels that the Catholic Church is out of touch?'

'That's not true,' said Quinn, 'The Church goes out of its way to ensure that couples are adequately prepared for marriage so that they don't avoid marriage difficulties.'

'I'm sorry Your Eminence, you can do all the marriage preparation that you like but it doesn't stop people drifting apart or developing psychological problems which can lead to physical abuse and financial hardship. People cannot remain committed in such situations. And how many marriages have been initiated because of un-planned pregnancies, where couples who may not be ideal for each other are forced together to legitimise the offspring?'

Johnson had to have his say. 'Again, if people followed the Church's laws, God's laws, these things wouldn't happen.'

Peter let out a big sigh. 'Look, this is what I mean about the Church's views being delusional. The Church needs to accept the fact that people will not wait until they are married to have sex. They may also maintain committed relationships without ever getting married. So instead of mandating that all sex outside of marriage is sinful, we should emphasise that sexual intercourse should signify the fulfilment of a relationship and not, as it is so often portrayed on television and in movies, as the initiator of a relationship.'

Again, the silent stares of his audience forced Peter to continue.

'You see, if people are allowed to base their morals on what is shown on movies and television they will be excused for thinking that most relationships are initiated by sexual intercourse. The Church's only means to counter this perception is to promote abstinence. We should instead be emphasising that couples should wait until they are in a relationship before engaging in the act or at least have considered the significance of the union. The issue is not whether a couple should be married before they engage in sex, it is that the couple should have formed a commitment or bond with each other before taking their relationship to that level.'

'But this goes against all of the teachings of the Church,' said a now-perplexed Johnson.

'No, it does not! The significance of the union is what the Church has been promoting all along; that sexual intercourse is first and foremost the act of human reproduction. It is right for the Church to continue to emphasise this.

'What is curious, however, is how in modern societies when couples fall pregnant unexpectedly, they call it an accident! How can it be an accident if they've performed the act of human reproduction and it worked? So before bedding down with someone, people need to at least ask themselves: firstly, is this the sort of person I would want to have a child with; and secondly, regardless of what precautions they may or may not be taking, am I ready to accept the possibility that a child will result from this union?'

The cardinals were now dumbfounded. The views that Peter was presenting were so far removed from traditional Catholic doctrine.

'But the Church cannot easily change its teaching on morality and sexuality,' Pancetti declared.

'Of course it can't!' Peter replied, 'Not until you are prepared to talk openly and honestly about human sexuality. But while you have a clergy and hierarchy who have actively denied their own sexuality, you have a serious credibility problem.'

Being presented with such a frank description of human sexuality made the cardinals uncomfortable. The Church's interpretation of the Bible's teachings on sexuality has been entrenched for over one thousand years. Certainly, they had all struggled with their vows of chastity at some point within their religious life, but they all saw this sacrifice as helping them to focus on their vocation.

Quinn took up the challenge: 'Yes Mr MacDonald, I understand your frustration, but the Church has over one billion followers on every continent, you cannot expect the needs of Western societies to be imposed in developing countries, for example.'

Peter didn't hesitate to reply, and he had now totally disregarded his initial urge to temper his opinions. 'Your Eminence, is it not in developing countries that the issues of birth control and contraception are most pronounced? People are told that it is a sin to use contraception and they end up producing more children that they can ever hope to support. And isn't it true in South Africa,' he looked at Mobutu for support, 'That the Church's stance on the use of condoms has contributed to the spread of AIDS?'

Mobutu nodded in agreement but then added, 'The Late Holy Father actually consented recently that the use of condoms to prevent the spread of disease was okay.'

'See? The late Holy Father was starting to see some sense. But when you talk about one billion Catholics in the world, how many of them do you think are actually putting the Church's pronouncements on birth control and contraception into practice? Just look around your own diocese, do you see many families with more than two or three children? I've got six and people look at my wife and me like we're a pair of rabbits! And I'll tell you now that we only have six because we always wanted to have a large family and not because we thought it was against our religion to use birth control.'

Peter thought of bringing his recent surgery into the conversation at this point but decided that it was probably not a good idea. Nevertheless, he was on a roll now.

'So, my point is that out of your one billion or so Catholics, most have chosen to ignore the Church's stance on birth control and are the better for it. Because here again the Church's views are out of step with both human physiology and modern medicine.'

'How so?' Quinn asked.

'The human animal is ready to reproduce in the mid to late teens and women remain fertile well into their forties while men may never lose their fertility. Advances in modern medicine have dramatically reduced infant mortality rates. So couples no longer need to keep producing children to replace the ones lost along the way. You only have to walk through an old cemetery to see that even in the early twentieth century, three or four children from the one family could have been wiped out by an epidemic of some sort. Thankfully that doesn't happen anymore. Yet couples still have the capacity to produce at least one child per year! The Church's only response to this phenomenon is abstinence and frankly, that doesn't cut it.'

At this point, Peter had the cardinals totally stunned. The only person smiling was Fr Mick, who was not surprised by Peter's opinions and was thoroughly enjoying the show.

Quinn then sought to get the conversation back on track. 'So how do you think the Church should tackle the abortion debate?'

'Well, the thing with abortions is that people's emotional response to assisted terminations is very different to their attitude to natural terminations or miscarriages. We live in interesting times where doctors can monitor human development from the embryonic stage. From within weeks of conception scans can reveal the living foetus in the womb and the parents can take home a photo or a video. So, if within the first trimester of pregnancy, the mother experiences a miscarriage, the child that they have lost is mourned almost as deeply as if it were still born at full term. However, at the same time we accept the practice of abortion as a societal right.'

'So why then do you consider that women should still have access to abortions if they want to?'

'Well, while I think that society is duplicitous in the way that it mourns miscarriages but accepts abortions, I think that most of the women who pursue abortions don't take their decision lightly and are often victims of the circumstance that they find themselves in. So yes, I believe that abortion is a terrible thing, but a woman should not have to risk her life to have one if she finds it is something she must do.'

'So, what are we to do then?'

'You have to be able to do what I was suggesting before: talk openly and honestly about human sexuality. Emphasise that sexual activity can result in pregnancy, and people who are sexually active need to be prepared for this. So regardless of whether people are married or not, the Church's position should be that a sexual union between a man and a woman can often result in conception of a child. Couples need to decide whether they are ready to accept a child into their lives before they enter into such a union.'

The cardinals just sat in stunned silence.

Peter broke the silence by adding, 'Look, it's not going to work for everyone but at least if you make the connection between miscarriage and abortion, you will go some of the way to changing peoples' views on the subject and get them to think more carefully about the responsibilities associated with being sexually active.'

'You have obviously thought about this for some time. How did you come to these conclusions?' Mobutu asked.

Peter had to think about this a bit. 'I guess I have never had an unquestioning faith.'

This remark caused a chuckle from Fr Mick. 'I can vouch for that!'

'But it was only in the past ten years that I started to realise that the Church's stance on a number of issues was so out of step with my own views and the views of many of my fellow Catholics. I had become so disillusioned with the Church that I was beginning to wonder whether I should remain a Catholic at all. But I figured that if the Catholic Church has made me what I am today, why should I have to leave it? Surely my form of Catholicism is as valid as everyone else's. So, I starting looking into things a bit more deeply and picked up a few good books written by respected theologians about what the Catholic Church should be about. I worked out that it was not me who was the problem. I also found out that there were many, many others who thought the same way as me – not only in Ireland, but in other parts of Europe and in Australia and the Americas. So, I was not the problem. The problem was that the Church hierarchy lived in fear of losing control and so were doing everything they could to prevent increased involvement of the laity in the running of the Church.'

Peter's response was then interrupted by cardinals Curiosa and O'Faherty re-entering the room with Declan O'Reilly.

'All sorted then?' Billingham asked.

'Yes,' Curiosa answered, 'Mr O'Reilly here has agreed not to print an account of anything that he has seen or heard here today until after the Conclave.'

'Is that wise?'

'I think that it's a good compromise. Given that the revelations that we have all experienced may result in an unusual choice for Pope, it would be good to have someone independent from the process to report on these strange events.'

Although the other cardinals were not comfortable with this, they couldn't think of any alternatives apart from keeping the poor journalist locked up. They were also more than a little confused as to how to interpret Peter's views on Church issues. It was clear that God had put Peter in their dreams for a reason, but to follow his ideas to the letter would cause tremendous upheaval. Surely, they couldn't have gotten things so wrong for so long!

Cardinal Quinn then looked at his watch. 'Shivers,' he exclaimed, 'it's just gone 11 am, we've all got a General Congregation to attend at 11.30!'

This made all the cardinals jump out of their seats and make ready to leave. Cardinals Curiosa and O'Faherty stayed behind while the others filed into the hallway to make their way back to the Vatican. Declan was still in the room as well.

Curiosa took Peter aside. 'This General Congregation may take a while, as it is the last one before the Conclave. But at 5 pm I've invited a few more cardinals to meet us here before we retire to the rooms that have been allocated to us in the Vatican to prepare for the Conclave. But in case we don't get the chance to talk again … can you, Fr Finlay and Mr O'Reilly come to the Basilica tomorrow for the mass before the Conclave? Just tell the security desk that you are my guests, I'll make sure that he has your names on his list and he should find some seats for you.'

'Look,' a nervous Peter replied, 'I'm not sure I need to hang around here. This is all a bit crazy. I've said what I have to say, and I think you now all have a good idea of where I'm coming from. So, if it's all the same to you I'd really like to get back to my family.'

'No, No! We need you to sit tight here!'

'But what can I do while you're all in the Conclave?'

'Granted, it would be very unusual for you to be invited into the Conclave – but given recent events I wouldn't rule this out. If, as we suspect, the other cardinals have seen you in their dreams, then I'm sure that some will want to meet you.'

'But I've promised my employer that I'll be home tomorrow night!'

'I'm sorry Peter, but I think we'll need you to stick around just in case.'

'My family needs me at home on Saturday as well! I can't put my life on hold indefinitely!'

'I wish I could give you some assurances Peter, but no-one knows how the Conclave will turn out and I think that you now understand that this thing is bigger than us and the Roman Curia put together. God wants something from us, and it must involve you in some way. We can't ignore this.'

Peter again suppressed the urge to scream but instead replied, 'I'll see what I can do. But it's not going to be easy.'

The power of a good priest

When the cardinals had all left, Peter, Fr Mick and Declan O'Reilly remained in the lounge at the Jesuit College.

'So, Mr MacDonald,' Declan asked, 'how does it feel to be the man of their dreams?'

'Oh, so they told you about that,' Peter replied. 'To tell you the truth, it scares the shite out of me!'

'You had no idea of the true reason for bringing you to Rome until this morning?'

'No fecking idea at all! I thought the cardinals were all fecking idiots the way that they were carrying on around me, but now I know why.'

'It's a pretty amazing story.'

'Tell me about it. I know that there is a mystery surrounding God that we may never understand but this is just too much. I mean, I'd convinced myself that the miracles in the Bible were just political spin.'

'How so?'

'Well, Jesus spoke in metaphors so the stuff about making the blind see and the deaf hear just meant that he was able to get through to people when others couldn't. But the Gospel writers translated these stories into real situations to make it clear to their readers that Jesus was someone special.'

'What do you think now?'

'I don't know what to fecking think! It can't be possible that I could be personally conscripted into what amounts to a direct intervention from God Almighty. If you and Fr Mick hadn't been told the story as well, I would have thought that I had totally lost the plot and was about to be locked in the loony bin.'

'All the cardinals are sure it was you in their dream?'

'You saw how they acted when they entered the room! I had no fecking idea who they were, but they certainly knew who I was! It's all so fecking unbelievable!' Peter looked over to where Fr Mick was sitting and noticed that the smile hadn't left his face. 'I'm glad that you're getting some enjoyment from this, Mick! What do you think is really going on? Is this just some sort of elaborate joke at my expense?'

'I'm enjoying this to no end,' Fr Mick replied, 'but I'm with you in that I wouldn't have dared to imagine that I'd witness a real miracle in my own lifetime – and make no mistake, this is truly a miracle. The way things have been going lately, I was beginning to think that I'd wasted my life in the priesthood, but this! This has more than restored my faith in God. It has left me in no doubt that we are being looked after and that my prayers at least have been heard. To see the cardinals finally being told, in no uncertain terms, that the Church belongs to the people and not the priests, bishops, cardinals and Pope … is fecking fantastic!'

'Is that what you really think the dreams are telling the cardinals?' Declan asked.

'I can't see how they could interpret it in any other way. To see the Pope presented as a layman – and not just any layman, but my wonderful, liberal, and progressive friend here – has got to be giving them a clear sign that they have no right to impose their belief systems on anyone. Their role is to guide people along their faith journey and not telling people how they are meant to behave or what they are meant to say.'

'That may be true of your friend O'Faherty and his friends Curiosa and Pancetti, but do you seriously think that they'd be able to influence conservatives like Mangiafuoco and D'Angeli?'

'You've got a point there m'boy. I'm not really sure how the cardinals will handle this in the Conclave. But the key will be getting them to make a connection between their dreams and our man. That's why we'll have to get a prominent spot at the mass tomorrow so that all of the other cardinals will have a chance to have a good look at Peter.'

'You're confident that the other cardinals would have had this dream as well?'

'We're running at nine out of nine at the moment so I can't see why they wouldn't have.'

'But when I spoke to Cardinal Doherty about Peter MacDonald, he didn't give any indication that there was any significance in him being in Rome,' Declan replied.

'How could he? He doesn't know that others have had similar dreams. He won't be able to read anything into his dream yet. But once he finds out about the other's dreams that will be a different story.'

While Declan was talking with Fr Mick, Peter, who was still reeling from the cardinals' revelation, slumped back into his chair. To be personally implicated in God's grand plan was doing his head in. *Why me, why me?* he kept repeating to himself over and over again as he held his head and rocked back and forward. Why him of all people? Why would God choose him as a messenger to the cardinals?

Then his thoughts turned to Mary and the children. She was expecting him home on Friday night. What was he going to tell her? He thought it best not to delay the inevitable so decided to call her now.

The children would be at school and there would only be Mary and Suzanne at home. He excused himself and left the room.

Declan was curious to find out a bit more about Peter, so once he'd gone he asked Fr Mick, 'So what can you tell me about Peter MacDonald?'

'I've known Peter and his wife Mary since they were teenagers and I'm pleased to say that they are now two of my closest friends. Peter and Mary were young catechists at the time, helping me with Sunday school classes.'

'So, they both have been actively involved in the Church for some time.'

'Yes; after Sunday school it was youth groups. Then when the children started coming along, Mary organised church playgroups for the little ones and worked in liturgy preparation, while Peter got involved with organising Eucharistic ministers and helped me to establish our first pastoral council. I couldn't have got by without them.'

'They sound like a pretty dedicated couple. What led them on the progressive path?'

'I'm afraid you will have to blame me for that, but it's only recently that we've felt obliged to label ourselves as progressive.'

'What do you mean?'

'When I entered the Jesuit seminary in Dublin, Vatican II was in full swing. Like other priests of that era, I was excited with the opportunities that the Vatican II reforms would produce, especially the opportunity to say mass in English. But I still held on to the image of the priests that I knew when I was growing up in the 1940s and 50s. A priest at that time was an authority figure who people would look to for guidance and support – no-one dared question that authority.'

'So what changed you?'

'Soon after ordination when I was still in my twenties, I joined the Columbian missionaries and was sent to Peru. It was like taking a fish out of water; I didn't know how to relate to these people and could barely speak a word of Spanish. But the people themselves treated me with the upmost respect and accepted me as their spiritual leader, even though I didn't have the faintest idea what I was doing for most of the time.

'I'll never forget the first big earthquake I experienced over there. It was just after mass, and I was standing outside chatting with his congregation when the ground started to shake to the extent that it was difficult to remain standing. My parishioners were screaming in fear and holding on to my arms and cassock looking for support. What they didn't realise is that I was more afraid than them. They'd interpreted my stoic stance as a sign of bravery but in reality, I was fecking frozen solid with fear.'

Declan had to chuckle at Fr Mick's tale before asking, 'So what did you learn from that experience?'

'I came out of it realising that our cultural differences meant that I couldn't really get to know the people I was meant to be ministering to. And for their part they couldn't care less if I was Irish, French, or Japanese. All they were concerned with was that they had a celebrant who could perform the functions that only a priest could perform. They didn't really need me to run the Church and school because they did all that themselves. Collectively they saw that everyone in the community was looked after and they organised all the weddings, funerals and feast days. All I had to do was turn up!'

'I suppose that would have made you feel pretty useless.'

'You're damn right it did! For the first year or so I felt as useful as an udder on a steer. But eventually I began to realise that it was the community that made the Church. To be truly effective, a priest needs to work with the community and not try to dominate or control it.'

'So how long were you in South America?'

'Oh, I think I was there until the mid-seventies.'

'You didn't work in the missions anywhere else?'

'No, that experience was enough for me. When I finished in Peru I came straight back to Dublin and worked as a chaplain in the prison system for a while before being sent to St Stephens as an assistant priest. By the late eighties, old Fr McGuire retired and I got the job as parish priest.'

'So how did the experience in Peru affect the way you worked at St Stephens?'

'Initially not much at all. So far, I'd spent most of my priestly life in Peru with people who couldn't understand me and then in the prisons with people who didn't want me near them. But poor old Fr McGuire was a priest from the old school and had kept things going pretty much the same for decades. So, there was a real need to get things moving. Most of the older parishioners were set in their ways as well, so I started working with the young ones like Peter and Mary. Together we started to liven the place up a bit.'

'Did you see any signs of greatness in Peter MacDonald during those early days?'

'Oh, I don't know about greatness! He was an ordinary young fellow, just seemed to have his head screwed on a bit better than some of the others, is all. But looking back I think his and Mary's involvement was the catalyst for others to join in and even got some of the older ones motivated. Frank O'Carroll was archbishop back then and he was a big one for getting laypeople involved in all aspects of the Church.'

'Sound very progressive indeed.'

'Well in today's world it does, but back then we were still acting on the reforms of Vatican II to keep the Church alive and relevant. It all started to go south around the time that Bishop O'Carroll retired. O'Carroll had made a recommendation for a replacement but the Curia went against his advice and promoted Doherty instead.'

'How did that change things?'

'Not by much initially, because I just ignored him for the most part. We had things running pretty nicely. My aim was to make the parish as self-sufficient as possible so that the parish would remain viable in the event that it found itself without a priest – which was a distinct possibility.'

'Didn't Cardinal Doherty see the value in these initiatives?'

'Outwardly, he'd say how wonderful it all was. Privately, he would keep giving me a hard time about how it was my responsibility to run all of these things and I was giving the people too much control. In my naivety I tried to get him to see the light and realise that priests weren't going to appear magically out of the woodwork, and the only way for parishes to survive into the future was to give more responsibility to the laity.'

'What was his response to that?'

'He just stuck his head in the sand and said that we had to keep praying for vocations. In the meantime, the fecking idiot starts to import priests from Poland and the Philippines. The Philippines for Christ's sake! I happen to know for a fact that there are fewer priests in the Philippines per head of population than there is in Ireland!'

'What would you have him do to address the priest shortage?'

'For a start there's a small army of good priests living in Ireland who had to leave the Church because they wanted to marry. Do you know that in America and Australia, they've let married Protestant priests convert to Catholicism and still function as priests? If the Curia supports things like that, why won't they let married Catholic priests resume their duties?'

'That does seem unusual.'

'And secondly, I don't want to be pushing my own barrow, but I thought that my parish at St Stephens was providing a pretty good example of what the future church could look like.'

'So, are you going to persevere?'

'I'm not parish priest anymore, so that answers that question.'

'Were you beaten down?'

'No not really, Doherty just took advantage of me at a weak moment.'

'Is anyone running the parish now?'

'Doherty had to get *someone* in, even if it was just to prove me wrong about the parish ending up without a priest. He eventually gets Damian O'Tool. I know Damian pretty well, and although he's not the sharpest tool in the shed, his heart is generally in the right place. But he is a bit short on courage. So he became Doherty's puppet and started to restrict a lot of the perceived liberties of my parishioners with the end result being a dramatic fall in mass attendance.'

'How did Peter MacDonald react to all of this?'

'He, Mary and a few others in the parish tried as best they could to keep things going but without Damien's cooperation they were doomed to failure. Peter even tried to help me to get back in charge once I'd realised that my situation was not as dire as I'd first imagined. But Doherty had got what he wanted, and he started spruiking the stories fed to him by the temple police that I was leading everyone astray.'

'So how do you really feel about the prospect of Peter MacDonald becoming Pope?'

'Oh, I doubt if they'll go that far.'

'You do realise that they can if they want to.'

'Yes, I know that any Catholic male can be elected Pope by proclamation. But I reckon they've kept that clause in there just in case Jesus happens to reappear in our lifetime. They couldn't very well say, "Sorry Lord, we'd really like you to lead our Church, but you need to spend seven years in the Seminary first and then spend twenty or thirty years working your way up to cardinal before we can consider you."'

'Isn't it also likely that a layperson could be declared Pope by acclamation if, by some miracle, a standout candidate was made known to the cardinals?'

'Oh, I guess if the cardinals were all sure they experienced a miracle, they would feel obliged to act on it, but I don't think we've reached that situation here yet.'

'Haven't we? Nine cardinals dream of a specific person as Pope and the distinct possibility that many more if not all cardinals have had the same dream. As far as miracles go that's a pretty good one I think.'

Fr Mick thought about this a bit. 'You may have a fecking point there. Oh shite! Poor Peter.'

How do I explain
this to the wife?

While Fr Mick and Declan were having their conversation, Peter walked back upstairs so that he could talk to Mary privately on the phone. He switched his cell phone back on and by the time he got to the top of the stairs, he found that there were no fewer than twenty-eight voicemail messages and several more SMS messages. There was no way he was going to respond to all of these but a quick scan through the list showed messages from his manager, some of his brothers and sisters, his father and Mary's mother. He hadn't even told his parents that he was in Rome. What would they be making of what the newspapers we're saying?

He walked into the room he shared with Fr Mick and made the call. It was picked up by the answering machine. This didn't faze him too much as they often used the answering machine to screen calls. 'Hello darling, if you're home can you please pick up?' He waited a few seconds before repeating the message again but only managed to get halfway through it before Mary picked up.

'Peter, thank Christ it's you! The phone's still been ringing off the hook all morning. I've had TV reporters at the door. I had to call my brother Gerry around to move them on, but the idiots are still parked across the road! Both your mother and my mother called asking why we didn't tell her that you were going to Rome; half of our other relatives have called; there are messages on the machine from countless others. I got sick of picking up the phone after a while. You're lucky I didn't pull the plug totally.'

'Sorry dear, but I'm afraid that this thing may get worse before it gets any better.'

Peter then proceeded to explain to Mary what had occurred. To which Mary incredulously replied, 'That's totally impossible! They're all probably senile old men who don't remember what they had for breakfast this morning, let alone remember what someone looked like in a dream.'

'I already thought that they were all crazy, but you should see how they act when they see me for the first time. Some didn't even know of the other's dreams but once they caught sight of me they couldn't keep their eyes off me. It's totally freaky alright, but it seems to be true.'

Mary was silent on the other end of the phone for what seemed like an eternity but, in reality, it was less than thirty seconds. Her voice was wavering when she finally spoke. 'This is totally insane. It can't be true. But if it is true then … it must be a miracle!' She couldn't believe the words that came out of her mouth. But the shock and awe didn't last long before being replaced by total panic. 'Peter, you have to come home this instant!' she screamed into the phone, 'I don't care who these people are, they're totally bonkers if they think they're going to make you Pope! Totally and completely fecking bonkers!'

'Don't worry darling, I've no intention of letting them make me Pope,' Peter said. 'Besides that, they've told me that they don't believe that their dreams mean that I should be Pope.'

'Well, what else could they mean?' Mary was now getting hysterical.

'That's what they've told me anyway. They just think that dreams are telling them that they should take into consideration my thoughts and ideas when choosing the next Pope. So that is why they now want me to hang around until the end of the Conclave just in case they need to speak to me.'

'Can't they call you on the telephone? You can still speak with them from here!'

'They want me to hang around,' Peter said calmly, 'and I find it hard to ignore a direct request from a cardinal.'

'What am I going to do with the children this weekend and what are you going to tell work? You don't have many leave days up your sleeve, you know!'

'Shite, I told Callan just this morning that I would be at work on Friday to attend a planning appeal hearing. I suppose I could still come home tomorrow night and fly back to Rome on Friday night. I doubt that the cardinals will need me just one day into the Conclave.'

'What?' Mary screamed back at him. 'Forget about work, what about your family? We need you here this weekend!'

'Sorry darling, but I have to do it. Can you ask your mother to help out this weekend?'

'I suppose so, but this is totally crazy! How long do you think it will be?'

'Well, given the unusual and controversial discussions that they will be having, they'll be lucky to wrap up the Conclave by the middle of next week! But nobody knows for sure.'

'The middle of next week! What am I going to tell everyone?'

'Don't say anything to anyone apart from saying that I am here with Fr Mick as a guest of Cardinal O'Faherty. That's all they need to know.'

'Okay, but the children are all missing you.'

'I'm missing you all as well. I'll try to give them a call tonight. Give them my love in the meantime.'

'Okay Peter, but you be careful. I still think that these cardinals are senile old fools who aren't thinking straight.'

'Well, perhaps they are but I'm afraid that I'll have to ride it out. I'd better go now and see what Fr Mick and that reporter fellow are up to.'

'Is the reporter still there? Can he be trusted?'

'Yes, I think he's realised the importance of keeping this one under wraps and he'll have the scoop of the Conclave once it is all over.'

'I'll let you go then. Bye my love, and please be careful.'

'Bye darling, love you. Talk soon.'

Peter was emotional when he hung up the phone. He had hardly spent more than a few days apart from Mary in the sixteen years that they had been married. He hated placing her in such a difficult situation – especially now that the media was involved.

He decided that he should call Cardinal O'Faherty's secretary to see if she could arrange some flights for him to get back to Dublin by tomorrow evening and back again to Rome the following day. She was not overly helpful, and he couldn't convince her that the good cardinal would approve. So, he resigned himself to the possibility that he would have to find his own way back to Dublin. He was on a good salary at the council, but six children and a mortgage did not leave sufficient spare cash for impromptu trips to the continent, so the cost of a flight would certainly stretch the family's finances.

Then he thought a bit more about his conversation with Mary. Dreams or no dreams, it was ludicrous to think that he could have any influence over the papacy. 'Feck it!' he said to himself, and he called Mary again.

Mary, knowing it was Peter at the other end, answered by yelling into the mouthpiece, 'Peter, you have to come home now!'

They agreed that Peter would stay in Rome for the mass at the start of the Conclave tomorrow but book the first flight back to Dublin straight afterwards.

'Feck em!' Peter told Mary. 'You're one hundred percent right. If they really need to speak to me they can call me in Dublin. I'm not going to be a pawn in their game anymore.'

With this decision putting them both at ease, they said their goodbyes knowing that they would be seeing each other again the following night.

There's something about Peter

Peter spent the rest of the morning responding to phone messages. But in the haste that he'd packed for his visit to Rome, he had forgotten to bring his phone charger. So, he just sent short individual messages to his parents, siblings, and a few of his closer friends. He then drafted an SMS to everyone in his address book alerting them that *The Irish Times* article was a beat-up and that there was nothing unusual about his trip to Rome.

He switched off his phone and joined Fr Mick in the kitchen. Georgio had prepared another simple but spectacular meal for them. This time it was thinly sliced veal in a white wine sauce served with polenta and steamed vegetables.

Fr Mick informed him that Declan O'Reilly had left an hour earlier to continue his coverage of the Conclave. Peter couldn't put his finger on it, but he was sure that Fr Mick was behaving differently towards him since the morning's revelation. He wasn't talking much and had a worried look on his face for most of the meal. Occasionally he would just stare at Peter – but when Peter returned his gaze, he would quickly lower his head and take another mouthful of food.

'Out with it Mick, what's on your mind?' he asked.

'You know this is a pretty big deal, don't you Peter?'

'Yes it's fecking amazing alright, but you don't think that they'd be foolish enough to make me Pope?'

'Well, I think you need to prepare yourself for that possibility.'

'Not you too Mick!'

'Sorry Peter, but you have to accept that what the cardinals have experienced is nothing short of a miracle! Granted, the current crop of cardinals would never in a million years have proposed a significant change at this Conclave. But despite their support for the Roman Church, they are first and foremost men of faith and none of them are likely to ignore what appears to be a direct intervention by the Lord God himself!'

'But just because they saw me as Pope in their dreams doesn't mean that I should be Pope. Cardinal Curiosa said as much himself!'

'Remember Peter, this is a new and strange experience for everyone concerned. Of course none of them ever thought that a layman could or should be Pope. But they also never expected God to speak directly to them either.'

Peter put his head in his hands again. 'Jaysus Mick,' he said, 'what am I going to do?'

Fr Mick had no reply for him. But Peter wanted to get as much distance between himself and Rome as quickly as possible. He had half a mind to leave there and then but decided to wait until the start of the Conclave as he had discussed with Mary. Once the cardinals were safely locked up he could make a clean get-away.

After their meal, Peter and Fr Mick went back upstairs to rest up before their encounter with more cardinals later that afternoon. The morning's events were still weighing heavily on Peter's mind but the delicious meal, accompanied by two glasses of white wine and another dose of painkillers helped him to sleep.

Presently however, he found himself back at home in Dublin. He was sitting at the kitchen table enjoying his morning coffee and reading the paper. Everything seemed back to normal but he looked at his right hand and saw that he was wearing an enormous gold ring. He then noticed that he was dressed totally in white, including white shoes and socks. Patrick and Connor then walked in the room. He was surprised to see that the boys were wearing what appeared to be altar boy outfits.

'There's someone at the door to see you Daddy,' Connor said to him.

'Who is it?' Peter asked.

'I dunno,' Patrick answered, 'He's a big, tall dark-skinned man.'

'I think he said his name is Banana?' Connor added.

Who the hell could that be? Peter got out of his chair and walked towards the front door.

As he approached the open door, he saw that there was indeed a dark-skinned man there accompanied by a dark-skinned woman. As he got closer he was shocked to discover that the man was actually Barack Obama, former President of the United States of America!

He stretched out his hand to greet him but instead of shaking his hand, Peter was embarrassed to find that the former president had got down on one knee and reached out to kiss his ring instead. Michelle Obama, who was wearing a black lace head scarf, took his hand and curtsied.

Dumbstruck, Peter invited them into the living room only to find that behind them was a procession of other dignitaries and famous people, including the Dalai Lama, Bono from U2, Oprah Winfrey, David Beckham and Madonna.

He led them all into the living room but wondered how they were all going to fit. He walked into the room to find everyone chatting with each other. Mary and Bridie were dressed in nun's habits serving tea and biscuits, while young Michael was sitting on the sofa dressed as a bishop chatting to the Irish President and Lady Gaga. He initially couldn't see Suzi and Lauren but looked up to spot them hovering near the ceiling, dressed in white with angel wings.

He woke with a start. Thank Christ it was only a dream. He looked at his watch and saw that it was 4.30 pm – time to prepare himself for the next interrogation from the cardinals.

✝

Given Curiosa's liberal leanings, there were not many cardinals who would accept a supper invitation from him on the evening before a Conclave, so he co-opted Johnson and Quinn's support as well. The bad news was that despite their best efforts they only managed to get three cardinals to accept their invitation. The good news, however, was that one of those three was one of the preferred candidates, Cardinal Jose D'Angeli.

When Peter and Fr Mick had made their way downstairs to the college lounge, Curiosa and O'Faherty called him over. 'Ah good evening Peter, please come over here. There is someone I want you to meet.' Curiosa took Peter by the arm and positioned him directly in front of the cardinal that he was speaking with. 'Peter MacDonald, this is Cardinal Francesco Pandamonio.'

'Pleased to meet you, Your Eminence,' Peter said as he extended his hand to the cardinal.

Pandamonio politely took his hand, looked up at Peter's face and froze on the spot. O'Faherty took the puzzled Pandamonio aside to fill him in on the phenomenon that they had all experienced.

Fr Mick helped himself to the Irish whisky in the drinks cart and found a comfortable spot to view the spectacle. He was not disappointed and soon witnessed the arrival of Cardinal Jessie Marcos, who casually greeted Curiosa but then froze at the sight of Peter. Billingham and Quinn took him aside as well.

For Curiosa, the evening was working out well. Two additional cardinals had made the association between Peter MacDonald and their dreams of the new Pope, and he was still hopeful of D'Angeli arriving before the evening was over.

Earlier that afternoon, Curiosa had discussed with the cardinals who had already met with Peter how they would handle the issue in the Conclave. After some discussion, they agreed that they didn't need to risk breaking protocol, or worse, by instructing the other cardinals to vote in a particular way. It was sufficient, they thought, for only a few of them to put Peter's name forward. The presence in the ballot of someone other than those present at the Conclave would surely prompt discussion on the significance of the dreams.

The Portuguese cardinal Jose D'Angeli knew that he was the least likely of the favoured candidates to be elected. His core support base was with moderate cardinals who appreciated his willingness to consult widely as well as the fact that he didn't surround himself with conservative sycophants. His presence at the Jesuit College this evening was his way of showing his appreciation for the support that he was likely to receive from the progressive cardinals. Frankly, he needed all the support he could get because a good number of the cardinal electors were, in fact, conservative sycophants.

He arrived at the function and walked straight up to Curiosa who was still standing with Peter next to him. 'Olá! Ricky, good to see you,' he said. Then he looked over at Peter and promptly exclaimed, 'Santa Maria do céu!'

'What's the matter Jose?' Curiosa politely asked.

D'Angeli couldn't answer. Peter, who was now starting to enjoy the reaction he was engendering in the cardinals, smiled back at him and extended his hand. 'Good evening Eminence, I'm Peter MacDonald from Dublin.'

Hearing that Irish accent was too much for D'Angeli, who put both his hands on his face and exclaimed; Impossivel! You ... I know you ... I saw you in ...'

Curiosa helped him out. 'In a dream perhaps?'

'Yes … yes … in a dream. But how could you know?'

'It's an interesting story Jose, and we'll be pleased to explain it to you.'

Curiosa gestured for him to sit down and then filled him in on the fact that they all had experienced a great miracle and that this miracle must have some significance on the outcome of the Conclave that they were about to attend.

D'Angeli agreed wholeheartedly. His ambitions to be Pope now took a back seat to consideration of what this revelation could mean.

He eventually composed himself enough to have a conversation with Peter. Peter's lament that progressive Catholics in the Western world were becoming disenfranchised struck a chord with him. Personally, he agreed with the need for the Curia to provide a clear direction for Catholics to follow but did not agree with the religious zealots in the Vatican, who were using these directions to promote a form of religious fundamentalism. For the Church to grow and remain relevant to society, he knew it needed to maintain its diversity. He was also a strong believer in church celebrations in each country reflecting the indigenous culture and was genuinely shocked at the way that the new English translation of the mass was being received at the grassroots level. He and others had been deceived by the body formed to produce the translation, 'Vox Clara', who publicly promoted how wonderful the translation was and how it was going to improve the understanding of the mass. Apparently, this was far from the truth.

The evening progressed with all the cardinals wanting to get to know Peter a bit better. Peter, for his part, decided to keep his more radical views on the state and direction of the Church to himself. It was enough that the cardinals appreciated that things needed to change. So, he tried as much as possible to focus the discussions on emphasising the need to avoid a shift to religious fundamentalism and for the Church to celebrate its diversity rather than impose strict directives.

The Conclave

The day of the Conclave had arrived, and all the cardinals were eager to read the morning paper as this would be their last chance to catch up on world events before they were locked away to make their decision. Some managed to get local newspapers delivered from their home countries but all of them at least had a copy of the official Vatican newspaper, *l'Osservatore Romano,* to read while having breakfast.

The front page was, not surprisingly, dominated with news of the Conclave. The paper also included a lift-out with photos and information on all the cardinals. But it was a small item at the bottom of page 3 which caught the eye of each of them. The article was in a section normally reserved for lightweight articles and told the story of how the Irish had sent a 'Pope-maker' to Rome. It ridiculed the article published by *The Irish Times* the previous day and included a quote from Cardinal Doherty saying that the whole thing was effectively a beat-up. However, the news item also included a photo of the man in question and reported that his name was Peter MacDonald.

The eyes of each cardinal who saw the article were immediately drawn to this photo. He seemed so familiar to them. Slowly but surely, each cardinal realised that this man had appeared to them in a dream as the new Pope!

Each had the same thought: This could not be a mere coincidence. The news item stated that this man could not have any influence over the papal election. Yet they each had dreamt of a similar looking Irishman, and in each of their dreams this Irishman was Pope. This was an amazing revelation to all of them.

Of course, apart from those who had already met Peter, each cardinal had no way of knowing that their colleagues had similar dreams. But the more they looked at the photo, the more they thought that they would have to act on this revelation in some way. Some made a mental note of the name but others, despite knowing that they were not meant to bring anything into the Conclave with them, wrote the name down or ripped the article itself out of the paper and placed it in one of their pockets.

For a few of the twelve cardinals who had met Peter, the article caused some initial angst. They wondered if this whole thing was a set-up. But there was no denying the veracity of their dreams so in the end it strengthened their resolve that divine forces must be at work.

The first stage of the Conclave involved the procession of cardinals into the Basilica for a mass. From there they would process to the Sistine Chapel, where the Conclave proper would commence.

Peter and Fr Mick walked to the Basilica and were met there by *The Irish Times* Vatican correspondent, Declan O'Reilly. Cardinal Curiosa had managed to arrange press passes for them and had also secured them excellent seats adjacent to the central aisle. He instructed Peter that he should sit in the end seat to maximise the chances of being spotted by most of the cardinals.

The procession began. Peter, Fr Mick, and Declan stood with the rest of the congregation and turned to look at the procession as it approached.

Leading the procession were two of the preferred candidates, cardinals Enzo Mangiafuoco and Giuseppi Mantovani. They led the procession in a sombre manner befitting their status within the College of Cardinals. Mantovani was walking on Peter's side of the aisle and was scanning the sea of faces for dignitaries that he knew so that he could give them a polite nod as he passed.

He was distracted by the sound of a bird fluttering. A white dove had found its way into the Basilica and seemed to be struggling to find its way out. He and the cardinals immediately behind and next to him had to duck as the bird flew directly towards them before turning and flying ahead, eventually settling on a man's head.

Mantovani smiled as he approached the poor man who was struggling in vain to get the bird to move on without causing a huge commotion. The dove seemed to be making a nest in the man's thick black hair. However, Mantovani's smile disappeared when he saw the nervous face of the poor man with the white dove on his head.

This was the man who was in the newspaper this morning! The man he now knew to be Peter MacDonald. Furthermore, a dove, the symbol of the Holy Spirit himself, had chosen to settle directly on this man's head. This could not be a mere coincidence.

As he walked towards Peter, he slowed his pace and was unwittingly holding up the procession. The cardinals walking behind him had resumed their normal pace after the commotion caused by the dove and assumed that Mantovani had done the same. All the time they were looking around them and nodding or smiling politely to people they may have recognised in the congregation. Not realising that Mantovani's pace had slowed, the cardinals proceeded to walk right into him and pushed him over. The fall had a domino effect and at least eight other cardinals fell over behind Mantovani.

As all this happened directly in front of Peter, he felt duty-bound to help Mantovani to his feet. For his part Mantovani just kept staring at him before continuing his way down the aisle. All the time, despite a concerted effort to remove it, the white dove remained stuck to Peter's head.

Peter was able to help a few more cardinals to their feet and in each case received stunned stares as a reward.

It was fortunate that none of the elderly cardinals were injured in the incident, but that was not the end of it. For just as the initial few rows of cardinals passed Peter, another group approached and, in each case, the presence of the white dove sitting on Peter's thick black hair drew their attention and the incident was repeated.

So out of the one hundred and fifteen cardinals in the procession, at least fifteen had stumbled and fallen in three separate incidents. These events didn't go unnoticed by the other members of the press who were standing nearby. They had all bought the explanation that the Pope-maker story was a beat-up. Declan O'Reilly, who had investigated the case, confirmed as much when they spoke with him the previous day. But after witnessing this spectacle they were all starting to think that the story might have legs after all.

Once the procession had passed, the dove finally left Peter's head and returned to its roost. However, once the service was over and the cardinals proceeded to progress out of the Basilica, the dove gave a repeat performance and swooped down low directly in front of the procession of cardinals again before settling comfortably on Peter's head.

The resulting commotion was more pronounced this time as the procession deteriorated into a meme-worthy farce. It was a miracle that no-one was injured again.

After the mass, the cardinals proceeded directly into the Sistine Chapel, where they would make their final oaths to declare that they had not been influenced by any external forces in the making of their decision and swear to protect the secrecy of the Conclave.

The formalities of Conclave having taken the best part of the day, it was late afternoon by the time the first ballots could be cast. This was the process followed at all Conclaves and it was therefore not expected that a result would be achieved at this initial ballot. In fact, convention dictated that the cardinals would submit their own names in the first ballot, as this would ensure that no-one could achieve the two-thirds majority required to become Pope and the Conclave will be forced to sit another day. On the second day of the Conclave there would be time for up to four ballots, allowing voting patterns to form and the favourites to be clearly identified.

Nevertheless, a significant crowd was gathered in the Piazza San Pietro waiting for that first puff of smoke to come from the chimney which, if white, would signify the election of a new Pope. But few expected that a Pope would be elected that night. In among this crowd was Fr Mick Finlay. Fr Mick had decided to stay in Rome while Peter returned to Dublin. He was not aware that Peter had no intention of coming back to Rome again.

Peter was booked on an 8.00 pm flight and had gone back to the Jesuit College to gather his things. He got a great deal on the airfare, as planes flying into Rome full of tourists wanting to witness history were returning to their destinations almost empty.

After the dove incident, Peter was more determined than ever to put as much distance between himself and Rome. He didn't know who the cardinals thought he was, but the actions of that preposterous dove might be enough to make some of them actually consider making him Pope, and that could just not happen! Cardinal D'Angeli seemed like a reasonable fellow; hopefully they would put him in, and all would be well.

✝

In the Conclave the initial ballot papers were being distributed. These consisted of relatively small pieces of paper with the Latin words 'Eligo in Summum Pontificem' written on them and a space for the cardinals to enter the name of their preferred candidate. The cardinals who had met Peter had discussed the need for Peter's name to be brought up at the Conclave but hadn't settled on how and when this would occur. All of that cohort concluded that the best way to draw attention to the topic was to write Peter's name on the ballot. Even Cardinal D'Angeli, who was still entranced by the amazing miracle that they all had experienced, refrained from putting his own name forward and put Peter's name down instead.

German Cardinal Conrad Klijn had not met Peter, but after seeing his face in the paper that morning and later seeing him in the flesh at the Basilica? He hadn't made much of his dream up until now, but upon seeing the picture in the paper the image of the young Pope in his dream became vivid. Then there was the dove in the Basilica. Why would God put the image of this man in his dream and then send a dove to highlight the fact that this man was in Rome? Had God chosen him to convey a message to the Conclave?

This was the closest that he had ever been to a direct message from the man upstairs and although he didn't know exactly what it meant he was not going to ignore it. So, he took the only option available to him at the time and wrote Peter's name on the ballot paper.

Cardinal Roberto Bagnato thought there was no mistake: it must be the work of God. But what could God want from him? There was only one thing for it; he would have to reveal to the Conclave that he had experienced a miracle and the ramifications of this miracle would have to be discussed. So, to initiate this discussion, he would write Peter MacDonald's name on the ballot paper.

Apart from those who had met Peter, every other cardinal thought that they and they alone had been blessed by God with a miracle. The significance of this miracle could not be ignored. They each independently decided that they must make the Conclave aware of the miracle they had experienced. Coincidently, the method they chose to do this was to write the name of someone who was not a cardinal elector on the ballot paper. Once that name was read out, they would be able to reveal the miracle that God had endowed on them and initiate a discussion on what the significance of that miracle might be.

The process for the election required the cardinals to write the name of their candidate on the ballot paper, fold the paper in half and then in half again, and walk to the front of the Chapel in order of seniority. Each cardinal then holds up the folded ballot, so that it can be seen, and carries it to the altar where there is placed a receptacle which is covered by a plate. When they reach the altar, the cardinal elector says aloud the following oath: 'I call as my witness Christ the Lord, who will be my judge that my vote is given to the one who before God I think should be elected'. He then places the ballot on the plate, with which he drops it into the receptacle. Having done this, he bows to the altar and returns to his place.

As the most senior of the cardinal electors, Cardinal Curiosa was allocated the key role of reading out the names on the ballots after they were drawn. The counting and scrutineering process was performed by three cardinals. The first draws the ballots from the receptacle in which they had been placed, notes the name, and passes it on to the second, who does the same. The second scrutineer then passes the ballot to the third who reads the name out loud before using a needle and thread to keep the ballots together.

The first ballot was drawn from the receptacle. Curiosa noted a strained expression on the first scrutineer. The second scrutineer had a similar reaction and nervously passed the ballot to him. Curiosa was taken aback. The name on the ballot was Peter MacDonald – but he was positive that it was not the ballot he had completed.

It is a requirement of the voting process that the cardinals disguise their handwriting so that votes could not be traced back to individuals.

The cardinals would therefore print the name of their candidate or even scrawl it with their un-favoured hand. Curiosa had chosen the latter method of encryption but was certain that this was not his scrawl. The ballot must have been completed by one of the other cardinals.

He braced himself for an uproar from the majority of cardinals and in a loud clear voice called out the name: 'Peter MacDonald.'

To his complete surprise, apart from some coughing and spluttering coming from the direction of Cardinal Doherty, everyone else sat in stony-faced silence.

Truth be told, they were all were a bit surprised that their individual ballot paper was drawn first, for apart from those who had met Peter over the past few days, they all assumed that they, and they alone, were chosen by God to deliver this message to the Conclave. Curiosa passed the needle and thread through the word 'eligo' on the ballot paper and waited for the next ballot to be drawn.

The first scrutineer then drew out the next ballot, unfolded it, and raised his eyebrows. He noted the name and passed the paper up to the second scrutineer, who was also taken aback by a second vote for Peter. He completed his task however and passed the ballot to Curiosa.

Curiosa couldn't believe it. How could two of the relatively few votes for Peter be the first to be drawn? He braced himself, and called out the name: 'Peter MacDonald.'

This time there was a bit more of a reaction from the gathered cardinals, but again, it was only Doherty who seemed visually put out. He was looking around frantically and seemed like he would jump out of his seat at any minute. Curiosa threaded the needle through the ballot and waited again for the next to be drawn.

This time the first scrutineer let out a gasp when he unfolded the ballot. Here was a third vote for Peter MacDonald and again it was most definitely not his vote. He composed himself, noted the name and passed it on to the second scrutineer, who stared wide-eyed at the paper before noting the name and passing the ballot to Curiosa.

Cardinal Doherty could not contain himself when Curiosa called out Peter's name for the third time. He jumped to his feet, drawing the attention of all the other cardinals. But the way that they stared back at him made him reluctant to voice his concerns and he sat down. It was not until the next five ballots opened were also votes for Peter that he felt enough was enough and he had speak up. 'Is no one going to stop this corruption?' he called out.

O'Faherty felt obliged to respond to his junior colleague. 'Sit down, Patrick! How can there be any corruption? We've all witnessed the ballots entering the receptacle and we had now witnessed them being drawn out! There is no question that the ballot is valid.'

'But this man, Peter MacDonald – who I assume is the same Peter MacDonald who is a layman from my diocese! Surely he is not a valid candidate?'

'I'm sorry Patrick, but if he is a baptised and confirmed Catholic and is an active member of the Church, he is a valid candidate.'

'To my knowledge, the only thing that Peter MacDonald is active in is the subversion of church values! He has been working with other liberals in my diocese against Vatican proclamations for changes to the mass! He has helped organise several petitions requesting the ordination of married priests, among other blasphemies!'

'I happen to believe that this man has a better handle on church values than you'll ever know.'

'How do you know? He is from my diocese and is on my Diocesan Council. Surely I know him better than anyone else here.'

'Someone disagreeing with your vision of the Church in Ireland does not make him blasphemous. To be frank Patrick, if everyone who disagreed with your vision of the Church was excluded from it, there would be no Catholics left in Ireland at all! A few of us have met with him over the past few days and we have found him to be a person who is true to his Christian faith and only wants the Church to become more relevant to the wider world.'

Doherty couldn't believe what he was hearing, and couldn't understand why anyone else was not taking O'Faherty to task. He went in for the kill. 'Met with him? Met with him! So, this is a conspiracy to subvert the Conclave, is it? You're on the fast track to excommunication, old man. You have allowed the influence of lay and secular forces to influence your decision! Who else has met with him? Let us expose these conspirators so that we can end this travesty and start the Conclave properly.'

Doherty's accusations had created a stir among the cardinals. Were they victims of a conspiracy? But how could they be? They all witnessed the conduct of the ballot; there was no room for error or deception. Even if Curiosa had read out the wrong name, the other two scrutineers would have picked up on it. And their dreams! How could conspirators possibly control their dreams?

Cardinal DiMattina, the Master of Ceremonies, decided to take control of the situation. 'Eminences, Eminences!' he called out, 'silenzio, silenzio!'

The hubbub eventually died down, but only after DiMattina banged his crosier on the floor several times while repeatedly calling for quiet. He then looked to O'Faherty to explain himself. O'Faherty looked to Curiosa for support. Curiosa felt obliged to help his old friend and addressed DiMattina. 'If I may Eminence, a few of us have met with this man Peter MacDonald over the past few days. But I assure you all that there is no conspiracy at work here.'

Curiosa's words only served to spur on Cardinal Doherty. 'Curiosa!' he called out, 'The last of the great Vatican II liberals! I might have known that you were involved!'

But DiMattina was having none of it. 'Please sit down, Cardinal Doherty, and let Cardinal Curiosa speak.'

This rebuke took Doherty off-guard. He thought that he had uncovered a great injustice and was adamant that most of the cardinals would see things the same way. 'But Your Eminence, it is clear to me that this is a conspiracy devised by our liberal colleagues!'

'Sit down, Cardinal Doherty!' DiMattina called out even more forcefully this time. 'Sit down or I will have you ejected from the Conclave!'

Doherty was totally floored by this reaction. It was not just DiMattina's rebuke that stunned him but also the fact that no-one else was taking issue with the fact that both Curiosa and O'Faherty seem to be involved with one of the biggest travesties in the history of papal elections. He frantically looked around for some sign of support but when it was obvious that none was forthcoming, he grumpily sat back in his seat.

DiMattina then looked back at Curiosa and signalled for him to continue.

'Thank you, Your Eminence. As I was saying, there is no conspiracy. Yes, a few cardinals have met with this man Peter MacDonald, and we asked him for his opinion on the state of the Church, but we have never discussed with him the issue of who should or should not be the next Pope. I agree it is highly unusual, but rest assured that there were some very special circumstances that led us to bring him to Rome in the first place. Given the way the first ballot is progressing I am now almost certain that you all will support why we had to make this decision. For although there are only twelve of us who have met with Peter MacDonald over the past few days, I believe that there are many more than twelve ballots with his name on them.

'I suspect that this man is familiar to everyone in this room … and not just because his picture happened to appear in *l'Osservatore Romano* this morning. It was only four days ago when four of us, including Cardinal O'Faherty, found out by accident that we all had dreams where we met the new Pope. Furthermore, we all commented that the Pope in our dreams was relatively young and Irish.'

The stir within the Conclave made Curiosa more confident that all cardinals must have seen Peter in their dreams. So, he continued. Curiosa's account could barely be heard above the gasps and comments from each of the cardinals as they realised that 'their miracle' had in fact been experienced by every individual cardinal!

To settle the cardinals once more, Cardinal DiMattina, as Master of Ceremonies, had to bang his crosier on the floor several more times before addressing the Conclave. 'It is true, I also have had such a dream. I did not think much about it until I saw the photo in the newspaper this morning. But when I saw him in the Basilica, I was certain that this man was the Pope in my dream. But now to think that others have had a similar dream!' He then addressed Curiosa directly. 'You know that all four of you had this dream?'

'Well, once the four of us made the connection between this man and our individual dreams, we agreed that we should at least bring him to Rome so that we can meet with him and try to understand what God was trying to tell us in our dreams. Over the past few days another eight cardinals have met with him and all immediately recalled their dreams. But we still didn't believe that a layman could or should be elected. After all, he is a married man with a family, and we didn't think that it would be fair to him and his family to impose the life sentence of the papacy on him. We knew that God was giving us a sign and proposed to use the Conclave to discuss what that sign might be. However, it now seems that the Holy Spirit has had other ideas.'

Cardinal Doherty couldn't hold his silence any longer. 'So it is settled then, this man should not be made Pope!'

Curiosa replied, 'I'm afraid that it is no longer a question of whether he should or should not be Pope. Because if we agree that as a confirmed and practicing Catholic man he is a valid candidate, and if we also agree that this afternoon's ballot is valid ... he may in fact already be the new Pontiff. For if more than two thirds of the ballot papers in this receptacle have his name on them, and it is highly likely that they do, he has duly been elected and all that remains is for him to accept!'

Cardinal DiMattina was floored by this possibility. How could they have elected a layman to the papacy? 'We have only seen eight votes. This is too much for me,' he said. 'I think that I will let the Particular Congregation decide whether the ballot has been correctly performed.'

The Particular Congregation is responsible for running the Vatican in the absence of a Pope, so they would have the final say in determining the validity of Peter's candidacy. The Particular Congregation presiding during the Conclave consisted of cardinals Jan Kaparovski, Ian Roberton, Lorenzo Bontempo and Roberto Gratziatanto, who was the Camerlengo.

It was Kaparovski who spoke first. 'I for one consider my vote to be valid, as I felt compelled to write down the name that I did. Even though I did not expect this outcome, I stand by my ballot as a clear indication of both my intentions and the intentions of the Holy Spirit, whom I called upon to guide me.'

To Curiosa's surprise, the other three members of the Particular Congregation agreed wholeheartedly. So Kaparovski then put the question to the other cardinals: 'If anyone here believes that they have not voted according to their free will and is not prepared to stand behind their ballot, they should speak now.'

Each cardinal then realised that the situation they were in was totally unintentional and unprecedented. But each also reconciled that the decision of what name to put on the ballot was theirs and theirs alone. This revelation only further convinced them that the eventual outcome would be God's will.

One of the preferred candidates, Cardinal Giuseppi Mantovani, then rose to his feet and said, 'My esteemed colleagues, I confirm that I have not broken the oath that I made earlier today. I have not been influenced by anyone either outside of the Conclave or within the Conclave – and although the outcome may not be one which I intended, I stand by my ballot and will accept the outcome as the will of God.'

One by one, each of the cardinals rose to their feet and declared, 'I too stand by my ballot.'

Kaparovski then addressed the congregation: 'So it is agreed. This ballot is valid. But whatever the outcome, I think that we must bring this man Peter MacDonald into the Conclave.' He then looked to the Cardinal Camerlengo and the other two cardinals who formed the Particular Congregation, who all indicated that they were in agreement. 'Cardinal O'Faherty, can you arrange for this man to come to the Conclave?'

'Well, I'm not sure where he could be at the present time, but our man at the Jesuit College may be able to find him.'

'Then go and make sure that you bring him here immediately. The Cardinal Camerlengo will go with you to make sure that you receive the cooperation of whoever we need. We will resume the counting of the ballots when you return.'

With those clear instructions, O'Faherty left the Chapel with the Cardinal Camerlengo to track down Peter MacDonald.

A momentous decision

It was almost 5 pm and not wanting to miss his flight, Peter said goodbye to Georgio and left the Jesuit College to make his way to the airport. He couldn't be bothered trying to explain to Georgio that he needed a taxi, so he planned to try to hail one on the street.

Peter had only been gone a couple of minutes before the college phone rang. Georgio was surprised to hear O'Faherty's voice at the other end of the phone. But his surprise paled into insignificance against O'Faherty's shock when Georgio told him that Peter was headed for the airport.

With instructions to bring Peter to the Vatican immediately, Georgio ran out of the college to find Peter getting into a taxi. He called out to no avail and the taxi entered the traffic flow. This being Rome, the traffic was not flowing very swiftly but Georgio knew that he wouldn't be able to catch up with Peter on foot. So, he ran down to the basement carpark where the college's Alfa Romeo Guilietta was parked. In one fluid movement, he brushed his security pass against the sensor for the carpark door, jumped into the Alfa, fired her up and sped out onto the road.

Georgio grew up on these streets and he knew how to move though Rome traffic faster than any taxi driver. He skilfully weaved his way through the traffic and spotted what he thought was the taxi carrying Peter about half a block ahead of him. He kept his eye on the prize and gradually gained on the taxi. Twice he had to swerve past police officers directing traffic and although they called out to him and cursed him, out of respect for his Vatican number plates, they let him go.

Finally, he caught up with the taxi and swerved in front of it to block its path – and in the process, blocked all the traffic behind him as well. He ran up to the taxi and threw open the back door only to find a shocked elderly woman looking back at him.

He apologised profusely but was sure that he should have caught up with Peter by this time. He scanned the area for other taxis and then saw Peter, who had stepped out to see what the hold-up was, standing about four cars behind him. Georgio ran up the road, threw Peter's taxi driver a fifty euro note, grabbed Peter and his travel bag, and dragged him back to the Alfa. Peter didn't know what to make of this initially, but when Georgio turned the car around to head back towards the college he started protesting; 'No Georgio, no! Airport … aeroporto … Fumicino!'

Georgio called back to him, 'No Signore, Vaticano!'

'Not Vaticano, aeroporto!' Peter replied to no avail.

Cardinal O'Faherty and the Camerlengo re-entered the Sistine Chapel. The Camerlengo left instructions with the security chief that if Georgio or Peter MacDonald were to arrive at any of the Vatican gates, they were to be brought straight through to the chapel. Although the security chief thought this request to be highly unusual, the Camerlengo had the authority to request whatever he wanted.

Once they resumed their places in the chapel, Cardinal DiMattina, as the master of ceremonies, directed that counting of the ballots should resume. Everyone waited with bated breath as the first scrutineer drew a ballot from the receptacle. This cardinal frowned but proceeded to write down the name and passed the ballot on to the second scrutineer, who looked back incredulously at his colleague before he too duly noted the name and passed the ballot to Curiosa.

Curiosa also seemed taken aback by what he saw but proceeded to announce the name. 'Patrick Doherty.'

The announcement of this name made all the cardinals but one sit up for a moment before turning to glare at Doherty, who was shrinking in his seat.

The mood in the chapel soon settled back to one of anticipation. The room issued a collective sigh of relief when the next name drawn was again for Peter MacDonald. But the seriousness of the situation soon took over as ballot after ballot came out with Peter MacDonald's name on it.

It was almost 6 pm when the eighty-seventh and eighty-eighth ballots were drawn and all but one of these ballots had Peter's name of them.

They had done the unthinkable. They had elected a layman to the papacy!

It was customary for the cardinals to clap and even cheer when a two thirds majority was reached by a candidate. But this time they all just sat there stunned.

Even Curiosa and his liberal colleagues couldn't believe that it had come to this. It was never their intention to have Peter elected, as it was not the intention of any of the cardinals to promote a layman to the papacy. The only way that they could explain their actions was that they were responding to what they thought was God's message to them in their individual dreams. God had taken the upper hand this time and there was no mistaking it. This was the first Conclave ever where the Holy Spirit had been running the show all along. So, whatever the consequences, they would have to live with it and trust that God knew what he was doing.

With a clear majority being reached, there was no need for the counting to continue but all were curious to see if, in fact, all but one cardinal had voted for Peter MacDonald. Kaparovski and the other members of the Particular Congregation instructed that counting should continue. As the drawing of ballots continued, the miracle of the Conclave was confirmed. Every cardinal apart from Cardinal Doherty had voted for Peter MacDonald.

Three loud knocks were heard coming from the chapel door. This was the signal that someone from outside needed to communicate with the Camerlengo. The Camerlengo approached the door to find Peter MacDonald and Georgio flanked by two Swiss Guards. The Camerlengo just stood and stared at Peter for a while. He had caught a glimpse of him in the Basilica earlier in the day, but at this distance there was no mistaking it; this man was most certainly the Pope in his dream. A broad smile came over his face.

The Camerlengo thanked Georgio and the guards, and escorted Peter into the Chapel. For a moment the room went totally silent before it erupted with applause and cheering. Though all the commotion, Peter was seen to mouth the words, 'Oh feck!'

The Camerlengo escorted Peter to the front of the chapel; Curiosa, O'Faherty and Pancetti were there to greet him. Peter looked at them and asked: 'What is going on?'

'Well, I'm not really sure how it happened, but we've just elected you as Pope,' Curiosa replied.

Peter's face immediately turned grey. He smiled and asked, 'No, really! What is going on?'

O'Faherty grabbed a nearby chair and positioned it behind Peter. 'I think you'd better sit down.'

Peter sat down and prayed that the cardinals were joking. Then O'Faherty crouched down in front of him, held both his hands and said, 'You see Peter, your presence in Rome has had a bigger impact than any of us could have imagined. Although none of us intended that you should become Pope, you have received the required majority of votes.'

'What?' Peter screamed, 'But you all agreed!'

'Yes Peter, we all truly believed that the purpose of our dreams was not to make you Pope, but I'm afraid the Holy Spirit had other ideas.'

'The Holy Spirit! How can you claim that this is the work of the Holy Spirit?'

'I can only speak from the point of view from those that had met you over the past few days. Our intention was that a few of us should put your name forward as a means of initiating discussion on the significance of our dream.' O'Faherty then noticed that all the cardinals were now gathered around Peter. 'Perhaps one of my other colleagues will share why they also put your name forward?'

Cardinal Giuseppi Mantovani was the first to respond. 'For me too, the decision to write your name on the ballot was because of a dream. So, I write your name so that I can let the other cardinals know about my dream.'

Cardinal DiMattina then spoke: 'I thought the same thing. I thought that God was talking to me and me alone, and I had to share this miracle with everyone to see what it could mean.'

Cardinal after cardinal confirmed that they had interpreted their dreams, coupled with the sighting of Peter, in the same way.

'So, what you're all saying is, that you all voted for me accidently.'

'No, it was not an accident,' Mantovani replied. 'If it was one or two votes maybe that could be an accident. But everyone voted for you! Everyone!'

'Well, almost everyone,' Curiosa felt obliged to add.

'Everyone?' Peter repeated incredulously.

'You see, that is why this could not be an accident.' Mantovani added, 'This could only be the work of God himself!'

O'Faherty, who was fast loosing circulation to his legs, was struggling to stand so Peter had to help him to his feet. 'Thank you, Peter,' he said, 'but you need to know that every cardinal but one put your name into the ballot. We have all agreed that you are a valid candidate and you have received in excess of two thirds of the vote. Therefore, all that remains if for you to accept the nomination and you will be the new Pontiff.'

'Accept? So, I can refuse?'

'Technically yes,' O'Faherty replied,

Doherty couldn't help himself. 'Yes, you don't have to accept. Do you really want to commit yourself to spending the rest of your life in the Vatican? Think of your family!'

The other cardinals quickly shouted Doherty down and the outburst left Peter in no doubt who was the one who didn't vote for him. But how could he possibly accept?

Peter slumped back into the chair and held his head in his hands. How did it come to this? Not four days earlier he had been lamenting to his friends how dysfunctional the Church was and now he was being asked to run it? The situation was so surreal he was beginning to wonder if something had gone drastically wrong during his vasectomy operation, putting him into a coma.

Yes, that was it! He was in a coma. It all makes sense. The past few days were totally imaginary. This wasn't really happening! It was like that TV show *Life on Mars;* he was living a parallel life. *Poor Mary*, he thought. She and the children would be beside themselves with worry. Perhaps he could simply think of something else and he would be removed from the situation.

He thought long and hard about being back at home with Mary and the children. Then he peered through his fingers to see if it worked. But all he saw was the smiling faces of one hundred cardinals looking back at him. *Oh feck!* This was real; the papacy was his if he wanted it. Poor Mary! He couldn't begin to think about how this would change their lives.

If he ran out of the Chapel now, he could still make his flight back to Dublin. But the cardinals were certain that some miracle had occurred, and they had a point. How else could he explain himself appearing as Pope in each of their dreams! And how else could he explain the fact that one hundred and fourteen of the one hundred and fifteen cardinal electors were so affected by these dreams that they wrote his name on a ballot? If this was truly the will of God, who was he to refuse? But did it have to be a life sentence? If he were to accept, he needed to know if there was some sort of out-clause available to him.

Curiosa broke his chain of thought. 'I'm sorry Peter,' he said, 'but we need an answer from you.'

'Wha? Sorry Your Eminence, this is a lot for me to take in. But if I accept, I need to know if I can leave whenever I want?'

'Well, it hasn't been exercised for some time, but abdication is an option.'

Abdication? Well at least that was something. He could take on the role, hopefully change things for the better, and then leave it to someone else to continue. He thought about this for a bit longer and then, still somewhat reluctantly, looked up to Curiosa and nodded his assent.

It so happened that the formality of asking the consent of the elected candidate fell on the cardinal who is first in order and seniority – which in this instance was Cardinal Curiosa. Curiosa asked the question: 'Do you accept your canonical election as Supreme Pontiff?'

Peter could not believe the words that came out of his mouth: 'In as much as it appears to be the will of God that I was elected, I accept,' he replied.

Then Curiosa asked; 'By what name do you wish to be called?'

Name? Peter hadn't thought of a name. He couldn't see why he couldn't keep using his given name so he replied, 'Peter, I guess?'

This caused a bit of a stir among the cardinals. Doherty had learnt to keep his mouth shut by this point, so it was Quinn who spoke. 'Of course you are free to choose any name you like, but Peter was the name given by Jesus to the disciple who founded our Church. Even though it is your Christian name, no Pope has ever dared to assume this name for themselves.'

'But that's my name,' Peter replied, 'I don't see the need to be called anything different.'

Despite his reservations, Peter thought hard about an alternative name. The only one that came to mind was the name that he had assumed for his confirmation, which was Simon. But that was St Peter's given name anyway. He didn't think he could carry one of the traditional papal names like Benedict or Pius. It was not his fault that his name was Peter, and he couldn't see himself being called anything else.

'I'm sorry, but I have always been Peter and I can't see myself carrying on with a different name. I wouldn't be true to myself if I chose a new name.'

Mantovani then spoke. 'Yes, Our Lord did give his apostle Simon the name Pietro, as he saw him as the rock on which the Church would be founded. But the Church today is very different to the Church that St Pietro started. And I think now we have laid a new foundation for our Church. So, it is perhaps appropriate for the leader of our new Church to have the same name as our original founder.'

Cardinal D'Angeli added, 'I agree. But I think also that although St Peter was never actually known as a Pope, you could acknowledge his significance as our original founder by using the name Pietro Secondo.'

Peter nodded his agreement, and everyone considered this to be a reasonable compromise.

'There is something else you must know, Your Holiness,' Curiosa said to him. 'It is necessary for all Popes to first be ordained bishops.'

Peter gave Curiosa a bewildered look. 'So how can I be Pope if I am not a Bishop?'

'That's not a problem because we're going to make you a bishop.'

'But doesn't a bishop need to be a priest first?'

'Well, we're in unchartered waters here but I presume that if a layman can become Pope, there is no problem with a layman becoming a bishop, so sit tight and we'll take you through the process.'

So, after a surprisingly short ritual, Peter was duly ordained a Bishop of the Church and once the ordination had been completed, the cardinals all lined up and paid homage to the new Supreme Pontiff of the Roman Catholic Church, Pope Peter II.

Adulation and distress

Down in the Piazza San Pietro, the crowd had been growing. The expectation had been that there would not be a result on the first day of the Conclave, so black smoke should have issued from the chapel by 5.30 pm at the latest. When by 6 pm no smoke was seen, the crowd and the media rightly suspected that something was up and there could well be a result that evening after all. So, either alerted by the media or friends present in the piazza, many Romans and tourists left their homes and hotels in the hope of seeing the new Pope for the first time.

It wasn't until 7 pm that white smoke rose from the chapel furnace and the crowd roared with excitement. Peter and the cardinals heard this roar from inside the Vatican just as Peter's ordination as bishop was completed. 'What was that?' Peter asked.

'We've just burnt the ballots,' O'Faherty replied. 'The crowd must be reacting to the white smoke. Wait till you hear their reaction when they see you for the first time.'

The thought sent a shiver down Peter's spine. Then he thought of Mary and the children, and his parents as well. He couldn't let them find out that he was Pope via the television; he would have to call them and tip them off. 'I need to make some phone calls!' he announced urgently.

Cardinal Quinn said, 'I'm sorry but the requirement is that no-one finds out until the result is officially announced.'

'I can't let my wife find out via the television!' protested Peter.

'Yes, but there are set protocols that must be followed,' Quinn replied.

Peter was becoming more and more agitated. It was not just that Mary needed to know before the announcement was made on Dublin television – she and the children also needed protection. The media would be swarming over the house the second the decision was announced. He thought about his dilemma for a while then it came to him. 'When exactly do I assume the authority of the papacy?'

'You could become Pope from the moment you accepted,' Curiosa answered, 'and now that you have been ordained a bishop you *are* the Pope.'

'Okay then. I need to make some phone calls before the public and the media find out what has happened.'

'But I already explained to you,' said Quinn, 'there is a process to be followed.'

'I don't care what the current process is, and I am not asking for permission. I need to make some phone calls. Are you going to deny me a direct request?'

'Oh!' Quinn replied, before quickly going to fetch the Camerlengo so that he could assist Peter with his request.

It isn't so bad being the Pope after all, Peter thought.

While this was happening, two men in dark suits with measure tapes around their necks had entered the room and promptly started measuring Peter up for his papal robes. Peter managed to pull out his cell phone and switch it on before he was required to raise his arms for the tailors. Holding the phone at arm's length he saw that he had barely enough battery life to make one phone call. Fortuitously, the Camerlengo had arrived furnishing another phone. Peter thanked him and quickly dialled his home number.

Expecting it to go to the answering machine, as it had earlier that evening, he was surprised to hear Lauren's voice: 'MacDonald residence, Lauren speaking,'

'Hello Lauren speaking, this is Daddy speaking here. Can I speak to Mammy right away please?'

'Okay Daddy.' Then Lauren called for her mother without moving the handset away from her face and yet again Peter had to move the phone away from his ear, lest he burst an eardrum. He slowly brought the phone back to his ear to hear that Lauren was still on the other end. 'Oh Daddy, have you heard the news? They've just chosen the new Pope! We're going to see him on the TV soon. Isn't that exciting?'

'Yes, it is darling,' was all he could say.

Then Mary came to the phone, 'Hello Peter, I suppose you'll be boarding your flight soon. I see they've chosen the new Pope, do you have any inside information as to who it might be?'

'Hello Darling … yes, funny you should ask that, because as a matter of fact I do.'

'Oh really! I'd love to know if this whole saga of yours has had some effect.'

Peter was struggling with his words. 'Well, firstly you have to know that I won't be home tonight after all.'

'Why, what's happened?' Mary asked cautiously.

'I'm afraid that this saga has had a bigger effect on the papacy than we could have imagined. You know how I mentioned about the cardinals and their dreams?'

'Yes,' now Mary's voice was breaking,

'Well, we now know for certain that every cardinal had a dream where I appeared to them as Pope.'

'So, what does that mean?'

'Well, the story of me being some sort of Pope-maker made it into the Vatican newspaper complete with a picture of me. Unfortunately, that meant that all the cardinals were able to make a connection between me and their individual dreams. They all put my name into the ballot to see what it was all about.'

'Nice try Peter. So, you expect me to believe that you have been elected as Pope?'

'Yes?' muttered Peter, realising how incredulous this story was.

'Stop messing about, Peter. Just tell me when your flight is expected to land in Dublin.'

'I'm sorry darling. I know this is almost impossible to believe, but they really have elected me.'

'Don't be daft Peter, how could they possibly elect someone who is not a cardinal?'

'I don't fecking know why, I just know that they did!'

His outburst caught the attention of the tailors, who although couldn't speak English, thought they understood the 'f' word when they heard it and paused their work to glare at Peter for a moment.

Embarrassed, Peter softened his voice and continued, 'This thing has got my stomach, brain, and knickers in knots! It was those fecking dreams. They all thought that they'd experienced some sort of miracle.'

'This really isn't funny, Peter.'

'I'm not trying to be fecking funny Mary, but I got a winning majority of votes in the first ballot which means they had to offer me the papacy.'

'That's impossible! Tell me that you haven't accepted.'

'I didn't want to accept! I was on my way to the airport when they sent their man at the Jesuit College to intercept me. He literally dragged me to the Vatican. Once they told me about the outcome of the ballot my first instinct was to run straight out of there.'

'But Peter, this isn't just a job with another Council; this is the fecking papacy we're talking about! You've turned our whole world upside down!'

'Sorry Darling, but it wasn't a very easy decision to make and if I thought I could get out of it I would. But all the cardinals think it's part of God's grand plan. I couldn't get past the fact that I have been given the opportunity to change things for the better. I don't know how I'm going to do it, but I'll need you by my side while I'm trying.'

'Oh Peter, this is just impossible, It's like we're in some sort of parallel world.'

'Tell me about it. If it's any consolation, there is the option to abdicate, so it need not be a lifetime commitment.'

'At least that's something. But the media, Peter, they won't leave us alone now.'

'I know; we'll have to arrange some sort of police protection or something. In the meantime, can you get your brother to come over right away? I'll call Niall Brodie and see if he and some of the lads can come over to help fend off the media.'

'What about your parents?'

'Oh feck! I'll give them a call now to tip them off as well. You'd better call your folks to prepare them for the shock. I'm meant to step out onto the balcony at any minute now so I expect that all hell will break loose once that happens.'

'But when will we see you again?'

'I don't know when I'll be able to get back to Dublin now. I suppose I'll have to get you and the children to come here.'

'I've always wanted to go to Rome, but I thought it would be for a holiday, not to live.'

'Sorry to put you through all of this, darling.'

'I just hope that God knows what he's doing.'

'Bye my love, talk to you again soon.'

The children had heard Mary's anxious cries and by the time that she had hung up the phone they were all gathered around her. 'What's up Mammy?' Michael asked.

'They've gone and made your father Pope!' Mary replied as she burst into tears.

The children went quiet for a while but then started cheering. This was amazing news for them. The younger children had failed to appreciate the adjustments that would be required of them and only an indignant Brydie looked up at her mother and said, 'Well I'm not moving to fecking Rome!'

Peter made a quick call to Niall Brodie and asked him to gather some of the lads together and go help Mary. He didn't tell him why, he just said that Mary would fill them in when they got there.

He then placed a call to his parents. It was his mother who answered the phone. 'Hello mammy,' he said.

'Peter! So you remembered your old mother then!'

'Sorry mammy, but things have been a bit crazy lately.'

'What's this about you being in Rome?'

'Yes mammy, that's what I need to talk to you and dad about actually. There have been some very strange things that have happened while I've been here.'

'Strange things, what sort of strange things?'

'Well, before I tell you, I need to know if you're sitting down.'

'You haven't gone and done something silly have you? You've already got a reputation as a troublemaker with Cardinal Doherty; you haven't gone and upset the rest of the cardinals now, have you?'

'No mammy, I haven't upset the cardinals. In fact, I've impressed them. But I may have made a bit too much of an impression on them.'

'There you go, I knew it, you've gone at them with your radical views and got them all riled up.'

'No, I haven't mammy! It's nothing like that. Now are you sitting down?'

'Yes, yes I'm sitting.'

'Okay mammy, you know how you always wished that one of your sons would become a priest?'

'Well, there's no chance of that happening now is there?'

'Perhaps not, but although it's totally unbelievable, the cardinals have gone and made me the new Holy Father.'

'Peter Collum MacDonald!' his mother screamed at him. 'Where do you think you get off interrupting my teatime to tell me lies like that?'

'No mammy, it's not a lie, it's true I swear!'

'Oh really? And how could they go and make you fecking Pope when you're not even a fecking priest!'

'No, but I am a bishop!'

'A bishop now, is it? You've skipped over priest and gone straight to bishop. Peter MacDonald, did you lose your brain when they cut off your balls? Yes, don't think I don't know about that as well. You couldn't tell me yourself, so I had to find out from Maree Brown of all people. Can you imagine my embarrassment when I found out that half of Dublin knew, and I didn't?'

'I'm sorry mammy but it's all true, they had to make me a bishop after they elected me as Pope. I just wanted to make sure that you and Dad knew about it before you saw it on the television.'

'Peter MacDonald, I always thought of you as the sensible one. Now I don't want to talk about this nonsense anymore. You get back to your family right away and go see a doctor to sort out that head of yours, you hear?'

'Yes mammy.'

'Okay, bye now.'

'Is everything alright?' O'Faherty asked Peter when he finished his call.

'That was my mammy,' Peter replied, 'I tried to warn her and Dad so they didn't get a shock when they saw me on TV, but she wouldn't believe me.'

'Well, that shouldn't surprise you. I find it hard to believe what's happened over the past few days myself! Now let's get ready for you to shock the world.'

To Peter's surprise the tailors had managed to put together a garment for him to wear over his jeans and casual shirt – so even though he didn't feel as if he should be Pope, he did at least look the part.

Peter and the cardinals made the relatively short walk to St Peter's Basilica, where the traditional announcement of the new Pope is made from the upper-level balcony.

It was agreed that the three candidates who were considered preferred at the start of the Conclave would go out on the balcony together, as this would provide a hint to the media that the Pope was not someone anyone expected. Giuseppi Mantovani would make the announcement.

Peter asked Curiosa and Pancetti what would be expected of him. They told him that the new Pope was expected to address the crowd in Italian. Peter didn't speak a word of Italian, but Pancetti was able to reassure him that it would be alright for him to speak in English, and he would be able to translate his words to Italian for the benefit of the crowd gathered below.

It was now almost 8 pm in Rome and news services around the world had been tipped off that the Conclave, which was one of the shortest in recorded history, had ended and the new Pope was about to make his appearance.

D'Angeli, Mantovani and Mangiafuoco walked out to the balcony to the cheers of the waiting crowd. Of course, most of the crowd had no way of knowing who they were because it was not possible to make out their faces, and the public address system was practically useless against the din from the masses. But the media had indeed picked up on the fact that the three favoured candidates had obviously not made the cut.

Then Mantovani walked up to the microphone and raised his hands in a vain attempt to silence the crowd. When he thought that things had at least settled a bit he made the announcement that everyone was waiting to hear.

He began with a greeting in several languages: Firstly, in Italian, 'Fratelli e sorelle carissimi,' then in Spanish, 'Queridísimos hermanos y hermanas,' in French, 'Bien chers frères et sœurs,' German, 'Liebe Brüder und Schwestern,' and finally in English, 'Dear brothers and sisters.'

The sound from the crowd was deafening and Mantovani again had to raise his hands to try to quiet things down enough to make the announcement proper. The crowd just kept cheering louder and ever. Mantovani had no choice other than to try to be heard above the roar of the crowd. So, he walked up to the microphone made the traditional Latin announcement. 'Annuntio vobis gaudium magnum,' *I announce to you a great joy.* 'Habemus Papam!' *We have a Pope!*

Just when he thought the crowd couldn't get any louder, they issued a most tremendous roar. Mantovani knew he couldn't hope to quell their excitement, so he had to persist.

'Eminentissimum ac ...' Mantovani had to pause at this statement. He was reading from the standard script for papal proclamations which assumed that the Pope would be a cardinal and he was not sure whether referring to Peter as 'The most eminent and most reverend Lord' was appropriate. The crowd interpreted his pause as a call for silence and dutifully obliged. Mantovani therefore had to continue; '... ac reverendissimum Dominum, Dominum Petrus.'

The crowd roared yet again at the revelation that the new Pope's given name was Peter. Media centres were taken totally by surprise, as there were only two possible candidates with this given name. They were the Australian cardinal Peter Quinn and the French cardinal Pierre Soutier – and neither appeared on anyone's list of probable candidates.

The cheering of the crowd at least gave Mantovani some time to think. The next statement, 'Sanctæ Romanæ Ecclesiæ Cardinalem', directly referred to the Pope being a cardinal of the Holy Roman Church, which Peter was not. The crowd were anxious to hear the full name of the new Pope as well as his papal name and had quieted down again in anticipation of the announcement. Mantovani decided to skip the cardinal reference and just say the name: 'Petrus MacDonald.'

He could have announced Mickey Mouse as far as the crowd was concerned because they just started cheering again. Some even got down on their knees and raised their hands in prayer.

The media, however, who had a direct feed into the Vatican's public address system, had no trouble hearing and transmitting the name and all commentators went suddenly silent. They frantically scanned their list of cardinals' names to no avail. It was only the Irish media who immediately made the connection between the name Peter MacDonald and the man that *The Irish Times* had dubbed the pope-maker only a couple of days earlier. But the thought that this man could have been elected Pope was too fantastic to contemplate.

Mantovani had not yet announced the new Pope's papal name. There was no way that the roar from the crowd would diminish now, so he just continued to speak into the microphone; 'Qui sibi nomen imposuit Petrus Secundius.'

Then Peter, wearing white papal robes and a white and gold papal mitre, walked out on to the balcony flanked by Pancetti and Curiosa, with O'Faherty and Billingham just behind them.

Again, the crowd, who just assumed that he was one of the cardinals, roared. Peter nervously walked forward while Pancetti and Curiosa each raised Peter's arms in the air, making the crowd roar even louder.

While most foreign media commentators were struggling to work out who he was, the Irish media commentators couldn't believe what they were seeing.

The Vatican had, of course, simultaneously issued its own press release informing the rest of the world of the incredible news that the new Pope was a forty-two-year-old, married father of six from Dublin in Ireland. The press release added only that the Holy Father had chosen to retain his given name as Peter for his papal name and made no comment on the manner of his promotion to the papacy.

As Peter was reluctantly led towards the microphone by Pancetti and Curiosa, word of the unprecedented appointment of a layman filtered through the crowd. The applause and cheering was gradually replaced by confused muttering and eventually complete silence as Peter moved towards the microphone to speak.

'Err … hello,' was Peter's hesitant start to his first speech as Pope, 'I'd like firstly to say that I'm just as surprised to see myself up here as you all are.'

Pancetti stepped in and immediately began translating Peter's remarks.

'Only a few days ago, I was an ordinary Catholic in Dublin and I fully expected that one of these cardinals would be elected as Pope. But all I can say is that some amazing things have happened over the past few days and my election as Pope is a result of these events.

'The cardinals and I don't fully understand why God has chosen me to take on this venerable position. But with your prayers and support, we hope to come to better appreciate what God's plan is for his Church.

'I know my appointment will be difficult for some to accept and could be interpreted as call for change. But rest assured that I will not make any changes without consulting with the cardinals and other church leaders, and I will work with the cardinals to ensure that the Church continues to listen and respond to the needs of all Catholics around the world. Thank you!'

Slowly but surely, polite applause emanated from the crowd intermixed with some raucous cheering from an Irish contingent.

Peter then motioned to walk inside but Curiosa stopped him. 'A blessing, you should make a blessing,' he whispered.

'Oh, okay …' Peter was not sure what to do, so he turned and hesitantly walked back to the microphone and said, 'God bless you all,' while making the sign of the cross in the same way he had seen so many Popes do before him.

This seemed to please the crowd and they all started to cheer again, and Peter and the cardinals moved indoors.

The event was quite rightly reported as one of the most significant in papal history. A quick scan of the list of previous Popes revealed that Peter was the youngest Pope for over five hundred years and the first married Pope for over seven hundred years. Furthermore, he was the first ever Irish Pope and the first Pope from an English-speaking country.

Not surprisingly, conservative commentators were having a lot of difficulty coming to terms with the decision. They were certain that the Church would continue the path back to its glory days, where the churches were packed with faithful and unquestioning believers. In their minds the debate surrounding married clergy was old news and there was no question that the celibate priesthood would be preserved long into the future. So, the appointment of a *married* Pope was unfathomable. Surely the cardinals had made some sort of mistake!

The fact that Peter was surrounded by the most liberal of the cardinals when he made his appearance led to the fear that this all could be part of a great conspiracy.

Were the cardinals acting on their own free will or were they pressured, perhaps by force, into choosing a lay candidate? Surely, the cardinals could only make such radical choice if they feared for their safety. The cardinals must therefore be in great danger. Some of these commentators openly called upon the Roman authorities to act. That the Vatican authorities seemed to be doing nothing about it indicated that the conspirators must have infiltrated the Swiss Guard as well as the Vatican security staff.

The general public and the mass media, however, did not buy this conspiracy theory. They only saw joy on the faces of three cardinals when they came out to announce the appointment. The only one who looked worried or stressed was the new Pope himself. So, if anyone was under pressure it was him.

Bishops from around the world looked on completely puzzled. They knew that it was impossible for the feeble liberal forces that had any authority within the Church to exert any influence over the College of Cardinals. Most bishops had been appointed by the two Popes prior to Pope Anthony; that was the main the reason that the Vatican had succeeded so well in winding back Vatican II reforms. Now the world of these conservative bishops had been turned upside-down. A layman had been given the papacy and the Roman Catholic Church may never be the same again.

In their Dublin home, Mary MacDonald was sitting in shock, holding her eldest daughter Brydie's hand for comfort. Apart from getting excited when she saw her daddy on TV wearing a funny hat, little Suzie was oblivious to what was happening, but Michael, Lauren, Patrick, and Connor were still dancing for joy. Mary's brother Gerry was there as well, along with Niall Brodie, Ian Brown, and Paul Tyson.

Within five minutes of the announcement being made, the front yard of the house was swarming with reporters and neighbours alike. The family had decided not to engage in any dialogue with the reporters and set about ensuring that the windows and doors were secured against intruders. Niall soon realised that it was impossible for them to get people to move on, so he made a call to the local police.

The local police chief was at first reluctant to step in. Apparently, he hadn't been following the news and therefore didn't believe Niall's story that a Dubliner had been made Pope. Niall eventually got him to escalate the issue with his superiors, who convinced the local chief that the story was indeed true and now that Peter was effectively a foreign head of state, his family were entitled to police protection while they were in Ireland.

It was still another twenty minutes before the first contingent of police arrived and they were hopelessly outnumbered. So, a contingent of Dublin's riot police had to be called to move the crowd away and keep the press corps off the property. This only provided minor relief to Mary, because it was now evident that she and the children were prisoners in their own home; she wouldn't even be able to go leave the house without being pursued by reporters.

At the other MacDonald house, Peter's mother Nora MacDonald had fainted in front of the TV when she realised that all that her son had told her was true. Her equally shocked but still conscious husband, Patrick MacDonald, was frantically trying to revive her while wondering what the feck was going on!

The stress of the past few hours has all been too much for Peter as well. No sooner had he re-entered the Basilica that his eyes rolled back and he collapsed. The cardinals initially feared the worst; could this be the shortest reign in papal history as well as the shortest election? But their fears were eased once they realised that Peter had just passed out and was still breathing. Nevertheless, a medical team was called, and Peter was taken to the Pope's private medical facilities for observation.

After about two hours in the medical centre, the doctors on duty were satisfied that Peter's turn was just a stress response and there was nothing seriously wrong with him. Curiosa and Pancetti had been waiting with him along with the Cardinal Camerlengo. Although it was traditional for the new Pope to share a meal with the cardinals on the evening of his appointment, it was too late for anything like that now. They all thought it best to take Peter to his apartment so that he could rest up and try to come to terms with the situation.

When he got to the apartment, Peter immediately asked for a telephone. He needed to speak with Mary again. The Cardinal Camerlengo managed to furnish him with a cell phone for his private use and then left him to settle into his new abode.

Peter initially tried to call home, but a busy signal confirmed his suspicion that the phone had been taken off the hook. He expected Mary's cell phone to be switched off as well. So, he managed to retrieve Niall Brodie's number from his own cell phone and dialled the number.

Niall answered and proceeded to fill Peter in on the situation at home, including the need to call the riot police. This information did nothing for Peter's stress levels. He thought that Mary would never forgive him for what he had done to their family.

'Peter!' was all that Mary could say when she took the phone.

'Darling, I'm so sorry!' was all that Peter could say in reply.

They both sat in silence for a while, each comforted by the other's presence on the phone.

'What are we to do?' Mary eventually said.

'I'm sorry,' Peter said again, his voice beginning to waver. A few more moments of silence ensued before Peter spoke again. 'I had to accept, I didn't want to, but I had to.'

'I know,' Mary replied as she burst into tears. But she managed to continue in between sobs, 'I know, Peter. This is an amazing thing … an incredible thing! People talk about receiving a calling from God, but they don't expect him to use a fecking megaphone!' Mary's comment lightened the mood a bit and they were both able share a laugh between their sobs. Then Peter told her about the dove, and she started laughing again at the thought of Peter trying to shake off this bird. 'Oh Peter, I thought God would be subtler than that.'

'Apparently it wasn't enough for God to have the cardinals see my picture in the paper, he had to send this fecking dove as well. I'm starting to believe that God is a real bastard!'

'Now, now, this is your new boss remember?' They both had a good laugh again but once they'd composed themselves, Mary said, 'But Peter, what are we going to do?'

'I don't know darling. We'll just have to see where this thing takes us. How did the children take the news?'

'They just think it's so fantastic that their daddy is such an important person. I don't think they realise the potential consequences just yet. All except for Brydie who has already said that she is not going to move.'

Peter laughed; it was the response he would have expected from his eldest daughter. 'I suppose it will be best not to change their routine right away.'

'Are we destined to live separate lives then?'

'No, we can't do that! This is a new situation for all of us and I think we need time to work out what's best before we make any changes.'

'I'm sure God's plan doesn't include abandoning your family! The children need to see you. I need to see you!'

'Don't worry, I'm not going to abandon you. I just haven't a fecking clue where I'm going to start. I think I'll need the following week to myself to come to grips with it. But the Church will also have to come to grips with the fact that the Holy Father has family obligations.'

'Oh Christ!' Mary exclaimed.

'What?'

'They're not going to refer to us as the Holy Family, are they? And if anyone refers to me as the Holy Mother, I'm going to scream.'

'I hadn't thought of that. This is going to be new territory for everyone. I suppose you could be known as the Pope's consort.'

'Consort, I don't like the sound of that. The Pope's wife will be fine or just plain Mary MacDonald will be better.' The Pope's wife indeed! Mary couldn't believe the words had come out of her mouth. 'This is so incredible Peter; I can't believe what we're talking about.'

'Look, I suppose that I could divide my time between Dublin and Rome until we work out a more permanent arrangement,' Peter said.

'Is that going to be possible?' asked Mary.

'It's going to have to be. And you and the family can come and stay with me on weekends as well.'

'How do you suppose we are going to pay for all this?'

'Well, I'm the fecking Pope aren't I? I've got jets and helicopters at my disposal, I think?'

'Well, I don't think you're going to win any friends if you start exploiting your position!'

'I don't have any intention of exploiting my position, but the Vatican is going to have to adapt to my needs.'

'Okay Peter, but just because you're meant to be in charge doesn't mean that you can do whatever you want.'

'This is going to be harder than I thought, isn't it? I don't even know what this job pays.'

'Actually Peter, I don't think the Pope gets paid anything.'

'Well, that puts us really in the shite.'

'You said it!'

He and Mary talked about their new situation for almost half of the night. Mary's brother Gerry had managed to break through the blockade to purchase a new sim-card for Mary so she and Peter could continue to communicate freely. So, when Niall's phone was in danger of running out of battery, they were able to continue their conversation.

In the end they resolved that it would be best if she and the children could stay in Dublin at least until the summer holidays. In the meantime, they would try to join Peter in Rome whenever possible, and Peter would try to get back to Dublin as often as he could as well. They knew this was not the way popes normally operated, but if they would have to adapt to the needs of the Vatican, the Vatican would have to adapt to the needs of a Pope with a young family.

New foundations

Peter didn't know how he did it, but he managed to get some sleep during his first night in the papal apartment. It was the early hours of the morning before exhaustion got the better of him. He wasn't allowed to sleep long, because he was soon woken by someone bursting into his room.

'Good morning, Holiness,' said a lady's voice in a familiar Dublin accent.

'Err … Good morning.' Peter muttered, having to shield his eyes from the daylight that suddenly bathed the room. 'Can I help you?'

'No, no, no … It is I who am here to help you, Holiness,' she said as she continued busying herself around the room. 'I'm Sister Kelly, Beatrice Kelly, and I'm the head of your household.'

'Oh,' said Peter, still groggy from his sleep and puzzled as to why the sister seemed to have no respect for his privacy. 'What time is it?' he asked sheepishly.

'It's just gone 6 am. I thought I'd let you sleep in a bit as it is your first day and all. All of the other Popes would have been well into their day by now.'

'Err … thanks,' was Peter's decidedly un-enthusiastic reply.

'Best be up with you now. To be sure you'll be wanting to say your prayers before breakfast.'

'Yes …' Peter replied unconvincingly. Reluctantly, Peter pulled back the bedsheets and realised that he was totally naked! He'd been out of clean underwear and clothes when Georgio intercepted him, so the only thing for it had been to find something clean in the morning. He quickly covered himself with the bedclothes.

The sister, who thankfully had her back turned to him when he pulled off the sheets, was starting to become impatient with him, 'Come on now, up you get. You've got an important job to get on with now, no time to loll about you know.'

'Err, excuse me Sister,' he replied meekly. 'You wouldn't perhaps be able to organise some laundry for me? You see I hadn't planned to stay in Rome for more than a few days and I've run out of clean things.'

'There's a hamper in the bathroom!' was her curt reply. 'Put your dirty clothes in there and we'll see they're cleaned for you.'

'Thank you, Sister,' Peter replied, 'but you wouldn't by any chance be able to find some clean things for me to wear this morning? I desperately need some clean underwear.'

'You'll find some clean robes to wear in the bathroom. As for your smalls, I'll see what I can find.'

'Thank you sister,' he said, again expecting that she would soon leave the room. But instead, she just stood there waiting for him to get out of bed. He started gesturing with his eyes that he would like her to leave the room and then pulled down the sheets slightly to show her that he wasn't completely dressed.

'My goodness!' A clearly shocked Sr Kelly remarked before dutifully turning around and leaving the room.

When he was sure she had gone, Peter got out of bed and made his way to the bathroom. He couldn't find any robes; all he could see was a white surplice and stole. He would have much preferred his old jeans and tee shirt, but they were now decidedly on the nose and had to be cleaned.

He looked around for some trousers or shorts but couldn't see any, so he covered himself with the surplice alone. It was tight around the shoulders and a bit short, but it would do. There was also a pair of shoes left in one of the wardrobes. These must have belonged to the previous Pope, as they were hopelessly too small for him to wear. He was out of clean socks and his sneakers were also on the smelly side, so he resolved to walking around barefoot.

Having covered his nakedness, he felt comfortable enough to explore his surrounds. He first investigated some of the cupboards in the papal suite to see if there were any other clothes that he could wear under his surplice, but all the wardrobes and drawers must have been emptied after the death of his predecessor.

The papal suite was huge. It was just one room with an adjoining bath, but it seemed almost the size as the entire ground floor of his Dublin house. The bathroom alone was almost as big as the room that he had been sharing with Fr Mick over the past week. But now, at least, he had a place to have proper salt bath. However, he didn't have the energy for that.

He then opened what he thought was just another wardrobe door and was surprised to find that the door led to a small chapel. The chapel contained a marble high altar with a gold tabernacle positioned centrally and gold candle holders on either side. The candles were already lit. Above the altar was a rough-hewn timber crucifix with a carved image of the suffering Christ attached. To the right-hand side of the altar was a statue of Mary, the mother of Christ, and to the left of the altar was a statue of a man whom Peter surmised must be Saint Peter. There were no chairs or pews in the room, only a couple of kneelers directly in front of the altar. *This must be where the Popes said their private prayers,* he thought.

Peter had been a practicing Catholic for all his life, but he was not really in the habit of saying private prayers. Mary and Peter encouraged their children to say prayers every night and Mary would often say prayers to herself before going to bed. It was not that he didn't value the importance of prayer; he knew that it was in moments of quiet contemplation and meditation that one could connect with the forces at work in the universe. The problem was that he felt self-conscious when he tried to pray on his own. It didn't help that he associated piousness with the conservative zealots who had brought the Church down to where it is today. This was a silly excuse, and he knew that it was holding back his spiritual development.

But if there was ever a time that he needed to pray, this was it. Furthermore, he couldn't use being self-conscious as an excuse, as this room was just for him and him alone. So, he knelt in front of the altar, crossed himself, and tried to meditate. There were a myriad of questions running through his head, but he tried to push them aside to free his mind and let the room speak to him.

He thought about how he had come to be Pope. Was there a plan or was this just a weird joke that God was playing on the Catholics to have a bit of a laugh? He surmised that all things must happen for a reason and his job was to make the most of it. That God had specifically singled him out by putting him into the dreams of the cardinals meant that He wanted a very different Church to the one that currently existed. This reality emboldened Peter to use his new authority to achieve some real change and not get too bothered about putting people off-side. After all, there are some people who will never be happy whatever you do. He was the Pope! He answered to no-one – well, no-one on earth anyway. Whatever he decided would have to be accepted. The responsibility was immense!

This resolve made him less fearful of the tasks ahead of him, and more confident that he could actually make a change for the better. But he also felt lonely.

He would have to make some significant changes. Surely people wouldn't have a problem with the idea of married priests now that there was a married Pope in the Vatican. The idea of women priests might be harder to get through, but it would certainly be on his agenda.

He couldn't do this alone and needed a trusted group of advisers around him. One definite thing was that he would invite Fr Mick to move into the Vatican. Fr Mick had been his trusted spiritual advisor for most of his adult life and he couldn't see how he could operate without him.

Then there were the cardinals. Although he had grown to trust them over the past week, he really didn't know any of them very well. It was also clear that Curiosa at least was seen as an extremist among his peers; having him too close may isolate others. O'Faherty didn't seem to have the stomach for high office and Billingham, who seemed inoffensive enough, didn't seem to have the right credentials to galvanise support either. Pancetti, he thought, was the only one who could have widespread appeal. He was Italian at least; the Italians had by far the biggest contingent of cardinals and he already proved that he could speak on his behalf. It would be a while before Peter would be able to master the Italian language, if ever. So, he needed someone like Pancetti to have a key role in his Curia. But what exactly were the roles in the Curia? He had absolutely no idea. That would have to be Pancetti's first job: to explain to him how the Vatican worked.

His thoughts were interrupted by the sound of someone entering the papal suite. He turned to see that Sr Kelly had returned. She smiled, impressed with finding him praying in the Chapel. He got to his feet and re-entered the main room.

'It was difficult on short notice, but I managed to find a few things for you,' she said.

Peter was very impressed with what the sister had managed to find. There was underwear, tee shirts and socks. Some of the items appeared to be from the Vatican souvenir shop, but that didn't matter. They were all new items and close enough to his size. 'Thank you, Sister, these will be grand.'

'Well, you put them on,' she replied, 'and I'll go and bring your breakfast in for you.'

Peter headed into the bathroom and took the time to wash and shave before getting dressed. There were no trousers or shirts for him to wear, but Sr Kelly had brought him a better fitting surplice – and at least he now had underwear and socks! Wearing a surplice was a bit strange, but it helped him reconcile himself with his new role.

He emerged from the bathroom to find that a breakfast table had been laid out for him. It was largely a continental breakfast, which was refreshing change from the heavy feasts that Georgio had been preparing for him at the Jesuit College.

Also delivered with the breakfast were some newspapers including the morning edition of the Vatican newspaper, *The New York Times* and *The London Times*. But his eyes were drawn to a copy of *The Irish Times* which someone had been considerate enough to include. Peter eagerly lifted this newspaper from the pile before him and saw immediately that Declan O'Reilly had had a busy night, for the headline read: 'Our Man: the Pope of the Cardinals' Dreams'.

The article went on to describe how Peter had miraculously appeared in the dreams of the cardinals and how this amazing revelation led to them to taking an unprecedented step of making him Pope. Reading the article, Peter thought that it should help people to understand why such a strange thing had occurred and hopefully trust him with the decisions he had to make.

It appeared, however, that *The Irish Times* had kept this exclusive to themselves. Both *The New York Times* and *The London Times* only reported on how amazing the decision was and speculated on what it could mean for the future of the Church. Thankfully, Peter could not find any references to his recent vasectomy, but he figured that it would only be a matter of time before that juicy titbit got into the papers.

Most of the pain and swelling in his groin had now disappeared but he was still irritated by his stitches and couldn't wait to have them removed. He would not be able to make it back to the clinic in Dublin by Monday as was arranged, so he would have to ask someone to do it in Rome. The cat would well and truly be out of the bag then!

His thoughts then turned to work and how he had promised his manager Callan Dyson that he would be back in Dublin that morning to attend a planning appeal hearing. This was obviously not going to happen now. Surely Callan would understand the change in Peter's circumstances. But Peter felt that he owed him the courtesy of a phone call to apologise.

It was now about 8.30 am in Rome, making it about 7.30 am in Dublin. But he knew from the numerous phone calls he often received from Callan early in the morning that Callan would be on his way to work if he was not there already. So, Peter made the call. 'Hello Callan, its Peter MacDonald here.'

Hello Peter, you'd better be on your way in if we're to make this hearing on time.'

'Err Callan, there may be a slight problem with that.'

'What? Don't tell me that you didn't make it back to Dublin last night!'

'Well, here's the thing, I was on my way to the airport when I was intercepted and dragged back to the Vatican.'

'I thought you were done with that Vatican business?'

'You don't watch TV or listen to the radio much, do you Callan?'

'No, I have no time for that rubbish!'

'Well, there's been some strange things going on here in Rome over the past few days and the upshot of it is, they've gone and made me the new Pope.'

'Pope! Pope! They've gone and made you Pope! Well, I don't know about that. You're a key employee of this Council, and your employment contract says that you must provide six weeks' notice before resigning and taking on another job!'

Peter couldn't believe Callan's incredulous response. 'I had no intention of getting a new job Callan, it just happened!' he replied.

'Well, that doesn't mean that you shouldn't serve out your notice!'

Peter had a lot more to worry about now than this planning appeal hearing and was rapidly losing patience with his manager, whom he now realised was totally psychotic. 'Look Callan, I think you'll just have to accept that being offered the papacy is a bit different to just getting another job, so it is extremely unlikely that I'll be able to get back to the council any time soon.'

'We'll see about that, but I still need your help this morning, so I'll give you a call when I'm at the hearing.'

'Okay Callan, I'll wait for your call.'

Peter then hung up, having deliberately neglected to advise Callan that his cell phone was out of action. Callan needed to learn that the world didn't revolve around him and Council business. There were in fact, bigger things in life.

Having finished his breakfast, Peter was now at a loss at what to do. Did he have an office or did people come to see him in his room?

Then there was a knock on the door. Peter was in the process of getting out of his chair when Cardinal Roberto Gratziatanto, the former Pope's Camerlengo, opened the door and walked in. 'Bon giorno Santo Papa,' he said as he walked towards Peter, 'I hope you sleep well.'

'I think that I managed to get a few hours, thank you Eminence, but I had a lot on my mind,' Peter responded.

'Yes … it was big shock for you. We think you die when you fall, but you okay now, no?'

'Well, I think I am still in shock, Your Eminence.'

'Please, not so formal anymore. You Papa now, so you can call me Roberto.'

'Oh … okay … Roberto. But what did you call me when you came into the room?'

'Santa Papa, it mean Holy Father.'

'Oh, well seeing we're on first name basis, you can call me Peter then.'

'No, that would not be proper. I call you Papa.'

It seemed a bit odd to Peter that a man in his sixties would refer to him essentially as 'Daddy', but he wasn't in the mood to argue the point. He had only met the cardinal yesterday, but he knew that he was personally appointed to the role of Camerlengo by the late Pope Anthony. So, perhaps he could be trusted. Besides, 'Roberto' was very helpful to him in the hours after his appointment. 'Well … Roberto, thank you very much for your assistance yesterday with getting messages to my family and providing me with a new phone.'

'No problemo Papa. What you want me to do for you today?'

Peter had no idea what he wanted to do or what he was meant to do. But he wanted some trusted advisers by his side. 'Can you please ask Cardinal Pancetti to come to see me? Also, my good friend Fr Michael

Finlay is staying at the Jesuit College. Can you please contact him as well and arrange accommodation for him in the Vatican?'

'No problemo Papa. I will do it right away.'

The Camerlengo left. Peter had just settled back into reading the newspapers when the Camerlengo returned. He couldn't possibly have personally attended to Peter's requests in such a short time; there was clearly a team of minions at the Camerlengo's disposal who did all the running around for him.

The Camerlengo then took the opportunity to show Peter around the papal suite and offices. He did indeed discover that he had a private office that was separate to his private quarters, and there was a myriad of other offices located on the same floor. Most of them appeared to be staffed by priests and nuns, but there was the odd person dressed in civilian clothes as well.

Strangely, although there were many people milling about, the Camerlengo didn't bother to stop to introduce him to anyone. It seemed to Peter that staff protocol was to avoid direct interaction with the Pope and use the Camerlengo as an intermediary. He was getting a lot of sideways glances though. If he caught someone looking at him he smiled back, but they always turned away quickly as soon as he made eye contact.

But the minions had done their job well, as within half an hour Pancetti arrived. Peter thanked the Camerlengo and then retired to his office with Pancetti so that they could speak privately.

Peter wasn't sure where to start. He needed a crash course in what was expected of him. Pancetti proved to be a good tutor and explained the daily activities of previous Popes, and then went through the structure of the Curia and the various roles of the staff that worked in the Pope's offices.

Within a couple of hours, they were joined by Fr Mick, who was able to provide his advice on what was right and what was wrong with the Roman Curia. Through it all Peter took copious notes and drew organisational diagrams where appropriate to retain some of this information overload.

They worked through lunch, which Sr Kelly graciously arranged. She was a lot more respectful with a real cardinal in the room. But by about 3 pm his brain wasn't going to take any more. To top things off the Camerlengo had been fielding calls from all around the world with heads of state and religious leaders from many other denominations wanting to personally congratulate the new Pope. Peter had been putting off responding to these calls and was hoping that the day's discussions with Pancetti and Fr Mick would help him to formulate how he would respond. However, there were some extremely important people wanting to speak with him. People who Peter thought he would never catch a glimpse of in person, let alone have them seek him out for an audience! So, it was not polite to delay responding any further.

He was still not sure what he was going to say to these people, but Pancetti and Fr Mick assured him that if he just remained himself and politely accepted their congratulations, everything would be okay.

The calls, arranged by the Camerlengo with a small army of assistants, came through thick and fast. Thankfully most were relatively short with the various dignitaries just passing on their congratulations, wishing him well and indicating that they would like to arrange a longer discussion at an appropriate time. However, there were others who wanted to have in depth discussions with him right there and then. All that Peter could say to them was that he was not ready to discuss any issues of importance concerning the Church until he had time to settle into the position. But he needed to say this several times before some of them got the message.

His conversation with the President of the Irish Republic was the most rewarding for him, as he was able to discuss his concerns for the security of Mary and the children. The President assured Peter that he would contact the Prime Minister immediately to arrange an appropriate security detail. Peter felt like a huge weight had been lifted from him and he immediately phoned Mary to let her know what had been arranged. She was not overly pleased with the prospect of having to be escorted everywhere, but at least it meant that she and the children were no longer prisoners in their own home.

After three hours and twenty-three phone calls, the Camerlengo had advised that they were done for now. But there were several more calls they would have to make later that evening when it would be morning in the Americas.

Thoughts of a quiet dinner were erased when he remembered that he'd agreed to dine with all the cardinals today. The dinner was an extended affair, with cardinals rotating tables between courses to ensure that they all had a chance to speak with him. They were all eager to find out more about this man who had infiltrated their dreams. Consequently, he was subjected to a constant barrage of questions and hardly managed to eat anything.

At about 9.30 pm the Camerlengo advised that it was time to get back to his office to receive calls from American dignitaries. Peter thus found himself chatting with the likes of the presidents of the United States, Mexico, Brazil, Argentina and Chile, and the Canadian Prime Minister. If he thought being elected Pope wasn't surreal enough, he found himself discussing the trials of raising young children with none other than the President of the United States!

It was almost 11.30 when he finally finished his phone calls. Physically and mentally exhausted, he returned to the papal bedroom suite, collapsed on the bed, and immediately fell into a deep sleep.

His second full day as Pope was much like the first. But instead of taking phone calls from dignitaries he spent most of the day having private audiences with the cardinals. He was surprised that more than a few of them seemed to be genuinely looking forward to changes that would increase the appeal of the Church to the wider world. However, over half of the cardinals he spoke to warned him against making wholesale changes and emphasised that the Church needed to stick with its traditional values. Initially, these cardinals were surprised to find that Peter wholeheartedly agreed with them. But he lost them again when he added that traditional values could co-exist with progressive views and the Church needed to be relevant to today's world if it was going to survive and prosper. These cardinals left openly wondering whether they had done the right thing after all by following their instincts at the Conclave and promoting Peter to the papacy.

These meetings also provided him with the opportunity to have his first private discussion with Cardinal Doherty. They had never previously spoken one to one. It was not a comfortable situation for either of them.

'Good morning, Your Holiness,' Doherty muttered as he entered the room, almost choking on his words.

'Good morning, Your Eminence,' was Peter's nervous reply. 'Look, I'm not really sure what protocol dictates and as this is new ground for all of us, I think it will be grand if you could just call me Peter when we're having a private conversation.'

'Well, that is highly irregular, but if you insist,' Doherty answered.

'Thank you, that makes me feel much more comfortable … and I should call you …?'

'I suppose you could call me by my first name as well, if that is the way you want it?'

Peter tried to lighten the mood. 'Well, this is a strange turn of events isn't it?'

'It certainly is,' Doherty replied. 'Never in a million years would I have thought that a layman could become Pope!'

'It wasn't exactly at the top of my mind either,' Peter assured him.

'So now that you have all this power and responsibility, what are you going to do with it?'

'Well, I haven't had much time to think about it but rest assured that I will aim to look after the needs of all Catholics.'

'And previous Popes haven't?'

Peter was slightly taken aback by the aggravation in Doherty's reply but felt that now was as good a time as any to let Cardinal Doherty know what he really felt about his running of the Dublin diocese. The discussion was full and frank and covered issues such as the enforcement of church doctrine, the idiocy of the new revisions to the English mass, and the suppression of any initiatives which would provide the laity with more control over parochial services. It didn't end well, with Cardinal Doherty effectively agreeing to disagree with Peter and storming out of the room.

It was now mid-afternoon and Peter's experience with Cardinal Doherty meant that he was no longer in the mood to continue discussions. This was Saturday and it was expected that he would deliver an Angelus prayer to the crowd in the Piazza the following morning, so Peter needed some time to get his head around what he was going to say.

He had absolutely no idea where to start, so he called together cardinals Pancetti, Curiosa and O'Faherty and Fr Mick to help him. After tossing around several topics for the best part of an hour without finding a topic that he was comfortable with, Fr Mick eventually asked Peter, 'What is it that you most want for the Church?'

Peter thought about this question and was surprised that the answer came to him almost immediately: 'Unity!' he said. 'I'm sick of different groups within the Church declaring that theirs is the only way to be a Catholic and anyone who behaves differently to them is not being true to their faith. I want people to understand that although we may have very many different means, we are all after the same end which is to spread the love of Christ.'

'Excellent!' Curiosa declared. 'That's the topic you should use for your Angelus. We'll help you write it.'

So together they worked on the Angelus until Peter was satisfied with it. When they had finished, the others left Peter and Pancetti alone so that they could work on the translation, and it was not until late in the day again that Peter was able to finally rest.

The Pope's private office was equipped with a surprisingly well-stocked liquor cabinet. So, before Pancetti left him, Peter asked if he could stay behind for a nightcap. Pancetti was very tired as well, but he obliged and Peter poured them both a small glass of amaretto.

Peter served Pancetti his drink, sat himself down and thought it would be a good opportunity to satisfy his curiosity. 'I know that my presence here is because of the dreams that you all had, but I have never had anyone describe what actually happened in their dream.'

'Well to tell you the truth, Holiness, I have never told my dream to anyone. All I told Cardinal O'Faherty that night was that I dream the new Papa was Irish, and later when Cardinal Curiosa asked what our dreams were about, all I say is that I was celebrating the wedding of my goddaughter, but that was not the truth.'

'Sorry Luigi, I didn't mean to pry, you don't have to describe your dream to me then.'

'No, it is alright; I think that I would like to tell you. You see, the girl who was getting married in my dream was the daughter of my housekeeper Cinzia. Cinzia has worked for me for over forty years and over that time I had become a close friend of her family. So, I have celebrated the weddings of her two older children as well as some of her nieces and nephews. Cinzia's husband left her shortly after her youngest daughter, Gina, was born. She could not support herself, so I arranged for her and her three children to move into an apartment near my house. That way she could have a place to live and could continue to work for me.

'In my dream, I was standing in front of the altar and Gina was walking down the aisle with her mother. She looked so beautiful.' Pancetti started to choke on his words as his eyes welled with tears.

Peter touched the old man's hand and said, 'It's alright, you don't have to go on if you don't want to.'

'No, I have to tell you! I need to tell you! You see, in my dream I was crying too.' Pancetti was struggling to get the words out again. 'You see, in my dream, I was thinking that Gina should not have to walk down the aisle with her mother; that should be her father's job!'

'And you were upset because her father wasn't there?'

'No, he was there!'

'So why didn't he give his daughter away?' Peter asked. Pancetti chin began to quiver again, and his eyes filled with water as he looked back at Peter. The penny dropped. 'Oh … you are Gina's father, aren't you?'

Pancetti could only nod as he began to sob. Peter sat down next to him and put his arm around him to provide some comfort.

Pancetti took some time to compose himself before explaining to Peter how he fell desperately in love with Cinzia from the moment he met her. Their love went unrequited for almost ten years before they could not hold back any longer, and Gina was the result. Her husband left as soon as he discovered that the child was not his. Pancetti wanted to leave the Church and marry her but Cinzia wouldn't have a bar of it, insisting that the Church needed him more than she did. So, he moved Cinzia and her children into an apartment nearby and looked after them as best he could. They managed to hide their relationship from all but a few close family members ever since. Once they were old enough to understand, he and Cinzia had told the children; Gina had known the truth since she was sixteen years old. Gina's wedding was in a month's time and the thought of not being able to lead her down the aisle was preying on him.

Peter then asked, 'So in your dream, what was I doing?'

'Well, in my dream Gina and her mother had only started walking down the aisle, when the Holy Father walked into the cathedral. Everyone stopped and stared, including the organist and Gina and Cinzia. Then he … I mean you … walk up to me and say, "Go take your place Louie."' Pancetti started to choke up again but pushed though. 'So, I walk up and take Gina's other arm, and her mother and me walk Gina down the aisle. When we reach the altar you make me put Gina's hand in the hand of her future husband. Then you take my hand and put it in Cinzia's and you marry us as well. I woke up so happy I thought my heart would burst.'

'Is this something you would want to happen in reality?'

'Very much so, I would like nothing more than to sanctify my love for Cinzia and spend the rest of my days with her at my side.'

'Well, let's see if we can make that happen … let's see.'

Come the following morning, Declan O'Reilly's story from *The Irish Times* had been picked up by all the international media services. Some of the more conservative commentators, who previously had questioned the results of the Conclave, were more accepting now that they knew that Peter's appointment may have been the result of divine intervention. These same conservatives were also pleased with Peter's decision not to celebrate mass. Most observers expected that Peter would automatically assume all the responsibilities of former Popes. However, Peter believed that the role of priest could not be assumed without some sort of formal training. Bishop he may be, but he was still a layman, so Peter resolved that it was not appropriate for him to take on the role of a priest when he was not trained for it.

With the theme of unity within the Catholic Church, his inaugural Angelus prayer was well received by most Catholics and largely achieved its intended purpose. He had managed to allay the fears of traditionalists who were worried that they would have to pursue a schism to maintain their current practices under the new regime.

In the ensuing week, Peter kept out of the public eye as much as possible and instead focussed on gaining a better appreciation for how the Vatican worked and what his role as Pope entailed. He was not yet ready to appoint new cardinals to individual roles within the Curia, so he decided to allow the previous representatives to retain their roles until he had a better idea on what he wanted to achieve.

He contacted Mary and the children at least twice daily but was missing them terribly. The novelty of being escorted to school and other activities by government security officers was beginning to wear on the children and Mary had never come to terms with it at all. Although the security detail was able to keep reporters off the property, they were always just outside and would bark questions at Mary and the children whenever they were within ear-shot. It eventually got so difficult to do simple things like going to the shops to buy groceries that Mary gave up and had to get others to do it for her.

So, Mary and Peter decided that the only place where the family could be free to move about without being hounded by reporters and the general public was within the walls of the Vatican itself. Easter was approaching and it wouldn't be a problem for the children to start their holidays a week early. Besides, Peter was certainly not going to be able to leave Rome during Holy Week.

Arrangements were made for the Mary and the children to join him from the following Sunday. They would then return to Dublin once school resumed after the Easter holidays. These arrangements caused some upheaval within the Vatican household. The papal apartment usually housed only one person but now it had to accommodate eight.

Peter made their job a bit easier when he advised them that Mary would not be requiring her own room and the boys and girls could each share separate rooms.

Most of the Papal Office staff were members of religious orders and they didn't fully appreciate the needs of a modern family. So, it was up to the few lay staff members to set them straight on a few things such as the need for computers and game consoles. Peter made a point of letting them all know that he was pleased with their efforts, and he was sure that his family would enjoy their stay at the Vatican.

It had been a tough week for Peter. He still felt he had a long way to go before he would fully understand how the Vatican worked – and after that, he still had to think about how he wanted it to work in future. He couldn't wait for Mary and the children to arrive and had dedicated his second Angelus prayer to the importance of family. This proved a bit more controversial than his first Angelus because he avoided the use of the term 'marriage' and instead focussed on commitment as the key to a healthy relationship. He stated that a marriage certificate signified a legal commitment, but the emotional and spiritual commitment between a couple mattered most. He also neglected to reinforce the Church's long-standing view that a family unit must have a man and woman at its head.

As he was finishing his Angelus he saw a helicopter flying over and heading to land within the Vatican grounds. Mary and the children had arrived. The second that he finished his Angelus, he ran down to the helipad to greet them. They were all excited as well and ran towards him so quickly they very nearly knocked him off his feet. The boys couldn't stop carrying on about how cool it was to travel in a jet to Rome and then ride in a helicopter from the airport to the Vatican.

They also had to laugh at the way Peter was dressed. Of course, they had seen him as Pope on television on a few occasions now, but to see him in person dressed in his papal robes was just hilarious. To hear the laughter of children within the private gardens of the Vatican was a real novelty and even the most ardent of the Vatican old guard could not help but be moved by such a joyful reunion.

Peter took the family up to the papal apartment and introduced them to the few staff that he was allowed to have direct contact with. They then settled down for a sumptuous lunch with Fr Mick and the cardinals Curiosa, Pancetti, O'Faherty and Billingham. After lunch, Peter and Mary stayed with Fr Mick, Curiosa, Pancetti and Billingham while O'Faherty took the children for a tour of the Vatican grounds.

At the end of the day the family were able to have supper together and Peter changed into his normal clothes. They all knew that their lives had changed forever but for now, they were just happy to be a family unit again.

Peter was so happy. He had never been away from them for so long. It had only been ten days since he became Pope and he had started to forget who Peter MacDonald was. But having Mary and the children close by was the reality check he desperately needed.

It was just after 10.30 pm. Peter and Mary settled the children into their own rooms before retiring together to the papal suite for the first time. Both were overtired. However, it was their first night together for almost two weeks and they'd missed each other terribly.

They were snuggling up together in the large four poster bed that sat at one end of the expansive papal suite when Peter had an interesting thought. 'Do you think that anybody has ever done the business in this bed?' he asked with a cheeky grin.

Mary turned to face him. 'Peter MacDonald!' she exclaimed. 'How can you think of such a thing? I'm sure all of the previous Popes lived up to their vows completely.'

'Well, not all, that depends on how far you want to go back. Some of the Popes in the Middle Ages were quite randy devils. But we're not under any limitations, are we? So … what do you think?'

'It seems that holy orders have done nothing to diminish your lustful ways,' Mary scolded. 'But do you think it will be okay? It's a bit soon after your operation isn't it, and my period just finished last week.'

'Don't you worry about that!' Peter replied confidently, 'I mean it's been a couple of weeks hasn't it? We should be alright.'

About the Author

B orn in Melbourne, Australia on the Feast of Stephen in 1962, Stephen is the fifth of his migrant parents' seven children. His ethnic background covers six countries. An Australian by birth but genealogically Italian and Armenian, his parents were born and raised in Alexandria, Egypt, and his grandparents were born in Turkey, Sicily, and Syria.

In his youth, Stephen balanced his interest in writing and performing against academic achievements in maths and sciences. The technical side eventually won out and in 1987 he completed a degree in civil engineering. A successful career in water supply, sewerage, and stormwater management has followed.

In 1992, Stephen met his wife Maria. Almost two years to the day later, they were married and went on to produce a family of three frustratingly fabulous children. Sadly, less than 20 years after their first encounter, Maria lost a six-year long battle with breast cancer.

Fostering the frustrating fabulosity and artistic talents of his offspring led Stephen to re-connect with his own artistic side. Over the past decade, as well as writing this novel, Stephen has contributed to three published anthologies in the *We Inspire Now* series (*Live Your Truth*, *A Message to your Younger Self*, and *The Spirit Within*). He has also written and performed comedy and prose for open-mic events, performed on stage in amateur theatre productions, and produced online content for YouTube.

www.stephendagata.au

Pope dreams
(bonus chapter)

When I came up with the premise for this novel, my mind immediately went to what the dreams of each cardinal would look like. Each dream had two objectives. The first was to illustrate the shared revelation of a strange young Irish fellow appearing to them as Pope. But the second objective was to humanise the cardinals.

In many cultures, religious leaders are often seen as demi-gods whose blessings can protect us from harm and evil spirits. I wanted to emphasise that cardinals are, in fact, mere mortals and their dreams would reflect their earthly loves and desires. Consequently, I came up with individual weird and wonderful stories for each cardinal representing their personal interests and ambitions.

Quite rightly, the inclusion of all these dreams within the narrative of the novel was seen by my editors repetitive. As once a couple of dreams have been described in detail, you know how all the others are going to end and it doesn't add much to the storyline. So, rather than deleting the dream sequences all together, I have included them in this bonus chapter for your enjoyment. Hopefully they will provide you with some insight into my weird and wonderful imagination through the subconscious of my characters.

Stephen D'Agata
St Helena, Victoria, 2022

Lorenzo Bontempo

Bontempo was game fishing off the coast of Argentina. He'd caught a big one and it was putting up a real fight. It took all his strength to reel in his catch but then, to his surprise, his catch had jumped directly on to the boat and was now standing right behind him.

It wasn't a fish that he had landed, but a man. Furthermore, this man was dressed in white robes and was wearing a papal mitre. He had landed the Pope! The Holy Father looked at him, smiled and said in a broad Irish accent, 'Now that's what I call being fishers of men!'

Jose D'Angeli

He was driving an Aston Martin DB4 on a mountain road. His mission was to deliver an important package – and he was being followed by a gang of villains in a black Mercedes who were preventing him from doing so. They were shooting at him with machine guns but the bullets were bouncing off the armour-plated Aston. On a straight stretch of road so he pulled out his Walther PPK, stuck his left arm and head out of the car window and took one shot at the Mercedes behind him. The shot pierced the radiator and the resulting steam blocked the driver's vision, causing him to lose control, crash off the road and burst into flames.

He arrived at his destination which, surprisingly, was a suburban house somewhere in the United Kingdom or Ireland. He walked to the front door with his parcel and was greeted by two young boys who, although not identical, where obviously twins. One of the boys took the parcel while the other said, 'Thank you, our daddy's been waiting for this. Come in.'

He walked into the house and was led into a kitchen where a man dressed in white had already opened the parcel, which appeared to contain a hat of sorts. But it was not a hat; it was, in fact, the papal mitre. This man was the new Pontiff and he, D'Angeli, had effectively crowned him.

Patrick Doherty

It was a Saturday morning, and he was participating in his favourite pastime: cycling through the hills of Dublin. He was excited to try out his new bicycle, a Jamis Xenith T2 with a carbon fibre frame and rims, chainstay-mounted rear brake, internal cable routing, and a seat tube with full rear wheel recess. It was the fastest bike he had ever ridden and cost more than a small car. Wearing his bike shorts, jacket and top, bicycle helmet and dark goggles, he could easily blend into a peloton. In fact, he was indeed riding his in a peloton, but he soon realised that this was not Dublin. It was in fact, the streets of Paris!

It was his turn to lead the peloton, so he lifted off his seat and pushed to the front. Following along with him was a rider who had been on his tail since the start of the race. This rider was dressed completely in white lycra save for a yellow jacket. This was the Tour de France, and he was being pursued by the current leader. But this rider had no decals at all on his outfit, and his bicycle and helmet were totally white as well. The only thing to break the white, apart from the yellow jacket, was the pale tan on his legs and arms and the tufts of black hair coming out of his helmet. But, he knew if he could remain ahead of this rider, the Tour de France would be his. However, the rider in white was not making it easy for him.

They were now on the final leg, and it was time to sprint to the finish. He lifted himself up off his seat and pushed the pedals as hard as he could. He managed to put a couple of lengths on the rest of the pack and the finish line was less than a kilometre away. He should have had the race in the bag, but the mysterious white rider was still on his tail.

He was peddling so hard now that the bike was pitching at a forty-degree angle with each push, and it took all his concentration to keep himself upright. But unbelievably, the white rider, who seemed to be using no effort at all, was slowly but surely passing him. He crossed the finish line a respectable second place but his dream of winning the Tour de France was over.

He dismounted and walked towards his opponent to congratulate him. The mysterious white rider had his back to him and was in the process of removing his helmet and goggles, revealing his healthy head of jet-black hair. But when the rider replaced the helmet with a papal mitre, he was amazed to discover that he had been beaten by none other than the Holy Father himself!

He immediately fell to his knees. Then, His Holiness turned to face him. But when he looked up at the face of the new Pontiff, he was shocked to see the familiar face of a relatively young man with bright blue eyes.

Stewart Johnson

He was surfing at Pismo Beach. Oddly though, it wasn't the present day. It was more like the early sixties. He was riding on a huge Malibu board, and he wasn't surfing as much as dancing. With him on the board was a young lady. But it wasn't just any young lady; it was actually Gidget, the character played by the actress Sally Field in her youth. He looked down towards his feet and noticed that he was wearing his crimson robes. He then glanced back to Gidget to find that she was now dressed as the flying nun!

They proceeded to perform several acrobatic acts together, all the time still riding the waves. The acrobatics culminated with the flying nun standing on his shoulders. He was holding tightly on to her ankles, and he felt himself being lifted off the board – before he knew it, they were flying above the beach. They hovered over the other revellers for a while before making a soft landing between movie stars Annette Funicello and Frankie Avalon.

They all immediately launched into a song and dance version of twisting on the beach but stopped abruptly to look at an amazing surfer making his way to the shore. This fellow was also on a huge Malibu board, but he was able to perform all sorts of amazing feats on it. The surfer entered a massive tube and after what seemed like an eternity, he came out the other end. This surfer was dressed in papal robes.

The white surfer manoeuvred his board gracefully onto the beach and when the board stopped he was able to walk off it directly onto the dry sand. This person, who he was now certain was the new Pope, walked directly towards him. He dropped to his knees and reached out to kiss the papal ring. When he looked up he was surprised to see a young man with thick black hair and deep blue eyes looking back at him. Then the Holy Father spoke to him in a broad Irish accent and said, 'It's grand to have a day on the beach, isn't it Stewie.'

Jan Kaparovski

He was lifting weights at what appeared to be his local gym. But there was no-one else training around him. He then noticed that he was in a large auditorium. An audience was seated in tiered benches all around him and four officious looking men were seated at a table directly opposite. He couldn't believe it; he had made it to the weightlifting world championships!

In front of him was a bar loaded with fifty kilograms on each side. His personal best for clean and jerk was eighty kilos, but he'd achieved that when he was in his early twenties. He was now in his late sixties so he didn't know how he would lift a full one hundred kilos. He looked over to his right to see a man dressed in white, whom he presumed to be his coach, giving him a double thumbs up. With this encouragement he approached the bar, squatted down, and gripped it firmly before effortlessly lifting it to his chest. Just as quickly and easily he lifted the bar over his head and held to roars of delight from the gathered crowd, who were being egged on by his coach.

The ease with which he accomplished this weight prompted him to ask for more. He was willing to go for one hundred and twenty kilos, but his coach instructed the officials to put another fifty-kilo weight on each side of the bar. He gave his coach a look of utter dismay. There was no way he was going to lift two hundred kilos. His coach came over and handed him a plate of his favourite foods: perogi, sauerkraut and Polish sausage. He wolfed the lot down and felt invigorated by this wonderful meal. His coach gave him a pat on the back and another double thumbs up.

He dusted his hands with talcum powder and squatted to pick up the bar. Again he managed to easily lift the weight to his chest before jerking it straight into the air. He had done it! He was surely the greatest weightlifter of all time.

He saw his coach throw his cap up in the air in celebration and run towards him to give him a big hug. But now he noticed that his coach was now wearing a papal mitre instead. He fell to his knees, reached out to kiss the papal ring and then looked up. This is the first opportunity he had to make out the face of the new Pontiff and it was not what he had expected. He was looking at a man who would have to be in his early forties and spoke to him in an Irish accent saying, 'To be sure Jan, you could lift the world on them shoulders.'

Enzo Mangiafuoco

It was the Eurovision song contest, and he was in the finals. The voting was tight and there were only a few points between him and the Irish entry, but he was leading. However, the votes from Italy had not yet been tallied. Surely his countrymen wouldn't give maximum votes to his main rival?

But it was not to be; his countrymen apparently adored this mysterious Irish troubadour who was dressed completely in white, with dark sunglasses and a white top hat. The Irish song was basically a re-write of The Furphys' 'Sweet sixteen' but the Irish contestant had translated the final verse into Italian. Although it was a very clumsy translation, the Italians loved it and voted in for it in droves. Ireland got the maximum points they needed from Italy and won the Eurovision Song Contest.

Being the good sport that he was, Mangiafuoco immediately went to congratulate his rival, who was in the process of removing his top hat and sunglasses. Then the crowd erupted in cheers and whistles for under the top hat was the papal mitre. His rival from Ireland was in fact the new Pope.

Eric Mobutu

He was running the one hundred metre sprint at the London Olympics. It was the final and he'd missed the start, but despite this and while still wearing his black and crimson robes, he managed to haul in his opponents to break the ribbon and win the men's final.

Presently, he was on the winner's podium waiting to be presented with his gold medal. He couldn't believe his eyes when the person who presented him with the gold medal turned out to be none other than the new Pope. And he couldn't believe his ears when this relatively young man, in papal robes with black hair and deep blue eyes, spoke with an Irish accent and said, 'You ran like the wind Eric. Truly you must be the fastest man alive.'

Francesco Pandamonio

He was standing on the high altar at the basilica in Perugia. He was walking up to the lectern to deliver his homily, but noticed that his shoes were clicking on the marble floor as he walked. He looked down and was delighted to see that he was wearing black tap shoes and white spats. It was his boyhood dream to dance like Fred Astaire and Gene Kelly. Where other boys couldn't get enough of westerns, Pandamonio loved nothing better than a good musical. When one was showing at the local cinema, he would go to see it as often as he could. Then he would memorise the dance steps, stick thumb tacks into the soles of his shoes and attempt to repeat every step back at home.

Presently, the organist had started to play one of his favourite dance tunes and he couldn't stop his feet from moving to the music, providing the rhythm accompaniment. In all these years he hadn't lost his touch. In fact, he was dancing better than he ever had before. He noticed that he was wearing a top-hat and tails and carrying a black cane with white tips.

Then he was joined on stage by a man wearing a white top-hat and tails, carrying a white cane with black tips. Their dancing was perfectly synchronised. At a break in the music he thought he'd take things up a notch and went into a brilliant solo routine before handing over to his dance partner, who was still able to match him and then add a few more steps of his own. The cardinal managed to match these steps before issuing another challenge to his mysterious partner. This duel continued for a few more rounds before they both stepped into a synchronised finale.

When the music stopped, the congregation rose as one and clapped and cheered. Pandamonio turned to his partner to embrace him, but stopped when he saw that in place of the white top-hat he was wearing the papal mitre. Pandamonio couldn't believe it. His dance partner was none other than the Holy Father! He immediately got down on one knee and took his hand to kiss the papal ring then looked up and was surprised to see the face of a relatively young man. The Pope then said with a broad Irish accent, 'Aye Frankie, to be sure you're the best dancer that I've ever seen.'

Peter Quinn

It was the Sydney Iron Man at Bondi Beach. He'd just completed the swim leg and was heading back into the water with his surf ski. Funny thing was that he had been dressed as a cardinal the whole time. Instead of a paddle, he held his crosier. There were a few young men ahead of him, but he had no trouble at all racing past them. It was like he had an outboard motor attached.

He made it back to the beach in first place. If he could stay in the lead during the run leg, he would win the competition. This he did with ease and no sooner had he broken the ribbon at the finishing line, he found himself on the winner's dais, patiently waiting for his trophy.

Then, onto the dais, walked the new Holy Father. Weirdly though, he didn't look anyone he would have expected to become Pope. He looked nothing like any of the other cardinals and he couldn't have been much over forty! Furthermore, when the Pope spoke to him and said, 'Well done Quinny, you really had the lord on your side for that one,' he discovered that the new Pope was Irish!

Ian Robertson

He was skating on a lake near his hometown of Vancouver. He had skated all his life and, in his youth, proved to be a very handy ice hockey player. But he now seemed to be living his dream of being a figure skater.

It was a quiet weekday morning and there were only a handful of people on the ice, a perfect opportunity to try out some fancy moves. He built up some speed and then launched himself into a double turn. To his complete surprise he executed the move perfectly. He had only attempted such a move once before and that was many, many years ago. On that occasion, he'd ended up flat on his back, but his success this time encouraged him to go further. So, he sped up again and this time launched into a triple. Again, he delivered a perfect execution and thought that he must be the best figure skater in the whole world.

He then noticed that although he was now alone on the ice, a crowd of spectators had gathered at the lake edge and their cheers and whistles echoed throughout the hills. In the midst of the crowd, on an elevated podium, sat a group of judges; they were holding up score cards, giving him a perfect ten for his previous move. It was then that he realised that he was competing in the figure skating world championships. This was his time to shine.

The success with which he executed the previous two moves emboldened him to try the impossible, a quadruple turn. He built up speed again and was now skating faster than he had ever skated before as he launched himself into the air. The crowd was totally silent. He spun once, twice, three times, four times, and then found he had still enough air and momentum for an additional turn, executing a perfect landing. He had gone beyond the impossible and landed a quintuple turn!

The roar from the crowd was deafening. People started running and skating towards him to offer their congratulations. Then the crowd parted to let a vehicle though. It was a Pope Mobile sliding gracefully across the ice. The vehicle drifted to a stop right in front of him and the new Holy Father, resplendent in his white robes, stepped out. Robertson immediately dropped to his knees to kiss the papal ring. He looked up and was surprised to see a youngish looking man before him. Then, with a broad Irish accent, the Pope said, 'You flew like an angel there, Robbo.'

Pierre Soutier

It was the world poker championships and he had been dealt two aces. He bet fifty euro and all but one of his opponents folded. The remaining opponent raised another fifty; he called this fifty and the dealer dealt himself an ace and two kings. He had what seemed an unbeatable hand and so took the punt and went all-in. To his delight his opponent followed suit and he proudly revealed his two aces, giving him a full house of aces and kings.

He looked smugly at his opponent but was taken aback when he noticed that this opponent was dressed in the white robes of the Holy Father. The Pope was holding his two cards in front of his face, but he could see that he had a head of thick black hair and seemed much younger than he expected the new Pope to be. His smiling face and bright blue eyes were revealed when he put his cards on the table, revealing two kings. Then, speaking English but with a thick Irish accent, said to him, 'Thought you had me there, didn't you Pierre?'

Phillip Suryani

He was playing Rachmaninoff's Piano Concerto No.3 to a packed house at the Palazzo Albrizzi in Venice. The brilliance of his piano playing had the audience in tears.

Then when his performance reached its final crescendo, the audience stood in unison and the cheers and applause literally lifted the lid of the concert hall. Amidst the roars of adulation from the crowd and the bouquets of flowers that rained down, a solitary figure dressed in white robes had stepped onto the stage and was now walking towards him with outstretched arms. As the person drew closer to him, he realised that it was the new Holy Father.

He fell to his knees immediately and reached out to receive the Pope's hand so that he could kiss the papal ring. He kissed the ring and, looking up to see the face of the new pontiff, was surprised to find such a young man in front of him with jet black hair and bright blue eyes. The Pope then spoke to him in English but with a broad Irish accent: 'That was beautiful Phil, you really brought a tear to my eye.'

Pope Dreams
Immaculate Conception?

Book 2 in The Pope Dreams Trilogy

The improbable election of an Irish layman, and married father of six, to the papacy has turned the Catholic church on its head. However divinely inspired his election was, many Cardinals can't help thinking that they have made a huge mistake.

The public disclosure that the new Pope had a vasectomy operation just prior to being elected, adds a scandalous edge to the situation. But an unexpected pregnancy suggests that divine forces are not done with Peter MacDonald, now Pope Peter II, just yet.

In Stephen D'Agata's second novel, *Pope Dreams: Immaculate Conception?* Pope Peter II finds that he can't simply impose his progressive views on the function of the church. Minor reform is possible, but major reform requires a paradigm shift which seems unobtainable.

The challenge of carrying on a *'normal'* family life in an environment not amenable to, and potentially not safe for, the raising of children, means that our young Pope really has his work cut out for him.

Coming in mid-2023!

www.stephendagata.au